CULT OF KU

Second Edition

D1560277

A   Grant   Kingsley   Novel

CULT OF KU

A HAWAIIAN MURDER MYSTERY

Bill Fernandez

TABLE OF CONTENTS

DEDICATION

I dedicate this book to
my loving wife,

Judith

"Hawaiian native history and the long-lasting effects of imperialism simmer beneath the surface in this Pacific murder mystery, with war hero Grant Kingsley racing to identify who's behind the ritualistic killings and the Cult of Ku."

Stanford Alumni Review "Shelf Life", online version, Sept-Oct, 2016

ACKNOWLEDGMENTS

EACH BOOK I write is the product of the Hawaiian ohana (family) value of working together. This, my first murder mystery, is no exception.

To my friend and editor, Bill Bernhardt, a big mahalo, thanks, for his patience and excellent seminars where I learned so much from him and my fellow students.

To my wife, Judith whose love, support, wisdom, and encouragement are so deeply appreciated.

CHAPTER 1

Honolulu, June 1920

FEAR GRIPPED GRANT Kingsley as Koko Head loomed above the morning mist. At the prow of the *Matsonia*, a pod of dolphins flipped from the sea, arched, and dove back into the water in a gay carousel of movement, drawing the luxury liner toward Honolulu and a confrontation with his step-grandmother Sheila Grant. His knuckles whitened as he gripped the ship's railing. Seven years ago he left Hawai'i for Yale believing he was the son of James Kingsley, a wealthy financier and sugar plantation owner. Today he returned uncertain of who he was, or where his place in the world might be.

His sister in Los Angeles warned him that Shiela was on a rampage. She read a deathbed note from his mother confessing to a love affair with a pure Hawaiian man at the time of the 1895 counter-revolution against the Republic of Hawai'i. Grant was born nine and a half months later.

Military duties and the flu pandemic prevented him from returning for his mother's funeral. In a curt Western Union telegram, his father advised finishing law school. He completed Yale on a scholarship and his army savings.

Grant watched the packet ship with its inspectors and reporters approach. He would not answer questions from newspapermen interested in scandal. He knew that Sheila was spreading gossip about his parentage. She hated Hawaiians and disliked him because of his brown skin. When he was growing up, she would say, "You're black as the ace of spades. Stay out of the sun or scrub it off."

The packet ship came about, tying onto the *Matsonia*. Several men climbed aboard as the graceful ocean liner edged into Honolulu Harbor. Canoes filled with natives and flowers raced to the ship. He heard a voice ask, "Do you know Mr. Grant Kingsley?"

He watched a steward escort a reporter toward the second class cabins. He smiled. His room was empty. A well-tipped seaman would deposit his valise on the dock.

Red, white, blue, and golden streamers flew from the ship onto Pier Seven. The Royal Hawaiian Band, led by its German conductor, played a Sousa march. As the gangplank trundled out, brown-skinned boys dove from the dock, seeking coins or favors from the passengers. He spotted a glee club dressed in white, the men with broad red sashes, the women with belts and leis of yellow. They strummed guitars and sang island melodies. Young women greeted each passenger with flower leis, and soon the arriving visitors were piled to their eyes with fragrant blossoms.

Grant hurried down the gangplank into a crowd. Someone jostled him. He thought he heard his name. He rushed from the causeway into a mob of greeters. By telegram, his father told him that Charles, a Hawaiian manservant, would be waiting at Alakea Street.

He pushed his way to the exit of the three-story port building. A dozen open-air vehicles were parked at the sidewalk. Two yellow electric trolleys stood in the middle of the street, their operators clanging bells, seeking customers for the trip to Waikiki. Several horse-drawn coaches were at the curb, the hitched animals munching in feed bags wrapped around their noses.

"You Mr. Kingsley?" a deep voice asked. "I'm Charles, the chauffeur."

A tall, rotund Hawaiian in dark clothes stood on the sidewalk. Grant nodded.

Charles took Grant's valise, stowed it into the back of a Ford three-door car, and headed up Nu'uanu Street. "This isn't the way to Waikiki," Grant said.

"Your step-grandmother wants to see you."

"Can't it wait?"

"No, she insisted you come immediately and your father ordered me to take you to her."

"Where is he?"

"On Mau'i. He'll be back in a few days."

He settled back, dreading the confrontation. He wondered if Dad had also turned against him. To lose his love was more than he could bear.

Charles turned the Ford touring car through the massive concrete portals of a two-acre estate. Iron fencing spiked at the top surrounded the grounds. Trees lined the border and flowers bloomed along the footprint of the building. Charles let him out at the entrance to the mansion, saying, "I can't wait, errands to do. When finished, to get home, go to the Young Hotel and catch the trolley to Waikiki." Grant nodded, took a deep breath and marched up the wooden stairs.

The house was imposing with its half-dozen white, Grecian-style columns supporting a second-floor veranda threading its way around the mansion. Its grandeur reminded all who saw it of the sugar wealth that controlled the islands of Hawai'i.

A Caucasian in dark clothes answered his rapping and asked him to wait in the foyer. The butler marched down a dark hallway, disappearing from view.

Grant grew impatient as time passed. Just like Sheila, demanding his immediate presence, then forcing him to wait. He glanced up the long stairwell that led to the second floor and decided on impulse to climb it and see if the window box was still there.

He ran his hand along the rail supported by a dozen balustrades, remembering his childhood when he whipped down the staircase escaping imaginary enemies. Sheila disapproved of his antics, scolding and spanking him.

At the top of the stairs Grant saw the window that opened out onto the side lawn. He rushed to the box below it, lifted its top and surveyed the interior. Invisible in this hiding place, he used to eavesdrop on the adults gossiping in the hallway.

He pushed open the window, ran his hand along the mosquito screen, and gazed at the large ohia tree branches overhanging the roof.

"Master Kingsley," a voice called. "Mrs. Grant will see you now."

He hurried down the stairs and into the opulent den of his dead grandfather. Its walls glowed golden brown. A magnificent Persian rug covered the floor. Behind a massive koa wood desk was a fireplace, its opening edged in Grecian marble. Above it hung a picture of his grandfather.

Robert Grant stood in a military uniform patterned after those worn by Union officers in the American Civil War. A saber scabbard rested against his side. His unsmiling face was wreathed in a full beard. A dark blue gold-braided kepi hid his hair.

Sheila sat at an ornate desk, writing. She did not look up. Instead she pointed to a luxurious red leather chair. Grant sank into it, relishing its rich comfort.

After many minutes, she placed her notes to the side. Her eyes narrowed as she gave him a piercing look, "I never liked your mother. Like a tramp, she came into our lives uninvited, claiming to be an illegitimate child of your grandfather. She played on Robert's guilt for dallying with a trashy Hawaiian woman. I told my husband long ago that brown women are immoral. That they would sleep with anyone and everyone. But no, he had to adopt Leinani, because he believed she was his daughter. I warned him when he sold her to Kingsley that she was not a virgin. That she was trash like all Hawaiian women."

"She was not trash. She was wonderful. You can't say ugly words about her." Grant stood. His lean six-foot, two-hundred-and-ten-pound body shook. His fists clenched and unclenched.

"Don't you shout at me. I'm not of your filthy dark blood, thank goodness. I'm of good New England stock. I married Robert Grant when he attended Yale. Your grandfather was a fine man from a missionary family in Hawai'i. He would turn over in his grave if he knew what I know."

"Why are you calling me filthy?"

"I will thank you to sit quietly and listen to what I have to say. I will speak my mind. If you don't want to hear it, you may leave knowing that I will disinherit you and ask Mr. Kingsley to do the same."

"Ask my father to disinherit me?"

"He is not your father."

"But he is my father. How can you say he isn't?"

"Because of this letter your mother wrote as she was dying." Sheila thrust a paper at Grant. "It is her confession to an adulterous relationship with a Hawaiian man. The man who killed my husband!"

"His soldiers shot him during the Queen's revolution!"

4

"I always suspected that was not the case. When I read the letter your mother wrote, I knew your traitorous, dirty, Hawaiian father killed him. You are his little brown bastard."

"Bastard, what are you talking about? I know nothing about this man."

"You are a bastard. You are not the son of Robert Kingsley, but the offspring of an illicit affair by a Hawaiian whore and my husband's killer. I will make certain that Kingsley disowns you and casts you from his life."

"You can't call my mother a whore. You can't take my father away from me and treat me like rubbish."

"Clarence, see this wild man out."

The servant entered and motioned Grant to leave.

"Please don't turn my father against me."

"I will."

The servant insisted, "Sir, please leave?"

Grant glared at him for a moment, then looked at the old woman. "If you dare spread lies about who my father is, I will do everything in my power to stop you. I love him and I will not let you destroy his love for me. I will do anything I can to stop you. Anything!"

He left the room.

CHAPTER 2

DAZED, HIS HEAD aching, Grant found himself in front of the Young Hotel. He took the trolley to Waikiki. The confrontation with Sheila more agonizing then the barbed wire he had fought through during the Great War.

At the Moana Hotel he met Jimmy Noah, a Punahou classmate. With him were a group of beach boys planning to practice paddling.

"This is Pahoa," Jim said, introducing Grant to a tall, very dark-skinned Hawaiian. "He is our leader. An outstanding surfer, they love him in California and Australia. This is my friend Grant. A war hero and a first-class paddler."

"You familiar with canoe racing?" Pahoa asked.

"Did it in high school and I was first oar in sculls at college."

"Good. We need another man. Big race Kamehameha Day. Big parade. Big competition. Come. Change at our clubhouse."

Grant worked with his new friends until nightfall. Reluctantly he left the *Hui Nalu* Canoe Club promising to return.

***

Grant watched a flotilla of canoes land on the sand near the Moana Hotel. A multitude of men with fourteen-foot spears thrusting into the sky raced to a platform where royal feather *kahili* rose above the ceremonial king and queen. The warriors wore full-length, dyed-brown union suits. Women dancing before the royal couple were covered by long white sacks. A Christian minister insisted on the heavy clothes saying, "It's immoral to show bare skin on Waikiki beach."

The dancing ended, and the king and his queen mounted a grand-stand. The parade began, led by *pau* riders, beautifully dressed women in long red gowns with golden capes flowing around their backs. They rode sidesaddle on garlanded horses. Hawaiian dignitaries in black suits, yellow capes, and top hats marched behind them.

At Pahoa's insistence Grant left the festivities. At the meeting house of Hui Nalu there were two canoes ready. With six men to each boat, Grant and Pahoa paddled to the start line where other vessels bobbed in the water.

"Why are we racing toward Ka'ena Point?" Grant asked.

"It's the jumping off place to Kaua'i," Pahoa answered. In the morning, we re-enact Kamehameha's landing at Waikiki and his conquest of O'ahu. This race depicts his attempt a year later to invade Kaua'i. His fleet was wrecked at Ka'ena. So we race toward it and return like he did a hundred and twenty-four years ago."

"You celebrate Kamehameha's birthday. But wasn't he a bloody man sacrificing humans to pacify some god?"

"He was given the Hawaiian war god Ku on the death of his uncle, king of Hawai'i Island. To be successful in war, Kamehameha believed that Ku demanded human sacrifices. Where you see the sun setting, Kamehameha re-built a temple and dedicated it to Ku. It was called Kaneaki. In that place he made sacrifices to the war god before invading Kaua'i."

"It didn't do him much good if he lost his fleet."

"Maybe, but fourteen years later, the king of Kaua'i surrendered to him. It just took a little longer for the sacrifices to work their magic."

The bullhorn ordered the vessels to "go," and forty-eight paddlers fought through the waves toward the midway point outside Ewa Beach. At the turn one canoe from Hui Nalu and another from the All Hawai'i Racing Club were ahead. The leaders increased their pace as they raced for the winner's marker outside Honolulu Harbor. Grant felt exhaustion setting in and saw the All Hawai'i canoe forge forward by the width of a prow.

"Give 'em," Pahoa yelled. "*Imua.*"

Six shafts plunged into the water. The strokes were short and powerful. The finish buoy loomed thirty feet away. Pahoa, Grant, and their companions shoved their vessel through the sea, closing the gap between canoes.

CHAPTER 3

"**S**AVAGES," SHEILA GRANT said, "parading like peacocks in black suits and fake golden feather capes. And King Kamehameha, whom they revere, was the worst of the lot with his pagan worship of Ku and twenty-one wives."

Sheila admired her slender figure, tummy and small *derriere*. She noted her barely wrinkled skin. "Not bad for someone who is seventy-five years old," she said with admiration in her voice.

Sheila let her night chemise fall over her shoulders, covering her nakedness from head to toe. "I laid into that bloodthirsty king and all his kind at the centennial. If it wasn't for the missionaries like my husband's father, those savages would still be sacrificing humans and fornicating like animals in perpetual heat."

The old woman snuggled under the sheets of her grand Victorian bed. The night was warm, and she had left the upstairs windows open. As she lay on her pillow she thought of Grant Kingsley. "I knew that he was not the same as Robert and Susan. Those two are my husband's grandchildren, fair-skinned and without the animal look of the Hawaiian."

Sheila dozed, the deep sleep of weariness escaping her. There came a sound from the second-story window. The slight noise did not come again. "Just the wind scraping an ohia limb across the roof," she muttered and closed her eyes. They opened again as scratching came from the hallway. "Must be the rat Clarence couldn't catch. Tend to it in the morning."

Her hand stifled a yawn. Was the bedroom door moving? Her eyes blinked away sleep as she tried to penetrate the darkness. Maybe it's

Kamehameha seeking revenge? Sheila rose from the covers, intending to step to the doorway and turn on the light.

A hand seized her throat. Another pressed a cloth against her nose and mouth. She struggled, flailing her thin arms. Grant has come to kill me, Sheila thought. She smashed her hands into her attacker. Scream, scream she willed her vocal cords to act, but the words died as the gag stifled her. Kicking, Sheila tried to thrust the man from her bed, but he pushed his body into her. She felt sudden pain as a bone snapped. Her panicked fighting weakened as everything became black.

***

Sheila woke with a start, a gag between her teeth, her wrists bound together. She shook her head to free herself from the restraint and yell. But words would not come. A hook lay embedded in her gums. A cord attached to it, forced her from the bed onto the floor. She heard a bone crack. Felt a sudden rush of pain in her leg. The gag halted her cry. Tears came.

A dark figure jerked the hook, forcing her to stumble through the unlit bedroom. The barbed shaft tore into her jaw. "What are you doing?" She tried to say but swallowed the words.

The killer pulled her down the staircase. Her injured leg gave way. Sheila stumbled. More pain came as the hook ripped her flesh. Blood gushed through her lips. Her body slid down the steps. The hooded man jerked her upright and dragged her into the hallway. Doors opened as the black-clothed figure looked into each room, finally pulling her into the den.

Moonlight streamed through the windows onto the koa desk where she had argued with Grant. The shadowy figure flung her onto the sleek brown wood. It hovered over her. She could see the hostile eyes, but not the face hidden by a black cloth.

Water sprinkled over her. She felt excruciating pain as razor-sharp points cut across her chest. More pain came as the salt water poured into her wounds.

Jagged slices slashed her breasts. Screams muffled in her throat. Thin points, like a comb of needles, plunged into her flesh and then ripped open her stomach. The pain was unbearable. Blood pooled under her back. Shock overcame her. Sheila closed her eyes.

A slap brought her awake. In the moonlight filtering through the windows, she saw Robert's picture. She pleaded to him for his help. A saw-like weapon slashed the portrait, smearing the unsmiling face with her blood. It whipped down and sawed across her body. She prayed for death. In the translucent moonlight, a pointed shaft rose, then plunged. Sudden overwhelming pain spread over her, then darkness.

CHAPTER 4

THE EERIE SOUND of a "daisy cutter" thundered in Grant's head. The explosion whipped away the barbed wire. He cringed when his squad charged across "No Man's Land" into a field of death. Drenched in sweat he forced himself awake.

Coconut leaves rattled outside his second-story window. Grant realized it was their noise, not artillery, that troubled his sleep. Early morning sunlight blazed on the sea, brightening his room. The air's warmth wrapped around him like a down comforter. He could use comfort.

He smelled the aroma of bacon and ham. A knock at the door and a soft voice said, "You awake Master Kingsley?"

"Yes, come in."

A tiny Asian woman entered with a tray of food and steaming hot coffee. Grant reached over and took the cup. "You didn't have to go to all this trouble. I could have taken care of my breakfast."

"No sir." Sue Watanabe, the Japanese house maid bowed her head. "I wait on you. You always kind to me and my family. Just like your mother. Thank you for the gift you brought from Paris. They say French perfume is best in the world."

"I hope you enjoy it. I searched all over the city for the special fragrance that reminded me of you and your gentle nature. Using it will make any man fall in love with you."

"Oh, Mistah Kingsley you so kind…"

A pounding at the front door interrupted her before she could finish. Sue gave him the breakfast tray and rushed downstairs as the pounding came again, louder and more insistent.

Grant heard the front door open, footsteps entering the hallway and an exchange of words. Sue rushed upstairs. "Policemen to see you."

"Who?"

A voice boomed from the lower floor of the home. "Tell him if he isn't down here right away, we'll come up and get him."

The harshness of the demand startled Grant. He walked to the bureau pulled on some pants and threw a shirt over his shoulders. "What does the cop want?"

"He no say. But there three officers downstairs. I scared. What you do?" Sue's hands shook.

"We're coming up. Don't try to run."

Grant brushed past Sue and out the bedroom door.

Three men dressed in dark suits mounted the stairs. One police officer, wearing a Panama hat banded with a multi-colored feather lei, said, "Are you Grant Kingsley?

"Yes."

"You will please come with me." He pointed to his companions. "You two search the bedroom."

"Who are you? What's this about?"

"Detective Asing, Honolulu Sheriff's Department. Put out your hands, please."

"Why?"

"Hands please," the detective said. His two assistants moved to each side of Grant. "No trouble, please."

Scowling, Grant shoved out his hands. Steel bracelets slipped over his wrists. He stared down at Asing, a foot shorter than him. "Why?"

The detective looked up, his lips twisted in a crooked smile. "Murder."

***

Except for the light shining onto his head, the room was dark. "Ugly," Grant thought. His hands chafed against the slats of a wooden chair.

Smoke from a lighted cigar twisted upward like rising fog when the sun warms the earth after a wet night.

Detective Asing stood in a corner, a bow tie dangling around the collar of his white shirt. His hat, tilted at a rakish angle, hid his eyes. A cigar parked on the corner of his mouth, flashed dim light on his sallow face.

"Talk, damn you," Lieutenant Hitchcock said, slamming his fist onto the bare table in front of Grant's chair. "What did you do with the weapons?"

"I don't know anything about any weapons."

"Look, fella, I can beat the truth out of you," Lieutenant Hitchcock, assistant Chief of Police said, clenching his fists and shoving his two-hundred and forty-pound body into Grant. "We know you did it. The butler told us that you threatened to stop her anyway you could. We found the second-story window broken into and your prints on the sill. We have the slashed corpse. Now we want the weapons and your confession."

"Go to hell. Don't know what you're talking about. I want a lawyer—"

Hitchcock's fist slammed into Grant's stomach. His head whipped forward, almost hitting the edge of the table. Hitchcock pulled his hair, smashing a rubber truncheon into Grant's side. "Talk."

"Maybe we shouldn't beat the kid up," Asing said, a cloud of smoke spiraling from his mouth. "Maybe he didn't do it. He's got an alibi. Several Hawaiians vouched for him."

Hitchcock sneered, "No jury of white men would believe a Hawaiian."

"Don't know about that," Asing replied. "This guy Pahoa's pretty credible."

"You mean the 'Duke'?"

"Yeah."

Hitchcock smoothed his palm over his hair. "Man's got a good reputation. How did he ever get that name, 'Duke'? He's not Hawaiian royalty, is he?"

Asing's craggy face smiled. "No, not royalty, a Hawaiian princess called the father 'Duke' after some British guy who visited Hawai'i. The name stuck to the son." The Chinese detective paused for a moment, watching Grant gasp. "This kid is some kind of war hero, his alibi might stick."

Hitchcock shook his head. "I think he killed her. We got the motive. All we need are the weapons and a confession."

"Better ease up for awhile. We've been pounding him for eight hours. Kid hasn't cracked yet."

"You could be right. Toss him into the big tank for the night. After those savages have their way with him, he'll want out so bad, he'll sing like a bird." Hitchcock laughed.

CHAPTER 5

GRANT LEANED AGAINST a concrete wall, the heat of the warm tropical night brewing a nauseating smell of sweating bodies, vomit, crap, and urine. Some air drifted in through a barred window at the end of a hallway bordering an iron cage. It was just enough to keep fifty men alive in the cell the inmates called "The Big Tank." He ached after hours of verbal abuse and physical beatings which failed to secure an admission of guilt from him.

Despite her hatred, Grant sat saddened by Sheila's death. But what caused her to insult him? What did his mother say in her dying message that outraged Sheila? Who killed her and why? These were puzzles he could not solve in this cell. He bent his head against his drawn up legs and dozed.

Scuffling in a corner brought him awake. Through an open flap of a makeshift tent, he glimpsed naked buttocks and another man mounting over them. With the flick of a hand, the flap was closed, followed by a gasp of "It hurts." and a grunt of "Shut up."

Despite the moans and the movements of the tent, the prisoners ignored the rape, except a tall, muscular, nut-brown man who licked his lips and gyrated his body in time with the animal thrusting inside the makeshift hovel. "Hey, leave a piece of the action for me," the man said.

"Get your own doxy," someone in the tent answered. "Ain't come."

Grant was repulsed by the rape in the big tank. How many in this cage had been violated? He realized that this is Hitchcock's plan, put fear of unwanted sex into him and force a confession.

In front of him, Grant noticed an old man, hair stringy, beard unkempt, scraping the dirty floor for food and shoveling what he picked up into his mouth. The sounds drew the attention of a big Hawaiian prisoner standing by the makeshift tent. Grant dropped his eyes, studying the floor. He sensed movement toward him as he heard inmates scurrying. He didn't want trouble. In front of him a kick and howl ended the scraping.

Grant had been in the trenches with thousands of men, men without women, men doomed to die. A release from stress for some came from choosing the path of the ancient Greek warriors. He never engaged in such practices, nor accepted them, but realized it is the price paid for forcing young men to fight without the relief that comes from the love of a woman.

Large toes drummed the floor dust. A deep voice said, "Gimmie your ass."

Grant didn't move.

A hand swiped his face, knocking him sideways. "Get up. Take off your pants and lean over."

"Okay, okay. Just don't hit me again." Grant raised his hands to his face as he rose from the floor.

The big man laughed, unbuckling his belt, and then gasped as Grant's clamped fists swung into his crotch. Twisting, he kicked the rapist's knee smashing the man's patella. The bully bent over from the shattering blow. Grant finished his opponent with a crisp right uppercut to the jaw and watched the man crumble to the dirty floor, howling in pain.

"Hey, what's going on?" The voice emerged from the tent. Its flap flew open and a half-naked man stepped out. He stared at the injured rapist rolling on the floor, then pointed a finger at Grant. "Jesse and I run the big tank. You trying to muscle in?"

The belligerent man buttoned his trousers and started across the room. Inmates pressed themselves against the walls and bars of the cage, clearing a path for him. He stopped a few feet from Grant, studying Jesse writhing on the floor. "You beat him. You think you going take over our territory. My name Mauloa." The man flexed his biceps, the veins of his arms popping out like long blue worms stretched under his skin. "You the rich guy, murder some old lady. Not very brave thing to do. I'm going bust you up."

"Before you do, maybe you should stick your limp dick into your pants," Grant said.

"You cocky bastard," screamed Mauloa. "I'm going to make you eat a mile of my shit." He spread his arms, rushing to crush Grant in his embrace. Some inmates began a rhythmic chant. Others banged metal against the iron bars. Grant thought the jail guards would hear the wild cacophony, come to his rescue, and stop the fight. But no one came. He understood what Hitchcock's parting words meant. Somehow he had to beat the odds, survive the night and the horrors of this cell.

Grant danced around the bully. He knew the man intended to grapple him and crush his lungs. He flicked his left arm in quick jabs, doing little damage to his adversary. Mauloa yelled, "You guys close in. So he no can run away."

Inmates crowded closer to the fighters. Mauloa smiled. "Hey rich kid, you got no place to run."

Grant backed against the wall, watching his opponent's feet. Mauloa stepped forward. Grant ducked under the ham-sized arms, struck a fist into Mauloa's belly, followed by a sharp left hook to the jaw.

Mauloa stumbled, crashing onto the concrete. Grant danced to the side, but the hands of waiting men shoved him into the big Hawaiian. Like an enraged beast, Mauloa tackled Grant, hurling him into the thicket of prisoners surrounding the fighters. Grant soccer-kicked, connecting with Mauloa's shin.

The bully shrieked losing his hold on Grant. But the inmates held him and he could not escape. Mauloa came again, seized him, and squeezed tight. He was seconds from blackness.

With a desperate effort, Grant smashed his forehead into Mauloa's nose. Cartilage broke. Blood flowed. The bully released his grip. Grant fell to a knee as the man backed into the crowd, his nose spewing blood.

Mauloa blinked several times. Grant rose, his chest heaving.

"You going die," the big man said, wiping his palm over his face.

His threat raised the noise level in the big tank into a roar. Metal dishes clanked along the bars. The inmates of the hell hole chanted "Kill, kill," and began a rhythmic clapping.

Grant stiffened against the cell wall. His ribs ached from Mauloa's grip, and he wondered if he had broken bones. The open space between the fighters shrank as the inmates inched closer. Mauloa clenched his fists. He stepped forward intent on ending the battle with his bare knuckles, pummeling Grant into a sack of broken bones.

CHAPTER 6

A WHIP CRACKED. "BACK away," Asing yelled. "Back, I say." The whip snaked through the bars. A turnkey rapped the iron with his baton. The prisoners retreated from the fight, crowding into each other. Men swore, shoved, and punched.

"Grant Kingsley, you will please come to the gate," Asing said. Two guards with shotguns stood by the detective as the gate opened. Grant weaved his way through the pack of prisoners, Mauloa uttered a curse saying, "Someday I'll get you pretty boy."

"Where are we going?"

Asing was silent.

At the intake room an elderly Hawaiian in a dark suit stood. You're Leinani's son," he said. "I can see her hazel eyes. I'm Joshua Kanakoa, I've come to take you home."

Grant looked at Asing, "You're free to go. Be sure to show up in court. Kanakoa will tell you when."

Parked outside the jail was a spanking new Ford Model T. "There's a hand crank by the radiator, give it a turn or two while I work the levers."

Grant grabbed the iron handle of the crank and heaved.

"Magnetos are firing. You can stop," Joshua said as the auto engine chugged into life. He abandoned the hand crank and headed to the passenger door. But Kanakoa motioned him to the driver's side of the Model T, saying, "Night driving is tough for an old guy." He slid over the hump of the drive shaft and onto the passenger seat.

"Where to?" Grant shifted the Ford into first gear.

"It's best that you stay at my house. Reporters will be all over your place tomorrow. Don't want you talking to them. Head to Alapai Street. I'll show you where I live."

Grant clutched and shifted the auto into another gear as he turned the Ford onto King Street. It was early morning. The ocean breezes sweeping through the two-seater were fresh and tangy.

"How did you know I was in trouble? How did you find me? What's going on?"

"One question at a time, I read the evening paper. Front page article about Sheila's murder and you as the killer. I've got friends in the sheriff's office. Found where you were. I got to the lockup as soon as I could, talked to Asing. He's a straight shooter..."

"Yeah, not his boss Hitchcock. He knows how to work a guy over without showing marks."

"Hitchcock is conviction happy. He has a ruthless reputation. Asing's different. He goes by the facts. That's why I convinced him to let you go."

"How did you do that? That jail house is a rat cage with the sheriff beating you until you confess."

"Territorial police are still bound by law, due process and all that. When I talked to Asing, he told me you were a prime suspect. Clarence, Mrs. Grant's butler, related a heated conversation you had with Sheila about being disinherited, and you saying, 'I will do all in my power to stop you.'"

"I admit saying something like that, but I meant to stop her from destroying my father's love for me. I wasn't concerned about any inheritance. I wouldn't kill her and I didn't."

"I believe you. Asing pointed out that you'd been through the Great War. You killed a lot of men. Maybe you snapped, went nuts."

Grant shook his head, "So I'm paying a price for doing my duty. I've become a headline. 'Crazed Soldier Kills Grandma.' Instead of a parade, I get the gallows."

"I understand your bitterness, but you have friends."

"Like you. Thank God for that."

"And thanks to five Hawaiian boys, who vouched for being with you on the night of the murder. Asing interviewed them all. They are unswerving in their declarations that you were with them, all night."

"Yeah, but Hitchcock says that white jurors won't believe Hawaiians."

"Asing believes them. He's Chinese-Hawaiian with a little white blood mixed in. It was easy to convince him that the sheriff's department must either charge you with a crime, so bail could be set, or release you. He released you into my custody."

"But didn't Hitchcock object?"

"It's Asing's case. He makes the decisions on booking and the charges to be made. There's my home. Pull into the driveway."

The gears gnashed as Grant's clutching failed to synch with his shifting. Without slowing, he swung the vehicle onto a path bordered by an unlighted single-story home. He stepped on the brakes, the hard rubber tires squealing as they slid on the dirt. The car came to a halt just short of a closed garage.

"That was exciting. You're out of practice shifting gears." Joshua laughed. He gripped Grant's arm. "One other thing Asing told me that cast doubt on your guilt. There was a note on the corpse. It said, 'Maki ka Mikanele kahuna nui o Ku.' It's Hawaiian for, 'Death to the Missionary, high priest of Ku.'"

CHAPTER 7

"THE NEWSPAPERS HAVE already found me guilty of murder," Grant said flinging a sheaf of papers onto the floor.

"That's why I didn't want you home," Joshua answered. "Reporters are snooping, searching for a story. Say the wrong thing, and you incriminate yourself."

"I can't hide with you forever."

"Let things simmer down for a while. I'll let it be known I'm your lawyer. Deny your guilt. Tell the papers you're innocent, you have an alibi. Pahoa is well liked. I'll suggest that people not jump to conclusions. Wait for the inquest."

"I appreciate that. But why are you doing this? How can I pay you?"

"Your mother was my client for many years. She was a beautiful woman. I loved her. In a platonic way, of course," Joshua added, his dark skin turning darker.

"Leinani came to see me shortly before she died. She did not have long to live and made changes in her will. Your mother also talked to me about a man we both knew, a former client of mine, John Tana."

Grant rose from his chair. "Marie d'Etienne, my mother's friend living in Paris, told me about him. Someone she and my mother both loved. What did Mom tell you?"

Joshua sighed. "There are some things I can't talk about. Attorney-client privilege. You went to law school and know the rules. But I will say this: your mother was wracked with guilt and worried about your future.

She gave me lots of money to hold for you. Made me promise to take care of you whatever might happen."

"You mean she saw the future. That someday I might be accused of murdering my grandmother?"

"No, but she was uncertain how her past might hurt you. She wanted to be sure you were protected should she die before you returned. Your mother loved you very much."

Grant rubbed his palms across his face. "My brother and sister were more than twenty years older than I. Mother always called me a 'love child.' Dad felt pleased that he could be so virile at his age. But Grandmother Grant never liked me very much."

"Not sure why. Except I know you were conceived and born in the year of the counter-revolution, 1895. The year your grandfather died from his injuries. The year John Tana disappeared."

"You think there is a connection between them?" Grant stepped up to Joshua's desk, his eyes searching the old attorney's face.

Joshua looked away. He closed his eyes as if resurrecting old memories. "Your grandfather was an enemy of John Tana. He stole his Kahului land. He had him hunted like a criminal. He accused him of raping Marie d'Etienne, which drove your mother into marriage with your father. Your grandfather may have killed John Tana's wife and son. He certainly squeezed him out of his Kaua'i land. Tana was in Honolulu at the time of the counter-revolution against the Republic."

"You think he was part of the revolt to put Lili'uokalani back on the throne? Do you believe, like Grandmother Grant, that Tana killed my grandfather during the fighting?"

"He had plenty of reason to do so, but I don't believe he did. The inquest found your grandfather died from accidental gunshot wounds inflicted by his men."

Grant fell silent, debating whether to ask the next question. Would Joshua assert attorney-client privilege and not answer? Would it create a rift between them?

Sensing his agony, Joshua said, "Time for lunch." He grabbed his hat and walked out the door, saying to his secretary—who was struggling to master the new Underwood typewriter--- "Back in a couple of hours."

Grant followed.

***

"Aloha, you naughty Hawaiian, you've been away a long time. Why haven't you come to see me? Who is this handsome man with you? Face is familiar."

"This is Grant Kingsley," Joshua said. "You remember him as a child. His mother was your godmother and namesake, Leinani Kingsley. Grant, this is Leinani Wong, long-time friend and owner of this restaurant."

Grant extended his hand to a pretty Chinese woman whom he judged to be thirty years older than he. Slender, she fitted tightly into a red silk dress slit at the knees. A large golden dragon wrapped around her hips and onto her chest, its mouth gaping. Her hair was piled high and dyed black. A string of white pearls, matched by earrings, hung around her tan neck.

"I'm so sorry your mother died," Leinani said, her brown cat-like eyes studying his face. "Our family loved her very much." Her eyes roved to the restaurant entrance. "Oh, there is my daughter and Selena."

Grant saw a beautiful Eurasian woman walk in. Men stopped talking, staring at her as she maneuvered between the lunch tables, following a young Chinese girl who came to Grant's table and said, "Hello, Momma."

"You're late," Leinani scolded. "This is Joshua Kanakoa. You've met him before, and Grant Kingsley, son of my godmother. Gentlemen, meet my daughter Lotus and her friend, Selena Choy. Come, let's eat."

Selena cast her eyes down. Grant ignored the chatter in the room as he strained to hear her soft greeting. He motioned her to the dining table and drew out a chair.

During lunch, Grant made table conversation with the others while learning more about Selena. At first the young woman was shy, but soon became animated as she spoke of her botany curriculum at the University of Hawai'i and the experiments she conducted in horticulture.

"Hawaiian sugar cane production is hampered by its excellent climate. Winters in other countries kills pests and diseases, but our constant warm weather allows them to thrive. I'm working on hybridization, the breeding of sugar cane from seed. By selecting the most resistant plants we can grow crops that are impervious to pests. Plus we are developing shoots that will produce more sugar per acre."

"That's good news for the plantation people," Grant said, "but there's more to life than academics. You need to go out and have some fun. Have you been wave sliding? Hawaiians call it *papa he'e nalu*. It's like riding Pele's lava rushing down a mountain - exciting and dangerous."

"That's intriguing, but isn't surfing done at Waikiki? Orientals are not allowed there."

"If you come with me, it will be okay. You should also try paddling a canoe, surfing in it, and racing other boats."

Selena's blue eyes sparkled when he launched into a description of the race on Kamehameha's day. "We were losing. The finish line was just ahead. Another boat had us beat. Pahoa shouted,' Imua,' and all six of us hit the water with our paddles so hard and fast that our boat shot forward and beat the All Hawai'i canoe by the length of this table."

The young girl clapped her hands, hopping up and down in her excitement. "Oh, I must try he'e nalu and canoe racing. You will show me?"

"Yes."

An old wind-up clock on the far wall chimed five. Selena put her hand to her mouth, gasped, and said, "I must go." She dashed out of the restaurant.

Grant called "Wait."

But Selena did not return. He wanted to arrange a surf riding date, learn more about her. Leinani and Lotus were in the kitchen, and Joshua had left for his law office. On an impulse, he dashed after the beautiful Eurasian. He caught a glimpse of her blue dress rounding King Street and followed her. Pedestrians slowed him. He barely saw Selena's slender legs turning onto Maunakea Street, the heart of Chinatown. Cloth banners with Chinese writing dangled over the roadway. Garish signs plastered store fronts of every building. Ignoring vendors hawking barbecued ducks and fresh fish, Grant searched the street.

Selena was gone. He ran on the hard-packed dirt, calling her name. A figure in blue disappeared through a door at the top of a second-story staircase. The building was enclosed by a wooden fence, painted red with a yellow railing along its top. He stopped at a gate suspended between two marble portals, each one topped by fiery Chinese devils. The facsimiles of evil stared at him with wide eyes and open jaws ringed with pointed porcelain teeth.

He knocked, but no one came. He tried again and called, "Selena."

From the darkness inside, a harsh voice said, "What you want?"

"I want to talk to Selena."

"What about?" someone behind him said.

Grant stepped back into the street, bumping into a man hovering by the gate.

"Watch it asshole," the man said.

"Who are you calling asshole?" Grant demanded, staring at a wiry Chinese, who stood a foot shorter and thirty pounds lighter. The man smirked and raised his hand, signaling.

Grant withdrew to the middle of the street, ignoring rickshaws trundling along the poorly paved roadway. A big man opened the gate watching him.

"Rudy Tang, that's who. This my street. Selena my girl. You no muck around with her."

"You engaged to her? Married to her?"

"You one sassy guy. No can take 'no' for answer. Maybe I cut off your balls. Stick them up your ass."

"You and what army."

"Me and those five guys coming at you."

Grant saw three men marching up Maunakea Street and two descending it. Rudy Tang smiled.

The man at the gate closed it. Two of the gang charged, one of them whirling a chain. Grant kicked, smashing his foot into the knee of an attacker who fell back into the man with the chain. Three others spread out in a crescent, hemming him in.

His opponents waited as the man wielding the chain whipped it onto the street spraying Grant with dirt. He grasped the links and pulled. The thug sprawled out on the roadway releasing his hold on the weapon. Grant seized it, whirled around, and swung it into an attacking Chinese who staggered and fell. Two others jumped onto Grant pinning his arms.

Rudy Tang came up to the struggling men, drew a knife, and said, "Now I cut off your balls and shove them up your ass."

CHAPTER 8

GRANT STRUGGLED WITH the two thugs, trying to avoid Rudy Tang's knife cuts. He managed to shove one of the men into the Chinese boss knocking him off balance.

"Hold him fast. Chow Ling grab him from behind," Rudy ordered.

Grant sensed someone at his back. He tried to swing around and fall into this new enemy with the pack of goons that held him. Before he could, a chain wrapped around his throat yanking him backward into a man's body.

"You finally locked in," Rudy said. "I do little surgery. After that, you no can love anybody."

"You will please all step away from Mr. Kingsley," a voice said.

The Chinese released the chain around Grant's neck. Grant saw the small detective Asing standing in the street.

"This is none of your business, punk," Rudy Tang said. "Get out of here."

The man with the chain flicked it out at the dark-suited man in the white Panama hat.

Asing stepped back and loosened the whip at his side. In one motion, he flung the rawhide snake around the wrist of his attacker and pulled. Tang's henchman sprawled onto the dirt of the roadway, screaming. One of the men holding Grant turned to attack the detective with a knife. The lash cut into his arm. The knife fell.

Tang gave commands in Chinese, and his men retreated from the fight. He shook his fist as he left. "Don't muck around with Selena. She's my girl." He glanced at Asing and scurried away.

"Thanks for helping. That's twice you've saved me. You're fast with that whip."

"Cowboy days. Learned to drive cattle with it. Best weapon I know. How come you're messing with Tang?"

Grant thought for a moment as to what to say, but decided he had better stick to the truth. "I was trying to see Selena Choy." Grant pointed to the house. "Tang claims Selena belongs to him. That's why his goons jumped me."

"She is very pretty. Her father is Dan Choy, maybe richest Chinese in Hawai'i and maybe biggest crook, too. I think Tang works for him. Maybe you better get out of here. More trouble could be coming."

"What about you?"

"Not to worry. Chinatown my beat, that's how I happen to see you in trouble. Nobody mess with me here. If they do, big *pilikia*." Asing laughed, pulled out a pack of cigarettes, and lit up. Grant thanked the detective and headed for Joshua's office.

***

"Dan Choy's a formidable character. He owns a lot of Chinatown. I didn't realize that Selena is his daughter," Joshua said, drinking coffee and munching toast at the breakfast table of his three-bedroom home. He was seventy-five. A widower who lived alone. "But you better forget about her. We have to find Sheila's killer. Hitchcock is under a lot of political pressure to solve the case. The killer threatened death to all missionaries and their descendants. Those are powerful people in these islands. If Hitchcock can't find another suspect, he might turn back to you."

Grant studied his hands. "We have nothing to work on. Only some note from the killer saying something about Ku. Who is Ku?"

"Ku-kai-ilimoku was King Kamehameha's personal war god, a blood-thirsty guy always wanting more human sacrifices. The man whose day we just celebrated gave him plenty of bodies to feast on. Asing didn't tell me all the details of the killing. We might have to wait for the inquest to learn everything, but he did say that Sheila Grant was killed in the traditional way that humans were sacrificed to Ku."

"That's bizarre. If you want to kill, just do it. Why go through some kind of ritual mumbo jumbo? It doesn't make sense. Besides, Sheila wasn't a missionary."

"But Robert Grant's father was. He came over on the third boatload of Christian ministers. The man was smart. He used his position as a missionary to acquire land and get rich. He made lots of money producing and selling sugar."

"You think there's a connection between the worship of Ku and Grant's father?"

"It's possible. The early missionaries were given credit for ending idolatry in Hawai'i and terminating the practice of sacrificing humans."

"But that was a hundred years ago. All the priests and worshipers of Ku must be dead."

"Old traditions and beliefs take a long time to die. There are still Hawaiians who believe in the old gods. You mentioned Pele, the volcano goddess, to Selena. So maybe you believe, too."

"Everybody living in Hawai'i has heard stories about Pele. That doesn't make me a believer in the pagan gods. How are we going to find a high priest of Ku among all the Hawaiians in Honolulu?"

"We have to find a *kahuna*."

"Where? In the phone directory?" His thoughts strayed to Selena, a beautiful woman with a mysterious father and a sinister boyfriend. He thought of Rudy Tang, his gang, and his threats. Maybe it wasn't smart, challenging him. He had to watch his temper. It was good to get angry in wartime, but not in peacetime, especially in Hawai'i.

A loud voice woke him. "Grant, did you hear what I said? We should talk with Malia Makanani. She's old and wise in the ancient ways."

"You mean Aunt Malia. Yeah, sure. Can you run me home on your way to work? My dad's coming in on the inter-island steamer this morning. He wants to see me."

CHAPTER 9

GRANT WATCHED HIS father stride off the gangplank of the *Manulani*, a small suitcase in his hand. There were no festive greeters for the inter-island ship like there had been on "steamer day." Visitors coming from far away were a novelty, but local travelers were not.

Grant had bought a lei from a vendor who squatted by the pier stringing flowers together. He hung it over his father's neck saying, "Welcome home, Dad." The older man scowled, gave him a curt nod, followed by a frown, and said nothing. Charles came to them and took the suitcase.

Except for the noise of the engine, complete silence blanketed the drive to Waikiki. Grant suspected that whatever his dad had to say would be said in private. He hadn't noticed any photographers or reporters at the pier, but he felt sure that at some time they would ask prying questions. Gossipers loved to be titillated by a family scandal and a murder.

Sue Watanabe greeted them, her face wreathed in smiles as she bowed several times to her master. "Many phone calls from newspapers. Want interviews. Do you wish breakfast, sir?"

"None will be given," Kingsley said. "Charles, you may go. Thank you, Sue, no breakfast needed. If you would return to the kitchen, it would be appreciated. Grant, follow me into the study, please."

His father's curt manner made him shiver. Was he to be denounced as a bastard, disinherited, accused of Sheila's murder? Trench warfare was easier. You knew what to expect: sudden death. So far his return to Hawai'i had been filled with accusations, tirades, and beatings, all for deeds that are not his doing. He felt alone in his fight to maintain his heritage. He needed someone who believed in him.

"Did you kill her?" his father said as they settled into chairs in the study.

He hadn't expected the accusation to come so quickly. It spilled out without preliminary words of affection or "I believe in you." It was a question Asing had asked with politeness. A query Hitchcock posed with brutality. Grant gave the same answer he had given many times before, "I did not." He fell silent, studying his father's face. Does he still love me?

"The newspapers said that after a big argument, you swore to stop her. Did you say that?"

"There was an argument. I was angry because of the accusations Grandmother made. The ugly words she used about my mother. The threats she made. I did say "I will do all in my power to stop you." I was emotional and spoke without thinking. I'm sorry for what I said. I did not kill her."

Kingsley sighed. His body sagged. He put his hands to his head, rubbing it. Tears welled in his eyes. Grant looked away, glancing through a window at Diamond Head, the dead crater where early European sailors had found large deposits of small crystalline glass they thought to be diamonds. He watched surfers far out at sea catching the waves at First Break. He wondered if Pahoa was with them, riding a wave curling toward shore.

"This has been a hard time for me. Your mother died from the Spanish flu. I loved her very much. She left an unfinished note on her desk, before lapsing into a coma. It was startling. I shared it with Sheila. That was a horrible mistake. When she read it, a blistering tirade followed. She made threats and demands. I never told you about them. I hoped we could have a sane discussion when you returned home from the war. I never expected she would be killed." Kingsley cupped his face in his hands, his body trembling.

Grant stood uncertain as to what to do. Comfort his dad? He feared rejection. Go away? But it would leave their relationship unresolved. "Dad, I promise you I did not kill Sheila Grant. Why she hated my mother and hated me I don't understand. But I did not kill her."

Kingsley looked up. Grant saw redness in his father's eyes. "I believe you, but the papers don't, and the police are suspicious. I would hate to see our good name dragged into the mud. Your mother's infidelity exposed for people to whisper about."

"What infidelity?" Grant said, though he suspected the truth from the letter he received on the battlefield. He saw his father hesitate. Tears brimmed and overflowed onto his cheeks.

"Let's not talk about it. Except you should know why Sheila was angry. In her last letter, your mother admits to helping a Hawaiian by the name of John Tana. It said that Tana was a revolutionary attempting to put Lili'uokalani back on the throne. It says that this man tried to kill your grandfather during the revolution. A revolt squashed in January 1895."

"And I was born October 10, 1895," whispered Grant.

"Son, we will talk about this later. I have to go to Sheila's funeral. After the burial, there will be a reception at the Grant mansion. I'll be gone all afternoon and into the night."

"Should I come with you?"

"I think not. There will be press at the funeral, sugar people, and missionary families. All are friends of Sheila. It could get ugly if you are there. She was well liked."

Grant watched Charles drive his father away. At the beginning of their meeting, he thought his dad would denounce his mother and disinherit him. Yet the anger that must have been building for months was gone.

Why did his mother reveal those ugly secrets instead of taking them with her to the grave? He knew she was a devout Christian. With death imminent, he supposed she wanted to confess her guilt, cleanse her soul. But she created an emotional dilemma for him and his father. He needed to ease the pain in his heart.

He thought of Selena maybe he would teach her surfing.

33

CHAPTER 10

HE TOOK A bus to the University of Hawai'i. Grant found the mom-and-pop store Selena described where students hung out after school. He waited for classes to end, bought sushi, and soon saw Lotus and Selena walking toward the Japanese shop. Lotus spied him first and came over, dragging Selena.

They made small talk for a while, but when Grant mentioned surfing, Selena became excited. "Come with me to Waikiki," Grant said. "Outside the Moana Hotel, at a place we call Queen's Surf, you can enjoy the greatest ride of your life."

"Lotus, let's go."

"Like to, but I got to return the car to the restaurant. Only one we have."

"Can you drop us at the Moana in Waikiki?" Grant asked.

"Sure can."

***

"Lie on the board, face down," Grant said, bobbing beside Selena dressed in a body-length bathing suit with a rubber cap covering her hair. As he looked at her well-shaped body, slender hips and legs, he thought it strange that the law required she be fully clothed to swim. Men and women in ancient times rode the waves naked, but when the missionaries came they frowned on this and prohibited surfing. Fortunately his friend Pahoa had brought the ancient art back to life, defying all conventions.

A wave washed over them, heading toward shore a quarter of a mile away. "Selena, when you see it beginning to break, kick with your feet and stroke like crazy with your hands. Try to stay in the wall of the curve and avoid the foam. Can you do it?"

Selena smiled, her blue eyes sparkling. "Watch me."

A wave came. Grant gave her board a shove. Selena's slim arms stroked furiously. The board skewered as the wave crested and she fell off. The surfboard bobbed in the foam. Grant swam to retrieve it, then returned to where Selena tread water. "Don't push," she said.

On her third try, she caught a wave, dashing on it halfway to shore. Grant urged her to try standing on the board. "Once you get going, kneel, check your balance, and rise up. Use your arms to avoid falling."

"Okay, boss man," Selena gave him a wicked smile. She caught the next wave, got to her knees, wobbled for a moment, then stood in a crouch, her hands behind her. The wave rose in height, white foam flecking the sides of the surfboard. Like a hawk diving for prey, Selena raced to the shore.

Grant swam after her, finally reaching the laughing, exhilarated woman where the waves washed onto the sand.

"That was great. Did you see me angle along the wave with my foot?"

"You rode like an expert."

"Hey, what you guys doing,?" Keoki asked, one of the beach boys of Hui O Nalu. "You like come with us? We are going paddle canoe."

"Let's do it," Selena said clapping her hands.

For the rest of the afternoon, four beach boys, Selena, and Grant caught the waves at Queen's Surf. Selena stroked with an effortless vigor, matching the strength of the male paddlers driving the canoe through the water. The sun was bending over the Waianae Mountains when they finally pulled to shore.

"I don't want to, but I guess I'd better head home," Selena said.

"Why don't you stay for dinner?" Grant asked. "The Moana has a great outdoor restaurant. The evening looks like it will be beautiful."

"The hotel will not serve Chinese. Besides all I have is my school dress."

"No worry," Keoki said. "Plenty good shops in the hotel. This guy got money. What you say, brother?" The beach boy laughed, giving Grant a nudge with his elbow.

"Clothes will not be a problem," Grant said, "and I think a beauty shop is still open and they can fix you up to be stunning. With the right makeup you can pass for white and I know the maitre d' so don't worry."

"But what will I tell my father?"

"How old are you?"

"Almost twenty."

"Then maybe this is the time to assert your independence."

Selena laughed, "You don't know my father." She frowned for a moment, and then her eyes brightened. "I'll do it. I'll telephone home right now and arrange it. After I call, shall I meet you in the dress shop?"

"Yes,"

***

The high oriental twang of the steel guitar filled the banyan tree-shaded courtyard of the Moana Hotel. The artist manipulated the heavy steel bar over the strings, dampening and bending the notes into a languorous combination of harmonious melody.

Selena closed her eyes as she listened. Grant studied her face. The trade winds blew strands of long dark hair across her cheeks. Beautiful, he thought. Her supple body, fitted into a red and brown tropical print dress, swayed in time to the music. A moon peeping above the Ko'olau Range silvered the waters of Waikiki. Slow waves swished up and back along the beach, adding a rhythmic background to the guitars.

"When you called your father and told him you were at the Moana Hotel with a date, what did he say?" Grant asked, as he circled his cut ahi in a sauce of soy and ginger root.

"I couldn't get through for a while. We have a party line. I finally spoke to my brother. He was unhappy, but I told him I am old enough to make decisions for myself. I said I would be home by ten."

"Did you tell him whom you were with?"

"I think he could guess. Come, let's dance."

At first there was a respectful distance between them. Grant didn't want to push his luck. He guided Selena along the spangled cement floor without holding her too tight, stepping in time to the music of the guitars.

"I had a wonderful time today," Selena murmured after a half hour of easy dancing. A male voice sang a song of love, and she drew Grant to her. The soft curves of her body melded with his, her cheek nestled into his shoulder.

Grant enjoyed her fragrance, her breath on his skin. The tensions Sheila created slowly eased. He felt relaxed. Selena's warmth relieved the stress that plagued him.

A hand tapped his shoulder. It broke Grant's dream. Angry, he stopped dancing and faced the hotel maître. "I'm sorry, sir. The blue laws of Waikiki do not permit intimacy."

Grant's jaw tensed. He wanted to shout at the man for spoiling the beautiful moment. He held his tongue, realizing that he did not want trouble. "What do you mean intimate?"

"The affectionate touching of skin between adults in public is intimate and prohibited by law," the maitre d'hôtel answered, his posture stiffening.

Flustered, Selena said, "Time for me to leave." She broke from Grant, gathered her bag, and rushed up the stairs toward the hotel exit. Grant followed her, leaping two steps at a time. Guests in the dining room smiled, some whispered to each other. One man stood and followed the fleeing couple.

At the bottom of the steps of the curved driveway at the entrance to the hotel, Selena stopped. "I don't have any money. How will I get home?"

"Taxi," Grant called as he came up behind her. He checked with the cabbie for the cost to drive Selena to Maunakea Street and paid the fare. When he opened the car door, she said, "I loved my day with you. Let's do it again." She ducked her head in, then pulled back and said, "To hell with the blue laws." She raised herself on her toes, reaching her hand to the back of his head, pulling his face toward her lips. They kissed long and hard. A honk came from the cab behind. Selena drew away and slipped into her taxi.

"Wow." Grant watched the car chugging around the driveway. In its turn onto the road, he noticed a Japanese man in a black suit standing by the pillars of the hotel entrance, staring at him. Tourist, he thought, or maybe a reporter. He rushed from the Moana, running along the roadway toward home.

Within a short distance, three men in dark pajamas blocked his path. He swerved to avoid them, but two other men rose from the bushes beside the road, hemming him in. A voice from behind said, "I told you to leave my girl alone."

Grant turned sideways and saw Rudy Tang with another man in dark pajamas. "She doesn't have a ring on her finger nor words on her chest saying Property of a Prick."

"You one cocky guy. I'm goin' slice you with this *leiomano* Cut off your balls and stick in your mouth. Then feed you to the fish."

Grant eyed the shark-toothed weapon held in Rudy's hand, its restraining cord wrapped firmly around his palm. The second man whirled a chain. The other men to his front and side closed in. He charged a pajama-clad Chinese on his left, knocking him down with a crisp right elbow to the face. A truncheon whacked his back. He pivoted and swung a left into the mid-section of his attacker. Two weak blows from the hard rubber club smacked him on his side. He kicked out the man's knee with his foot. Someone grabbed his arm. Another man tackled him, bringing Grant down onto the roadway. He struggled up, but two men seized him and pinned his hands behind his back.

Rudy swaggered to him, stopping a short distance away. He waved his shark-toothed knife in Grant's face. "I'm going to slash your body, then stick my knife between your legs and rip upward." He smiled and raised his leiomano across his shoulder, poised to slice it across Grant's chest. Grant tried to twist away from the shark-toothed knife.

"Hold him steady," Rudy ordered. Three men gripped Grant tight, one of them entangling his legs. Helpless, Grant watched a smiling Rudy Tang raise his leiomano for the killing sweep of the shark teeth.

CHAPTER 11

GRANT HEARD RUNNING feet and a crisp, "*Baka.*" Rudy Tang's smile vanished as he smashed into the men in front of him. The razor-sharp shark's teeth sliced across Grant's shoulder and upper chest. He stumbled into the three accomplices. All four men fell backward onto the road.

Tang recovered his balance. A voice said, "So sorry." The three thugs and Grant struggled to their feet, blood coloring his shirt from the shallow cuts of the shark knife. He smashed a fist into the belly of one of the men followed by a right cross to the jaw. Something hard struck the back of his head, and he sprawled onto the ground.

Tang yelled, "Get that son of a bitch," pointing his leiomano at a heavy-set Japanese standing in the road. Grant recognized him - the same man who stood outside the Moana Hotel. "Watch out," he yelled as four of Rudy's henchmen closed in.

A whirlwind of movement followed, as the Japanese kicked, slashed his hands, twisted his body. In moments, four attackers lay on the ground, groaning. Only Rudy, the man with the chain, and one other remained standing.

Grant sat in the dirt. His head ached. His shirt wet with blood.

Rudy tensed his body, the leiomano slicing the air like a woodcutter. The man with the chain swung its links. The other goon drew a knife. Someone among the fallen started to rise, then fell back.

The Japanese emitted a loud, "*Baka,*" leaped, pivoted and slammed a foot into the stomach of the chain-wielder. In a smooth twist of his body, he stabbed his foot into the side of the man with the knife, smashing his open palm onto his neck.

Rudy watched the last of his men falling. He stared at the Japanese, scowled, and lowered his weapon. "Okay, you win. No more trouble. We go." He issued orders in Chinese. His gang slunk off into the night. Shouts came from the hotel. Someone yelled, "Call the police."

The Japanese walked up to Grant. "Are you all right, Mr. Kingsley?"

"Head's bursting. Blood all over my shirt, but I'm okay. Who are you? How did you know who I am?"

"Your name and picture were in the newspapers. I am Noboru Sato."

"Thank you for saving me. What is the method of fighting you used to beat Rudy's gang? I have never seen anyone move so fast."

"It is called jujitsu, a Japanese martial art. May I take you to a doctor? Hospital?"

"I'd be obliged if you helped me to my home. It is not far away."

Sato placed an arm around Grant's chest and walked him the short distance to his house. At the door, he placed Grant into Sue Watanabe's care, pressed his card into Grant's hand, bowed, and left.

"Japanese Counsel Attaché, Noboru Sato," Grant read the card. "Mr. Sato, you are some kind of fighter. I wouldn't want to mess with you in a dark alley."

***

"Glad you're up and about," Joshua said, as he stood outside the court-house. "You spent time in the hospital?"

"Yeah, hurt worse than I thought from the fight with Rudy Tang. Charles took me to the emergency room. I had a lump on my head. Doctors said I had a hematoma, maybe under the skin or inside my skull. They kept me for observation."

"Why the attack? Who is the stranger that saved you?" Robert Kingsley asked.

"The man who helped me is attached to the Japanese Consul in Hawai'i. He happened to be at the Moana Hotel the same time I was with Selena."

Joshua chuckled. "It's always a girl, and a beautiful one at that, who gets a guy in trouble."

"Stay away from her," Kingsley warned. "You're in a serious predicament. I don't want you involved in petty jealousies."

Joshua put his hand on Grant's shoulder. "You need to prove your innocence. The inquest today is important. Stay away from distractions. Concentrate on finding the killer of Sheila Grant."

Grant listened but did not agree with them. He could find a way to solve the crime and still stay in touch with Selena. The three men filed into the courthouse and entered the hearing room.

"All rise," the bailiff ordered. "This inquest is now in session, the Honorable Christopher Wright presiding." A tall, slender, white-haired man assumed a seat at a wide desk at the front of a crowded room.

"Who's the judge?" Grant asked.

"Wright is from an old-time missionary family. He was an attorney with one of the kamaina law firms. He served in the House of Nobles during the monarchy. After the revolution, he became a leader in the Legislature of the Republic of Hawai'i. After annexation, he was appointed by Governor Dole to the Court. He's retired but comes back to handle special cases like this one. I know him. He's a good Christian."

The inquest began with Clarence the butler testifying that Mrs. Grant had returned home from the Kamehameha Day celebrations exhausted. She dismissed him at nine o'clock in the evening. His custom was to lock all the doors, secure the front driveway gate, and retire to the servant's cottage behind the main house.

His wife, the maid and cook, entered the home at six o'clock the next day, June 12, to prepare breakfast and clean. She alerted him that something was amiss, and he found Mrs. Grant's dead body in the downstairs den. He called the police.

Detective Asing testified that he was first on the scene from the sheriff's office. He found Mrs. Grant in a pool of dried blood on her koa desk in the mansion's den. The woman's mouth was held open by a cloth tied between her teeth. A bone fishhook was anchored in her jaw, a cord of sennit attached to it. Apparently she had been hooked in her bedroom and dragged down the stairs to the den. The body had been ripped in three long cuts by what appeared to be razors. There was a deep penetration wound at the heart. Weapons were not found at the scene. Dried salt covered her body. There was a mat of seaweed and coconut fiber at her feet. "Above her head," Asing testified, "was a note in red ink. It read, *'Mikanele make kahuna nui o Ku.'*

"What does it mean?" Judge Wright asked.

"Death to missionaries, High priest of Ku," Asing answered.

Grant nudged Kanakoa. "The killer is the high priest of Ku. Not me. How do we find him?"

"If such a person exists, it would be like seeking the proverbial needle in a haystack," Joshua answered. "Really don't know what to make of it. Let's listen to the coroner."

Jonathon Small testified that he had examined the body and found three long cuts, two in the shape of an X across the breasts and a third cut in a straight line from the pubic hair to the throat. "The cuts were painful, bled a lot, but none caused death," Small said. "The cuts were not made by a razor. The wounds were jagged like a crosscut saw sliced the body. Death was caused by a single penetrating wound into the heart. There was something curious that I found at the site of the killing wound." The coroner paused in his testimony, looked at the judge, and then at the audience. Grant wondered if he was holding back something incredible, beyond belief.

Judge Wright fumed. "Well, out with it. What did you find?"

"A broken piece of the death weapon."

"What kind of metal? Iron? Steel? Brass?"

"No. It was the tip of the bill of a swordfish."

***

Outside the hearing room, Grant shook his head. "Have you ever heard anything so bizarre? The killer dragged someone to her death with a fishhook. The murder weapon he used was the bill of a swordfish."

"It is unusual," Joshua answered. "The killer went to a lot of trouble to make it look like a ritualistic killing by a Hawaiian high priest. I can see why Asing let you go. It wasn't just your alibi witnesses."

"There's the detective right now. Let's speak with him," Grant said.

"You men talk to Asing. I'm going to say hello to Wright, then I'm off to Sheila's home. I need to start the inventory."

"Inventory?" Grant said. "Why?"

"I'm the new trustee of Robert Grant's estate."

"New trustee," Joshua said. "He's got the same powers to disinherit that Sheila Grant had."

Asing lounged by a large banyan tree, a cigarette dangling loosely from his mouth.

Grant reached out his hand. "I want to thank you again for saving me from Rudy's gang and letting me out of jail."

The ruddy face of the Chinese broke into a slow smile. His eyes twinkled as he said, "You didn't fit my image of the high priest of Ku. That's why I let you go."

"It wasn't the alibi witnesses?"

"They helped. But to tell the truth, I couldn't see why a man like you would go through all that craziness to kill Sheila Grant. Stab her with a knife, and it's over. There is something about this murder I haven't figured out yet, but I will."

"How was entry made into the residence if all the doors were locked?" Joshua asked.

"Someone broke through a screen covering an open second-story window. The killer climbed onto a window seat and padded down the hallway to the bedroom. You know the rest."

"How did the killer get to the second story?" Joshua asked.

"We don't know. A man would need a twenty-foot ladder and help pulling it over a spiked six-foot iron fence. Drag it to the house without leaving marks."

"You think two guys did it?" Grant asked.

"Maybe, but in the absence of evidence of two or more men doing the killing, you and Clarence became the prime suspects. He had a key to everything and you knew the house and maybe knew a way to get in."

"Well, I didn't do it and I never had a key. What about Clarence?"

"Like you, he's got an alibi. His wife vouches for him. We searched his cottage, no weapons or bloody clothes. So far he checks out."

"Did Hitchcock beat him like he beat me, or did he lay off because the butler's white?"

"Don't push it. It's not Hitchcock's case, it's mine. If you're the guy, I'll get you from the facts, nothing else."

"You know I'm not the guy. I'm going to get the killer, whoever he is."

"Stay out of it. Let me handle the investigation."

"I appreciate that, but my life is on the line. Your buddy Hitchcock is sure I killed Sheila. My fingerprints are probably all over that love-seat. I was in the second-story hallway the day I saw her. I've got to find that high priest. Goodbye."

"Where are you going?" Joshua said.

"I'm paying a visit to Sato. Then I'm off to Aunt Malia to find out about kahuna."

CHAPTER 12

GRANT PAUSED AT the entrance to the Japanese Consulate, not far from the shipping piers of Honolulu. The building had deteriorated over the years from the heavy salt air blowing in from the sea. The harbor was quiet, with only two freighters off-loading cargo.

In the building, he inquired of Sato, but learned that the Japanese attaché was off to Kaimuki working on a festive project. Grant left a thankyou note and a present and headed to Moiilili, on the outskirts of Waikiki.

He drove his new Studebaker with its canvas top down along a roadway bordered by rows of coconut trees. He headed around Punchbowl Crater, an extinct volcano that created the land upon which the town of Honolulu was built. The area around the tuff cone was sparsely settled, and Grant thought the reason could be the talk of turning the crater into a cemetery. So far the people of the town had rejected the idea. Nobody wanted a city of the dead looming over a city of the living.

The macadam road changed to dirt. He passed patches of rice fields with neat rows of slender green stalks poking through muddy water. He saw two yoked buffaloes pulling a wooden plow, guided by a thin Japanese in a straw hat.

Used to be Hawaiians growing taro, Grant thought, then Chinese with their ducks. Now Japanese had transformed from plantation workers to rice farmers.

The fields ended, and he motored by a string of shanties bordering a running stream. Clotheslines of white laundry hung out in long strings along the waterway. He noticed enclosed sheds hanging over the stream and guessed that none of the hovels had indoor plumbing. He steered onto a dirt lane. Chickens pecking on the roadway scattered, clucking and crowing in protest of his passage. He braked to a stop at a well-kept green-painted cottage.

Grant opened the white gate of the picket fence and climbed the steps to the front door. He knocked, and a young girl opened it. "Is Aunt Malia in?" he asked.

"Who dat?"

"It's me, Auntie. Grant Kingsley."

"No stand outside, come in. Come eat. Lehua, get some food for the boy."

Grant stepped inside. On a rocker in the room sat an ancient white-haired woman. She smiled a toothless smile. Her chair became agitated, producing crackling sounds from the woven lauhala leaf mat covering the floor. Grant thought Malia to be at least eighty-five, but her eyes sparkled with life as she motioned him over. "Long time you no come see Auntie. Where you been? Come give kiss. Lehua, where food for nephew?"

"Please, nothing to eat. I came because of Sheila Grant, my step-grandmother. She was murdered a few days ago. The killer might be a Hawaiian high priest."

Malia's chair rocked fast. In a reedy voice, she said, "I know her. She no like me. She no like your mother. She no like any Hawaiians. She too high class for brown people. Too bad she die. Why you say killer Hawaiian priest?"

Grant told her about the evidence at the inquest. He also admitted to being a suspect. He finished, saying, "I don't understand what all those strange rituals mean. Joshua Kanakoa said you might know or that you could direct me to a kahuna who could explain them."

Malia closed her eyes, rocked slowly in her chair, and said, "When I born old gods all gone. I raised Christian. No believe in them, but many people still believe. Dis Ku-kai-ilimoku, name means 'Destroyer of Islands,' worshipped by Kamehameha. Every time he go fight, he build *luakini* he-iau. *Lua* means hole, *kini* means forty thousand. The lua was placed by the altar and statue of Ku so da god could watch the sacrifices being pushed into the hole. Get two temples to Ku by Diamond Head, near where you live, maybe one more out by Waianae."

The old woman paused, catching her breath. Grant studied her, noticing the frailty of her hands, the mottled skin of her feet. She was ancient, but wonderful. She raised his mother when her Hawaiian mother died in childbirth. On an impulse, he asked, "Did you know John Tana?"

Malia's eyes opened. Her rocking stopped. "Yes. He was my nephew. Good man." Through eyes rheumy with age she studied Grant, as if thinking of what more she should say. She sighed. "No find kahuna in Honolulu. They outlaws. You go Kaneohe. Makanani family live there. Plenty old Hawaiians live there. Long trip, come early tomorrow. Take Lehua. She show you where."

Malia's eyes closed. Her rocking stopped. Grant left, whispering to Lehua that he would return in the morning. Driving home, he thought of Malia, her relationship with John Tana, and his mother. She knew something. He would speak to her again, but first he must solve the puzzle of Sheila Grant's murder.

***

"Windy road," Grant said as he zigzagged along the curves of the mountain highway. "Scary too. Six-hundred-foot drop on the other side."

Lehua sat beside him, ignoring the spectacular views spreading out beyond the dangerous Pali Highway. The backside of the Ko'olau range sparkled golden green in the early morning sun. Waterfalls sliced ridges into the stone as they fell onto the floor of the valley. For miles, the land was covered with fields of sprouting rice and broad-leafed taro plants. Copses of banana and coconut trees grew among the fields, with an occasional dwelling beside them.

"Which way?" Grant said as his Studebaker coasted into Kailua.

Lehua pointed the direction and continued to point as they traveled out of the small town and drove along the magnificent sweep of Kaneohe Bay. Minutes passed, and they saw only an occasional fisherman along the shore. Finally, Lehua pointed towards the mountains and Grant steered onto a dirt path that soon became a packed earth berm between taro fields. They traveled into woods of coconut trees and banana tubers. Lehua screamed, "Stop the car. Rose, Lukela, it's me."

Two children near Lehua's age emerged from the brush as Grant stopped. His companion popped from the car and spoke to them. "Hey, Lehua," Grant called as the young girl walked away with her friends, "where do I find the Makanani house?"

"Just follow that path."

Grumbling, Grant left the car and found a narrow trail into the woods. He walked until he became confused when he faced a wall of banana trees. He pushed his way into the tall tubers, and burst into a small clearing. He saw a still for making alcohol.

"Hey brah, what you doing here," an angry voice said. With a menacing stare, a big Hawaiian rose from a stool and stepped away from the broad green branches that hid him.

"Just looking for the Makanani house."

"What you want with them? I think you one cop. Come snooping around."

"I'm not a cop."

The Hawaiian reached over and grabbed Grant's shirt and belt. He tried to resist, but his attacker held him. The giant lifted Grant and flung him into the banana trees. The slender, pliable tubers crackled as his body plowed into them. Juice from the bent stalks covered his clothes and body with sticky slime. The air from his lungs escaped. He lay on the ground gasping.

Grant saw the man clenching his fists. They were as big as hams and lethal.

The Hawaiian stepped toward him. Desperate, he scrambled deeper into the brush saying, "Hold it. Aunt Malia Makanani sent me. I brought Lehua with me."

The giant stopped, "You brought Lehua, my sister?"

"I think she might be, although I don't know who you are."

"Abel Makanani. Where is she? Lehua," he yelled.

"Over here, brother," the young girl answered.

The big man smiled. "Sorry about that. What you want?"

"I'm looking for a kahuna."

"Okay, brah, come with me."

***

Grant drove slowly along the curves, the late afternoon sun catching his eyes with flashes of painful light. The cliff dropped sheer on the right side of his car.

He pondered what he learned from the kahuna. It had cost ten dollars. The information from the old woman had not identified the killer, but she had explained the meaning of the rituals. He needed to talk with Asing, share what he learned.

His Studebaker chugged to the summit of the Pali Highway. The wind from the sea blasted with a force so strong that Grant thought it would turn the car over. This was the point where Kamehameha's soldiers pushed the Oahu army over the cliffs many years ago. He bent low, peering at the road descending toward Honolulu. The shaman had given him information about sacrifices to Ku. Somewhere in all that he learned there must be an answer to the murder.

CHAPTER 13

"**W**E ARE AGREED," Judge Wright said as a referee, dressed in the robes of a Shinto priest, his voice high and nasal, announced the upcoming bout. The sumo wrestlers, squatting like crabs, lifted their legs high in the air, stomping hard on the purified sand and clay of the ring.

"They stomp hard on the ground to frighten the demons away," Dan Choy said, avoiding a direct answer. He glanced to the side and gave a nod to Rudy Tang, who stood and walked through a crowd of Japanese waiting to see the beginning of the match between two first level *rikishi*. "Those wrestlers are young. I'm sure they will try hard to make it a good fight." Choy observed.

"You're a slippery man, won't give me a direct answer to my questions. The HSPA wants to know, will you bring more Chinese laborers into Hawai'i?"

Choy gave Judge Wright a scornful look. "For years you sugar people brought Chinese to work at dirt cheap wages. When they protested, you stopped importing my people. You discriminated against them and flooded the sugar fields with other races. 'Divide and rule,' HSPA said. Now that the Japanese and Filipinos are striking you want to bring in Chinese again. More divide and rule."

"You have made lots of money from the sugar people," Wright answered. "Don't kill the goose that lays the golden egg. Have we got a deal?"

Choy grimaced. He looked out at the audience, then up to the canopy overhead, studying the four different-colored tassels on each corner that signify the seasons of the year. "Yes. My usual cut?"

Wright stood. "I've had enough of watching overweight men bash each other. Time for some fun." His smile broadened into a grin. "We have a deal."

***

It was dark when Grant dropped Lehua at Malia's cottage. Driving home, he thought of Selena. He hadn't called her, worried that phone calls were being intercepted. Instead, he reached out to Lotus, who promised to arrange a date. Grant heard nothing. He debated whether to call Selena. But would he appear anxious? Get her into trouble? Instead, should he play it cool, hold his desire in check? Make her contact him?

Dreaming, Grant found himself at his Waikiki house. He parked and walked in, his mind fogged with a mounting desire to see Selena. Sue Watanabe met him saying, "Letter for you."

His name and address were on the envelope. He parted the seal and opened it.

Ku will have his missionary where the sea meets the heiau and kites fly on high surf. Kahuna nui.

Another murder was imminent! He thought. Should he call Asing? But where's the temple? He decided to call Malia. Lehua answered, saying, "Auntie asleep."

"Wake her."

"No can." Lehua hung up.

Though he felt frantic, Grant forced himself to be calm. He thought back on what Malia had said yesterday, "Two Ku temples at Waikiki and one out in Waianae."

The one in Waianae was in the hills. It left the two Ku temples below Diamond Head. But which one was "by the sea where kites flew?" Pahoa would know. He raced for the Moana Hotel and the Hui O Nalu Canoe Club.

CHAPTER 14

WRIGHT WAS EXCITED by the woman. He had not known such love-making was possible. It had started with play in the hot tub. Then gentle massaging raised a passion that he thought dead.

Wright lay on his back, exhausted but exhilarated by the pleasure of the evening. The woman caressed his toes, rubbed his thighs. Oh, God, he would like to try again, but he couldn't perform.

"Curfew time," he said, saving himself from embarrassment. "I have to go home, nine o'clock."

"*Hai. Go-men na sai. Sayonara,*" the nude prostitute said.

"Yes, I'm sorry, too. *Arigato.*"

The geisha got to her feet, wrapped a kimono around her body, and helped the Judge dress. She did not kiss him, instead bowing many times and saying, "*Arigato. Sayonara.*"

Wright entered his 1920 Packard Phaeton. He started the engine and listened to the six cylinders purring. The car had set him back more than $3,000. He could afford it, settling the labor strike for the HSPA had made him a ton of money.

He drove onto Kahala Street, motored around Diamond Head crater and lurched onto Monsarrat Road. He felt and heard rubber thumping and pulled to the curb, a short distance from Kapi'olani. Night hid the trees, only a sighing of leaves made him aware of the park. He felt the tires wondering how both could have gone flat at the same time.

Headlights approached. Wright stepped into the roadway, waving. The driver turned off his lights and coasted to a stop in front of him. A dark shape exited the vehicle.

"Thank the Lord you came," Wright said, extending his hand.

The stranger slapped his ears. Stunned, the judge choked, unable to yell. A chopping blow slammed into the back of his neck. His hands and legs became useless. Bolts of jagged light flashed through Wright's head. Fingers seized his throat, pressing hard. Everything became black.

***

Grant raced into the Moana Hotel and grasped the arm of an attendant dressed in a white coat, black bowtie, and dark pants, "Where is Pahoa?"

"Sir, you are not dressed in proper evening attire."

"Look, a murder is about to be committed. I need to find Pahoa."

"I'm sorry, sir, but the rules are that unless you are on the beach all those who come to the hotel at night must have a coat and tie."

"I don't have time to argue," Grant said, brushing past the attendant. He shoved into a group of tuxedo-suited men and women dressed in white silk gowns garnished with pearls or diamonds around their throats. The hotel servant pursued him. Grant ignored his calls. From the beach came the pleasant music of guitars, a ukulele, and the singing of a Hawaiian song.

He raced through the dining area, crowded with supper tables spaced in a crescent around an open courtyard and a large banyan tree in its center. Waiters in crisp white coats and starched stiff shirts moved between the tables. Grant barely avoided colliding with them. Diners paused to stare as he dashed past in his colorful short-sleeved shirt and tan pants.

Following the sound of the music, Grant stepped onto a slatted walkway. His eyes caught the flicker of a small beach fire beyond a copse of coco trees. Outlined in the darkness were silhouettes of swaying bodies hovering near the flames. He raced along the wooden path, drawn to the burning wood by a singer's voice blending smoothly with the strumming of guitars.

A crescent moon shone onto the calm waters of Waikiki. In the far distance Grant could see the winking light at Ka'ena Point at the apex of the massive Waianae range. A Ku temple lay out there, but he knew that the heiau he sought had been built behind him, below the slopes of Diamond Head.

"Pahoa," Grant shouted as the song ended. His feet crunched into the sand of the beach, slowing his run to a walking pace. "Hey, Pahoa," he called again. Some of the small crowd toasting wieners at the beach fire grumbled, "Don't make noise. Listen to the music."

Grant searched the musicians. He saw Keoki with a guitar. Pahoa rose, "Hey, what's up Kingsley?"

"There's a murder that's happened or is about to happen. You have to help me. I got a message saying, 'Ku will have his missionary where the sea meets the heiau and kites fly on high surf.' The temple's below Diamond Head, but where?"

"Maybe somebody having fun with you?"

"But why use 'Ku' and sign the message, 'kahuna nui'? I learned that those Hawaiian words signify the high priest of Kamehameha's war god. It can't be a joke."

"But why would you get a message about a sacrifice to Ku? Why not just kill the missionary and let the police find the body?"

"Yeah," someone said in the small crowd around the fire. "Let the sheriff handle it. Let's hear more music."

Keoki interrupted, "My grandfather told me that there was a luakini temple at the beach across from the intersection of Monsarrat and Kalakaua Avenue. It was called Kupalaha, the spread of Ku. The heiau is gone. Only a few stones left. "

"First Break is outside that spot," Pahoa said.

Another beach boy chimed in. "I was told that in the old days, the priests at a Waikiki temple would fly kites to alert people that the surf was up."

"That's it. First Break, first surf, it means the same," Grant said. "Pahoa, call the sheriff. Find Asing. Tell him to get to Waikiki right away. I'm heading out to find Kupalaha."

"Hey, wait up," Pahoa called as Grant raced away. "Let us put out the fire. Take care of our instruments. Then we help you."

"No time," Grant answered, running to a path leading onto Kalakaua Avenue.

***

Wright blinked as he awoke. Rocks pierced his back. His broken arms and legs ached. He wanted to yell, but a gag stifled his voice. He thought of Sheila Grant and the testimony at the inquest, but there was no pain in his mouth. He tried to feel for a hook, but his hands were tied.

He heard waves smashing the shore. Spray from the roiling sea fell on his feet, mixing with the tiny droplets of rain pattering onto his body. Why am I alive? He shuddered, remembering the testimony of the shredded body of Sheila Grant, ripped by a saw-like weapon. Her pain must have been horrible. Is that what will happen? Dozens of raw cuts and then salt water cast over my body?

A figure hovered above him. Water sprinkled on his chest. An arm swung down. Razor-sharp knives created fissures through his skin like a plow furrowing a field. Not deep cuts, the coroner had said. Not enough to cause immediate death.

Another ripping sliced his body. Pain soared as salt water from a waving fern sprinkled the cuts. Wright screamed, but the gag muffled his voice. He knew that the slashes did not tear through the muscles of his stomach. If someone came to save him, he would live.

He drew up his feet to ward off the swift cuts crisscrossing his belly above his scrotum. He tried to howl, but the cloth in his mouth stifled his cry. Something moist and soft draped over his stomach. Hands tightened a cord, girdling it to his loins, covering his privates he knew were forever useless.

Far away he heard shouting. Help is coming. Lord in heaven let them come and end this agony. He felt the knife plunging into his heart. Before he slipped to eternity, Judge Wright bellowed, blowing away his gag.

***

Grant shouted as he ran along the beach bordering Kalakaua Road hoping that Ku's victim still lived. His eyes searched the darkness. The moon cast feeble light on the ground. There came a muffled cry, just steps away. He leaped from the sand of the beach onto the shoreline grass. A man-sized lump thrashed on the ground like a hooked fish flopping on the bottom of a boat. He ran to it.

A wraith-like figure appeared from the rocky ground. "What? Who are you?" Grant said, raising his arms to defend himself. A closed palm smashed into his neck, paralyzing him. He felt the arteries of his throat being squeezed. His knees buckled.

Grant heard shouts. Something hard was placed in his hand. "*Gago estupido*" his attacker said. Grant slipped into blackness.

CHAPTER 15

SOMEONE KNOCKED YOU out and put this dagger into your hand," Detective Asing said as he walked with Grant on Kalakaua Avenue. Behind the two men were sheriff's cars and an ambulance. Pahoa and the other beach boys were being interviewed. The remnants of the heiau of Kupahala had been roped off, and police officers were restraining reporters and curious neighbors from trampling the ground.

"Yes, and he said something odd, the words '"*gago estupido*,"'" Grant answered. He looked back at the death scene lit by the lights of police vehicles. He was dizzy from the blow to his neck and the fingers that had choked his throat. Despite the fogginess in his brain, he knew his answers in this part of the investigation were crucial.

"A figure appeared like magic, hit you, and gave you the murder weapon? It is the same dagger that killed Sheila Grant. See? Its tip is broken." Asing pointed to the blunted end of the slim swordfish poniard.

A vehicle passed by them, the driver honking his horn, a red light flashing on its side. "Lieutenant Hitchcock. It might be difficult to convince him that you are not the murderer."

Grant shuddered. He remembered Hitchcock's methods. Could he survive another night in the Big Tank? He shook his head, dispelling the fuzziness from his brain. "Asing, you must believe me. I didn't kill Sheila. I didn't kill Judge Wright."

"You have a motive for killing Mrs. Grant, but I do not see a motive for killing the judge. The circumstances of the killings are strange, ritualistic, as if done by a member of a religious cult. But this time, we found no message at the murder scene from the kahuna nui. Only some words as the killer slipped you the weapon. "*Gago estupido.*'"

"There is a message at my home. It came from the kahuna nui."

"That would be helpful in proving your innocence."

The conversation ceased. They crossed the street and climbed the stairs into Grant's home. A police car raced into the driveway, a red light flashing. Hitchcock got out of the black Ford. "They told me I'd find you here, Asing. What are you doing with this killer?"

"Mr. Kingsley said he was drawn to the murder scene by a message saying 'Ku will have his missionary at a heiau by the sea.' He says it was signed by the kahuna nui. I'm coming here to retrieve it."

"I don't believe there is any such message. This kid is a liar. He concocted the whole scheme about Ku. He's trying to throw us off track with another murder by a fictitious high priest."

"You mean within three days of returning to Honolulu I came up with this cult of Ku, planned the murders of Sheila, and then Wright?" Grant answered.

"I wouldn't put it past you," Hitchcock said. "Let's see this message."

They entered the home. Sue Watanabe had retired for the night. Noone else in the house.

The large picture windows in the salon revealed the sweep of Waikiki. From Diamond Head past the Moana Hotel and its three-hundred-foot-long causeway over the sea, continuing to the winking lights of Honolulu Harbor, and ending with the grim outline of Ka'ena Point.

"Magnificent," Asing said, his voice filled with admiration of the panoramic view.

"Where's the letter?" Hitchcock grumbled.

"It's here on this table where I left it," Grant said, turning on the room's light and reaching for an envelope on a table centered in the drawing room.

"Don't touch it." Asing scanned the envelope and the paper inside. Without a word, he showed the documents to Hitchcock.

Hitchcock looked at the paper. Scowling, he said, "Take him to the station and book him for the murders of Sheila Grant and Judge Christopher Wright."

"Why?" Grant asked.

"There is nothing written on the envelope or the sheet of paper inside," Asing said.

***

"You killed the judge?" Hitchcock snarled.

Grant forced himself to stay awake. He was exhausted by a day that had taken so many twists and turns. The green shaded light hurt his eyes. He suspected that its purpose was to confuse him. Hitchcock stood hidden in the shadows of the windowless room, clammy from the sweat of the interrogation. The sheriff had not resorted to brutality. Grant thought it odd. Maybe the man had doubts.

"Answer me, why did you kill the judge?" Hitchcock asked again.

"I told you. I didn't kill him. Somebody set me up."

"Yeah, well, you seem to know all about the rituals. You told me that the mat of sea-weed and coconut fiber over Wright's groin is an *aha*, symbolizing a prayer before the sacrifice. The cuts on the body were made by a leiomano, a crescent of wood with sharks' teeth sewn around it. You got Hawaiian blood, Kingsley. You're the kahuna nui. Admit it."

"I told you. I talked to a Hawaiian kahuna in Kaneohe. That's how I learned about the rituals."

An officer knocked and entered the room, then whispered to Asing. Hitchcock moved out of the light and joined the conferring men. Grant heard snatches of their conversation. He became hopeful. But his hopes shifted to despair as he saw Hitchcock shaking his head. He couldn't hear what he said, but from his gesturing he knew the lieutenant did not believe what he was being told. After many minutes Hitchcock stomped over to the table and into its spotlight. Asing came with him, his ever-present cigarette hanging from the corner of his mouth. Smoke curled from it, climbing in spiraling white vapors into the darkness above the green lamp shade.

"Your alibi checks out," Hitchcock said. "Lehua told the officer who spoke to her that she was with you until 9:00 p.m. Some woman at a party that Wright was at said he had been to a sumo wrestling contest during the day and with her until nine when he left for home. The Hawaiian beach boys confirm your story. They claim they saw someone running from the crime scene. Heard a car start and leave in a hurry. What we can't figure is why the note you got didn't have writing on it, as if the ink had vanished."

Vanished? Grant thought over the word for a moment. "Have either of you heard of Mata Hari?"

Hitchcock shook his head. Asing was impassive, his eyes narrowing.

"When I was in France during the war a big spy trial took place. An exotic dancer, calling herself Mata Hari, entertained French officers. She was accused of spying for Germany. There were all kinds of interesting stories about spies, secret codes, invisible ink, and even vanishing ink."

"Yes," Asing said. "I read her story in the paper. Vanishing ink, that's been known to the Chinese for a long time. Was the ink on the note blue?"

"It was," Grant answered. "The bluest ink I have ever seen."

"I smelled the envelope, the paper," Asing said. "There is a faint trace of alcohol on it. Vanishing ink uses a chemical that is blue when mixed with another chemical and alcohol. Blue color will stay one hour, maybe one week, all depend. Once alcohol evaporates, the color fades and is gone. Litmus paper is the same idea."

"That explains why the message vanished," Grant said. "But why set me up like this?"

"I don't know. You can go, but come see me tomorrow," Asing said. He paused for a moment, "When he slipped you the weapon you're sure the man said "gago estupido?""

"Yes. What do the words mean?"

"It is Tagalong for "stupid fool.""

CHAPTER 16

"GET UP, MISTER Kingsley," Sue begged.

"Why?" The early afternoon sun shone brightly into the room, its warmth creating a girdle of sweat on Grant's brow.

"You told me to call any time Lotus made contact. She is on the telephone."

Grant raced downstairs and grabbed the phone. "Hi."

"I thought you were never going to answer," Lotus said. "I was about to hang up."

"No! Don't hang up. You have word from Selena?"

"Her father tells her not to see you. But Selena is independent. At two o'clock, we go to the movies at the Princess Theater downtown. It's on Fort and Beretania Streets. Get there early. Sit in the back row. Save a seat for Selena."

"What about you?"

"You two enjoy the movie without me. I'll go in and then leave by a side exit."

The phone clicked before he could say more. He thought of the events of the night, the murder, and the strange words the killer used. He should see Asing, not pursue romance. But...

"To hell with it," Grant said, raced upstairs, dressed, and hurried out the door. It was twenty after one. He just had time to make it downtown.

***

Grant saw Selena peering into the back row of the auditorium. The organist played an overture while the opening credits for the silent movie flashed in bold white letters on the silver screen. He raised himself from his seat and beckoned her. She smiled. Selena stepped along the back row. Only one other customer sat there, he groused as she slid by, saying, "Next time get here early."

"Sorry we have to meet like this," Selena said as she slipped her warm hand into his. "But my father is keeping a close watch over me, and so is Rudy."

"Quiet," the grouch said.

Grant pulled Selena along the row to the furthest corner. No one sat near them. They watched the movie. The organist played soft passages of music. Then he increased its intensity as the Queen of the Nile began her dance. The melody swelled to an exciting pitch as Cleopatra stroked the Roman General's cheek and slid her body onto his. Selena's hand reached to Grant's. She squeezed it as the organist's fingers flew across the keyboard, replicating the passion on the silent screen. Selena leaned into Grant's shoulder, her fragrance overpowering him. He bent his face to hers and they kissed.

* * *

Morning came. Grant rolled from bed, satisfied at his good fortune. Selena had told him she did not love Rudy Tang. Even her father believed he was not the man for her. They promised to see each other again.

Exhilarated, Grant surfed, spending hours catching waves. He learned to steer the board along the wall of the wave with his foot. As the morning progressed, his rides became longer and he could slide the waves a half mile from the deep water to the shore. Returning home, he asked Sue Watanabe where Charles and his father were.

"I think he took Mr. Kingsley to the pier. Your father catch a boat to Mau'i. Left message he will be back in a week. Say to you, 'stay out of trouble.'"

Grant smiled. He didn't want trouble, but somehow it found him over and over again. "Did Detective Asing call?"

"Yes, he say come to his office today."

Grant headed to Honolulu, eager to see the detective. At the sheriff's station, he was relieved that Hitchcock was not there.

Asing invited Grant into his office. Cigarette butts littered the desk. The room reeked of tobacco. The detective offered a cigarette and Grant refused. Asing lit up and sent two smoke rings into the air. "Perfect circles," he said. "As you watch them they get wider and wider and then disappear. Just like our murderer. We know he exists, but every time he vanishes without a trace."

"Have you checked out the missionary angle?" Grant asked.

"Yes, the year 1920 marks the centennial of the arrival of Christian missionaries to Hawai'i." Asing cleared files from his desk and spread a newspaper across its center. "The *Thaddeus* brought them around the Cape and the group landed at Kohala, Hawai'i, April 14, 1820. They split up and a missionary family came to Honolulu in May. This news article describes the May first celebration six weeks ago. Sheila Grant spoke as a representative of Robert Grant's father, an early missionary. She talked about the worship of Ku, human sacrifices, and likened ancient Hawai'i to Sodom and Gomorrah. She said, 'The missionaries ended idolatry and human sacrifice.'"

"The article said she spoke as 'a representative.' That's very interesting."

"How so?"

"The kahuna in Kaneohe told me that Ku is both a war god and a god of fishermen. Before sacrifices began the temple priests would fish for the *ulua* and offer it to Ku. But if they couldn't catch one, they would find a human as a substitute, hook him in the mouth, and drag him to Ku's altar to be sacrificed. Was there a hook in Wright's mouth?"

"No. Maybe Mrs. Grant might have been killed as a representative of her dead father-in-law?"

"Maybe, or her dead husband. Did Judge Wright speak at the centennial ceremony on May first?"

"Yes, he did," Asing answered. He paused. "And if there are more victims of this kahuna nui they could come from those who participated in the ceremonies. There was one interesting aspect about the judge's body different from Mrs. Grant. A girdle of cloth and coconut leaves was wrapped around his belly. The 'aha' you called it. Why did Wright have a girdle and not her?"

Grant became wary. An innocent conversation could turn accusatory. He liked Asing. He had not booked him as Hitchcock ordered. But the man is still a detective sworn to uphold the law. "I don't know," he answered firmly then asked, "What do you make of the killer saying, "*gago estupido*?"

Asing shrugged, a sly smile crossing his face. "It is very strange that he should speak Filipino to you. It suggests several things, either you lie and want to divert suspicion, or the man is from the Philippines, or the killer wants to mask his true identity."

"I didn't lie. He said those words to me. I don't know why."

"Hitchcock would like your confession so the cases can be closed. For him, with a dead body nearby and the death weapon in your hand, it is an open and shut case." Asing laughed. "But I can see you will not grant him his wish. We have no clues to the murderer. What would be his motive to kill? You had a motive to kill Mrs. Grant, but what about Judge Wright?"

Grant thought that Asing's question posed danger. Seemingly innocent probing could lead to admissions that implicated him in both crimes. "I did not kill either of them."

"If you did not then all we have is a ghost rising from the rocks, attacking you, and placing a swordfish dagger into your hands. He is a man of mystery calling himself the kahuna nui. What is his motive? Revenge on the missionaries for ending the worship of Ku and human sacrifices?" Asing paused for some moments studying Grant intently. "The Filipino angle may be promising."

"Like what?"

"I've been doing some background checking. Judge Wright was a big time negotiator for the Hawaii Sugar Planters Association, the HSPA. The Filipinos unionized a year ago and are fighting the HSPA for higher wages, better working conditions. They went out on strike in January of this year. The Japanese went out with them. Bad blood developed between labor and the plantations. The HSPA hired strike breakers, called on the police and National Guard to beat up the union people. Deaths occurred."

"How does Wright fit into this turmoil?"

"It is the plantation method of controlling its labor force. When the Chinese made trouble, they brought in Portuguese, then Japanese. When these folks complained, they brought in the Filipinos. These were poor, illiterate peasants, who the labor agents lied to about wages and life on the plantations. What happened when they got here? Their pay was miserable, their life regulated, and they owed what they earned to the company store. Why is labor exploited? Profits. In the past ten years, the return on investments in sugar stock has been over one-hundred-seventy percent. Not to speak of stock dividends being earned."

"That's how Grandfather Grant and my step-grandma made their money. And I guess I have to add my family, too," Grant said shaken by the revelations. "And Wright had a role in this money-making?"

"Yes, he was one of the architects of divide and conquer. Because of the strike in January, he had been negotiating behind the scenes for the importation of cheap Chinese labor to Hawai'i. In my investigation, I learned that the night he died he met Dan Choy and concluded a labor deal to bring in workers from China."

Grant whistled. "You're thinking that the Filipino union hired some guy to do in my grandmother and Wright?"

"If you are not the killer, then it is a possibility that we must investigate."

An officer knocked and came into the room. He huddled with Asing. The Chinese detective took his whip from the wall. "I must break up a gambling ring. We will speak again of this matter." Asing planted his white panama hat on his head and hurried out the door.

Grant thought to visit the university, to find Selena, but realized classes were over. He could stop by her home, but Selena said it was dangerous for him to be near Maunakea Street. She promised to arrange the next meeting.

Grant headed for Waikiki. He would surf and sort out the puzzles as he fought the ocean, a power he understood.

When he arrived home, there was a message to meet Selena at six o'clock at an address near the shipping piers. Sue said the woman who called identified herself as Selena.

Grant felt uneasy driving toward the harbor, an unusual place to meet. The address was at the waterfront, next to the mouth of two streams that had built the Port of Honolulu. He considered calling Lotus, but thought it foolish. She could only confirm or say "I don't know." As he passed Alakea Street, he decided to visit Sato to ask about the strike. It was not yet five.

The consular office looked more like a residence than an embassy. It had a wide porch lined with several coconut trees in front. Two flags with the large red ball of the rising sun set on a white field draped from a second-story porch. Near the entranceway lay a small pond with a waterfall. Red, orange, and golden fish swam between the rocks set into the water. Stunted bonsai trees were cleverly arranged around the enclosure.

Grant entered the building and found the reception room cool and clean. A clerk snapped to attention. The man, dressed in a white suit and dark tie, approached, bowed, and said, "Your business, please?"

"Is Mr. Sato in? May I see him?"

"*Hai*. Name, please?"

"Grant Kingsley."

The clerk telephoned, spoke in Japanese, then directed Grant to a second-floor office. Stepping onto the upper level, he noted several large windows facing the waterfront. He knocked at Sato's door and a voice invited him in. Entering, Grant saw a large bay window facing the water-front and a tripod-mounted telescope trained on the sea. In the distance, smoke curled into the sky from Pearl Harbor.

Sato stood, bowed, and pointed to a chair. Grant noted a muscular Japanese of medium height, with short hair, wide face, and full cheeks. His slanted eyes peered at Grant through razor-thin brows that matched a small moustache.

"Thank you for your gift," Sato said indicating a polished brown *ipu* richly decorated with line drawings of long slender leaves and flowers. The calabash was shaped like a nude tan woman without limbs or hair.

"A small payment for the debt I owe you. These bottle gourds are very rare in Hawai'i. No one grows them anymore. In olden times it had many uses, vessels for holding water, storing food for eating, masks for the king's warriors, and drums for dancing the hula. The other night you saved me with a special art you called jujitsu. Where did you learn it?"

Sato did not answer for a moment. He studied Grant through narrowed eyes. "In Iga province, Japan. What brings you to Nu'uanu? Certainly it is not to see me."

"My lady friend, Selena, the one you saw at the Moana Hotel, tele-phoned my home. She left a message to meet at the waterfront where the streams meet the sea. Since it is nearby I thought to stop and ask a question that might help solve a puzzle." Grant stood and went to the bay window. Sato came up to him, and Grant pointed toward the harbor. "That is where we are to meet."

Sato stroked his thin moustache, studying the area Grant indicated. In a soft voice he said, "I know the building you are going to. It is a strange place for a romantic meeting."

Grant barely heard his comment. He was more interested in the telescope and the area of the ocean that it trained upon. He knew that Japan had seized Germany's Pacific Island Empire. Rumors suggested that America's next war would be with Japan. "You have a magnificent view of the harbor and the Waianae Mountains. You use the telescope to study the beauty of O'ahu?"

"Yes," the diplomat answered. "Sorry to hurry you away, but I must attend to my duties. What is the question you wished to ask?"

"The Filipinos and Japanese went out on strike in January of this year. Do you know of any threats by union people to harm sugar planters?"

"No. Please, I must return to work," Sato said, waving his hand toward the door.

Grant could not tell from the curt dismissal whether he knew of labor threats. Surely he must know something. But he would gain nothing by arguing. "Thank you for your hospitality. I hope we can arrange a supper in the future?"

Sato said, "*Hai*, yes," opened the office door, and ushered Grant out, saying as he left, "the building you pointed out is a strange place for a romantic meeting. Be careful."

CHAPTER 17

GRANT DECIDED TO leave his car parked by the consulate and hurried to the waterfront and the address Selena gave. Sato's concern disturbed him, but he wanted to see Selena wherever she might be. Approaching the two-story building, he realized it was one of the few structures that had escaped the devastating fire that wiped out the old Chinatown.

Precisely at six, Grant walked to the front door, knocked and heard a female voice say, "Come in." He entered and saw a garishly painted red room with the massive face of a Chinese warlord glaring from the far wall. Military figures on horseback pranced around the caricature. Tall lamps set in the corners, emitted low reddish light. Lounging on a sofa, two flimsily clad women smiled.

Grant smelled incense and another sweet odor. From a corner of the parlor, a fat Chinese stood up. His lips, protruding beyond a moustache and goatee, parted in a thin smile.

Grant backed out into steel points shoved in his back. A voice said, "Get inside." He tried to turn his head, but another man, pushed a knife into his side and said, "Inside, asshole. Rudy Tang wants to see you."

The four men walked through the bordello, the two prostitutes eyeing Grant as he marched up the stairs. They were young. Orientals maybe Chinese or Japanese, Grant was not sure. He heard the sound of gambling from an apartment on the lower floor. The bettors' yells muffled by the enclosing walls. Somewhere on the upper story came the plucking of a Japanese samisen. Grant speculated that a geisha prepared to entertain a rich customer.

At the second floor landing the thugs pushed him into a room. Large windows faced onto the ocean giving a grand view of the sun beginning its evening descent behind the Waianae range, its glowing golden orb shading red around its perimeter. Sand Island, built by dead coral creatures, loomed out of the sea. It formed a convenient breakwater for ships using the port of Honolulu and served as a quarantine station.

Rudy Tang sat at a desk. Set into the wall behind him were two leiomano. A long slender dagger was fixed beneath the shark-toothed weapons.

The Chinese gang lord rose. "Welcome to my business office." He waved his hand to the windows. "Enjoy the view. It will be your last."

Grant's eyes shifted around the room, gauging his odds of escape. Three men stood by him. The door had been locked after they entered. Only the windows offered an escape route. But they were closed and he could not tell how far from the building lay the sea.

"I told you to leave Selena alone. But you are one hardheaded guy. No pay attention. Now nobody around to help you, except us. We not going help you. Only drown you." Rudy laughed.

"Drown? You're not going to cut me up with your leiomano like you did Sheila Grant and Judge Wright?"

"No marks. The police will just find another dead body floating in the sea. Grab him."

Three thugs seized Grant. He fought, but two men held him on each side, and a burly Chinese picked him up from the waist and manhandled him toward the wall. Rudy pressed a button. An opening appeared. Shoved through it, Grant hurtled down a chute onto a trap-door that sprung open, and he splashed onto a rock floor covered with water.

At the far end of a six-foot-long tunnel dim light filtered through a grate. Crawling to it, his head scraped the ceiling of his prison. At the barrier, Grant rattled the bars. They held firm. He jack-knifed, using his feet to kick the metal gate. It did not budge. He searched the edges, but could not find an unlocking mechanism. He yelled. No answer. He called again. Only silence. The water rose, brackish to the taste. His prison lay where the sea met the fresh water of a stream. He crawled back to the trap door, tested its edges to find a finger hold where he might claw it open. He found none.

Grant leaned against the tunnel wall. Rudy Tang's voice filled the small cavern. "In the old days, smugglers brought opium from boats anchored in the harbor into this passageway. I use it to get rid of pests like you. When the tide fills the tunnel, you will drown like the rat you are. Then I open the grate and you float out to sea with the outgoing tide. Not a scratch on your body, except where the sharks might tear into it. Everybody will believe you committed suicide because of the murders." Rudy cackled, his laughter echoing through the tunnel.

Minutes passed. A rising tide flooded water into his prison. Grant hammered the trap door until his fists were raw. He returned to the gate, grasped the bars, and shook them, seeking to tear the barrier by the strength of his arms. Water rose to his shoulders, moving upward, the tide drawn higher by the rising moon.

Grant took a breath, submerged, and kicked back to the trap door. He lifted his face, inhaled, went under, and pushed off from the wall, slamming his feet into the grating like a battering ram. He tried the maneuver several times, but the metal would not give. He could not escape. Rudy had won.

Water lapped his chin. Grant shivered. Light, filtering through the bars, disappeared, blotted out by the rising water. He called for help again and again until the water rose to his lips. He had moments to live.

CHAPTER 18

SEA WATER SALTED his mouth. His forehead bumped the ceiling. Metal scraped against stone. Grant reached with his hand, felt nothing. He inhaled the little oxygen left and submerged. Through the murk he saw that the metal gate had opened. Stroking, kicking, he burst out of the cavern, swam past rock walls, and rose to the surface.

Above him, puffs of clouds floated across the heavens like hundreds of cotton balls. Moonlight filtered between the gaps, barely piercing the mantle of darkness that shrouded Honolulu. Lights twinkled along the shore and in the hills.

Treading water, Grant searched the boulders and saw no one. He glanced at Rudy's building, its second-story windows gleaming with light. A woman screamed. He could not tell if the scream was in pain or ecstasy. From one of the rooms came the discordant sounds of the samisen. A Japanese courtesan plucked and drummed the banjo-like instrument. One of the rituals geisha performed prior to copulating. The rules were strict—music, stylish dancing, and the proper serving of tea.

Boulders disappeared into the darkness on his left. Other rocks bent along the coastline to his right until they joined the first of the concrete piers marking the port of Honolulu. He crab-crawled toward them, his head swiveling above the water.

Uncertain how long he had been trapped, Grant judged it to be close to ten o'clock. Distant sounds of auto traffic drew him to the harbor. The only light came from a window in Rudy's building. He wondered how the man could operate a bordello, opium den, and gambling casino with impunity. But this was post-war Honolulu and he surmised that someone high in the sheriff's department could be bought. Maybe Hitchcock. He was the kind of mean scum who might be on the take.

The breakwater effect of Sand Island kept the ocean within the harbor calm. Plopping sounds startled Grant, as the sea erupted in small fountains. He dove to escape, but soon realized that rain pummeled the sea.

He rose. Sudden light came from the back door of Rudy's building. Dim shapes scurried out heading to the water's edge. "Rudy's men know I escaped," Grant said. He stroked faster, searching the rocks for a path to the harbor road. The rain weakened. Men called to each other. Hand torches switched on, illuminating the rocks.

Grant saw a metal ladder embedded in concrete. He swam to it, reached an iron rung, and pulled himself up. A torch beamed, the outer limits of the light reaching the ladder. Grant lowered himself to the sea. Hyper-ventilating, he submerged, grasping a sunken rock to prevent his body from bobbing to the surface. He could see the light probing the stones near the ladder. After an interminable time with bright spots darting through his head, the beam disappeared.

Grant surfaced, exhaled slowly, and sucked in clean air. He looked above, saw no one. Grasping the ladder he pulled himself up. At the top rung, he stopped, searching. To his right, a concrete wall, to his left shrubs grew out of the boulders.

A body sprawled on the ground, a torch beaming onto the grey walls of a warehouse that extended from the edge of the wharf to an unlit street.

Puzzled, Grant climbed onto the landing. Bending, he raced along the warehouse wall and reached the dark roadway. He started across. Light from a roof lamp caught him in its glare. A voice yelled, "There he is."

Grant raced across the street for his parked car. Men shouted. He heard running behind him. He thought to turn and fight. Someone screamed. Grant looked back and saw a man staggering with a dart in his thigh. Without pausing he leaped into his Studebaker, fumbling for the keys. Grant shifted into gear and sped toward Joshua's home.

***

"You believe that Rudy Tang is the murderer of Sheila Grant and Judge Wright. What is your proof?" Asing asked, rising from his desk and leaning his back against the wall of his office. The room reeked of cigarettes.

"He had twin shark-toothed knives fixed onto his wall and a long thin dagger beneath them. When I confronted him with using the leiomano to commit the murders he implied that he did."

"What would be his motive?"

"Joshua told me that it could be the Chinatown arson. The Chinese blamed the sugar people for setting it. They say it was retaliation for failing to renew work contracts and leaving the plantations to start competing businesses with Caucasian merchants. And you know that the rich sugar people and merchants are all descendants of the missionaries."

"But the big fire was many years ago. The reason for it was to end a plague by burning buildings corrupted by disease."

"Isn't it strange that before it happened, a law had been passed that Chinese could only engage in agricultural work? Then the arson occurs, consuming acres of Chinese-owned buildings and ending Chinatown in Honolulu. Dozens were dead from the fires and thousands of Chinese homeless. Later a law was passed by a plantation and business-controlled legislature that Orientals could not own property."

Sucking in his breath, Asing said, "I know about the fire. I was a young boy when it happened. It was terrible for Chinese families. You think Rudy Tang's family suffered from the fire and he is seeking revenge?"

"Yes. It is the centennial year of the coming of the missionaries. What better time to make them pay and blame it on the Hawaiians and their war god?"

"Maybe. You say there are prostitution, drugs, and gambling going on. A secret passage used to dump victims into the sea."

"Yes. I was one such person and lucky to be alive."

"I heard about those hidden tunnels. In olden times, there were whorehouses by the sea. Prostitutes would drug their clients, rob them, and shove them into a hidden room. Ship captains would row in and take the drugged victims to crew their ships. Tang has many friends. But we will take a look and see what we find."

"Right now, without a search warrant?"

"Yes." Asing removed his whip from the wall. He strode from his office, calling another officer to follow him. Perplexed by what seemed a rash decision, Grant went with them.

When they arrived at Rudy's building, Asing pushed open the door, Grant, and the police officer following him. The smell of fresh paint permeated the entry hall, its walls no longer red, but tan in color. Gone was the warlord and prancing horses. In their place stood rectangular black framed line drawings of mountains, trees, and flowers. A fully dressed woman sat at a desk where Grant had seen the lounging whores. She looked up saying, "What is the meaning of this entry without permission?"

"Where is Mr. Tang, please?" Asing said, showing his police badge.

The woman paused for some moments, "He is not here. Go away."

Asing smiled, "I know he is here. You betrayed his presence by the tone of your voice. Mr. Kingsley, show me the way to his office."

Grant mounted the stairs with Asing. The secretary came after them. "You can't go up there." As the men continued to climb she called, "Ho Chin, stop them."

A burly Chinese emerged from the darkness of the second floor landing. Grant noticed he limped. The slender Asing reached the second floor. He faced the big Chinese. Grant judged the goon to be thirty or forty pounds heavier than the detective. "I'm Officer Asing. We are here to see Mr. Tang. Step aside, please."

The big man hesitated, eyeing the small policeman. "No can go in."

"We can and we will. Step aside, please."

"Wait." He knocked on the office door. A voice barked, the words muffled by the wood panel. Chin opened the door and announced, "Detective Asing to see you."

"Let him in," Rudy Tang said. The gang lord's smile turned into a scowl when his eyes fixed on Grant. To a side of the room, by the harbor windows, a henchman lounged in a cushioned chair. Affixed on the wall behind Tang's desk, were the leiomanos and poniard.

"Why are you here?"

"There are many reasons for coming. The primary one is to investigate the attempted murder of Mr. Kingsley. Do you deny you tried to kill him last night?"

"The man is a liar. Would you believe an accused killer over my word and those of my men who say he was not here?"

"Yeah, then how come your goon, Ho Chin, is limping from a dart in his thigh?" Grant said.

"An accident, nothing more," Tang answered.

"And your goon by the window got the bruise on the side of his head by the same accident?"

"Somebody cold-cocked me," the henchman said, rising from his seat. "Maybe your friend did it."

"Shut up, Soong," Tang scolded.

"Show me your secret passage," Asing said.

"There is none."

"Grant, find it."

He searched the wall behind Rudy's desk, unable to locate a seam that would outline a door. He looked for the button that Rudy had pushed. He saw nothing obvious. Frustrated, Grant stole a glance at Rudy. His eyes were fixed on a point on the wall.

Grant pounded the wall where Rudy had looked. Asing joined the search. His fists smashed against the papered wall. A flap sprung loose. He pulled, and the wall paper came away. The rectangular lines of a low door became visible.

"Soong, Chin, get them," Rudy screamed.

Asing's uncoiled whip crackled, disarming the knife-wielding Soong. Chin limped forward with a cudgel. The whip lashed again. The henchman howled. The whip struck him once more. The club fell from Chin's hand. Rudy rushed to his desk, thrusting his hand into a drawer. Grant shoved it closed. The Chinese howled, pulling out his bruised fingers. Grant head-butted Rudy, and he fell to the floor, writhing in pain.

"You will please line up against the windows without your weapons," Asing said.

The henchmen obeyed. He reached to the floor and picked up the knife and club. "Mr. Kingsley, you will take those shark knives from the wall and put these cuffs on Mr. Tang. I think we have enough evidence to accuse Mr. Tang of attempted murder and possibly the murders of Mrs. Grant and Judge Wright. Officer Reuben, come upstairs and help me take these criminals away. As for you, Mr. Kingsley, give the policeman the weapons and visit me in the afternoon."

CHAPTER 19

"THANKS FOR PUTTING me up for the night," Grant said.

"I will always help you. I never married. No children that I know of." Kanakoa chuckled. "I have looked upon you as a son."

"And you are a special person. Since Rudy Tang is in jail, I think that it is safe to return home."

"What about the homicides of Sheila and the judge?"

"Tang hasn't been charged yet. But I'm sure he will be."

"I don't know about that. The man's a slippery character. He's got friends."

Grant shrugged. "If it wasn't Rudy, then I'm out of suspects, except maybe the Filipinos."

"Filipinos?"

"Yeah Asing's got a theory Wright was heavily involved with the HSPA. Filipinos started the labor war in January. Wright brokered a deal the night he died to bring in Chinese as strike breakers."

"The plantations are harsh with the workers. But hiring an assassin to get even is unbelievable."

"If Rudy isn't the killer, then the labor angle is something Asing wants to pursue. I'll see you soon."

"Before you go, I've been meaning to ask you. Would you join my law firm? I have some interesting clients. I'm sure you will find it worthwhile. I need someone young to take over when I'm gone."

"Thanks, I'll consider it."

Grant drove home. When he got there, Sue had a message from Lotus to call. When he reached the young Chinese, she said, "We got the news. Selena is happy you are safe. We want to come to Waikiki tomorrow, swim, surf, and have fun. Tomorrow night, you come to the restaurant for dinner. My uncle wants to see you."

Grant offered to pick them up.

"No. HRT is real easy, only a nickel to take the bus to Waikiki."

Grant couldn't sleep. At sunrise he ran to the Hui O Nalu and selected three surfboards. Arrangements were made with one of the beach boys for a canoe. He ran to the bus stop near the Moana Hotel. Three buses went by before the girls arrived. He took their hands and escorted them to the beach.

They spent the morning at Queen's Surf. Selena caught waves with ease. Lotus had problems and Grant spent hours helping her learn the steps: kick with the feet, stroke hard with the hands, and catch the wave before it turned to foam. By noon Lotus had mastered the art. Grant suggested lunch.

Pahoa lounged at the club. "Hey, Kingsley, let's do canoe racing."

"Like to, but I got the girls to tend to."

"No problem. We'll split them up, each in a different canoe. I'll take your girlfriend." The course was set from Queen's Beach to the harbor and back. The race started well for Grant's canoe, Lotus trying hard to catch the rhythm of paddling. But it soon became evident that Pahoa and Selena made a great team. Her effortless paddling matched the pure Hawaiian in rhythmic power. By the time Grant's canoe reached Honolulu Harbor, he knew they would not win. He called off the heavy beat of the chanter, and they coasted back to the Moana Hotel. Selena and Pahoa met them at the beach. "This wahine is terrific," Pahoa said. "She can paddle with us anytime."

Grant nodded. He meant to say something sarcastic, but held his retort in check. Selena was entitled to her victory. "Bathe and get dressed. I'll have Charles take you home."

"Come by seven o'clock," Selena said, blowing a kiss.

Grant raced home. Sending Charles to the Moana, he bathed, dressed, and put on his best summer suit then headed for Merchant Street with the top of his Studebaker down. The engine purred its power. The cool air whipped around his ears. He sang, his rich baritone belting out songs that he had learned during the war. He ended his nostalgic moments with the closing verse of a popular war song, *"That you loved me, you'd always be, My Lilli of the lamplight, My own Lilli Marlene."* He parked the car and leaped out, landing easily on his feet whistling *"Over There."*

Leinani met him at the door. Her face beamed. "You look very happy and you are humming a tune."

"I should be happy. Two murders are solved. I have a beautiful girl-friend. Life could not be better."

Leinani smiled and inclined her head. Over fifty, Grant thought as he followed her, but still beautiful. The restaurant was crowded. Waiters hustled among tables set around an inner court. Leinani led him past the cashier and tobacco counter, its wide rectangular opening decorated with ivory frescoes of scenes from Chinese mythology. They walked by the fenced garden. In its center, a waterfall spilled over shrub-covered rocks into a rectangular pool. Large gold and orange carp swam lazily along its perimeter.

Leinani took Grant to a private room. Her brother, Waihoku Sam, and his wife sat at a long rectangular teak table decorated in its center by a golden dragon with flower-filled brass urns at its mouth and tail. The men embraced. It had been years since their last meeting and they quickly caught up with personal news.

Leinani opened the dining door and ushered in a man dressed in navy whites and a woman in a yellow dress, with large white beads around her throat, matching ear rings, and bracelet. Sam stood and came to the couple. "Captain and Mrs. Trask, thank you for coming. This is long-time family friend Grant Kingsley. He fought for America in the Great War. He is a hero and a former army officer." Sam went on to explain that the captain had recently been assigned to Pearl Harbor. He and his wife had purchased furniture from his import and export shop. "I thought that you military men should meet."

Selena walked in, dressed in a shantung silk blue gown that tightly fit her from neck to ankles. The dress enhanced every curve of her body, accentuating the flatness of her belly. Her hair flowed over her shoulders, draping like a short brown cape onto her back. She stood tall in her blue high heels. Her entire aspect overwhelmed Grant. "You're beautiful."

Grant took a seat next to the captain and dinner talk quickly reverted to a discussion of the U.S. Navy in the Pacific. "For too many years," Trask said, "our country has had a one-ocean navy. But because of the war, we are now committed to two fleets, one in the Atlantic and the other in the Pacific."

"Is that because the politicians are concerned about the Japanese seizure of Germany's islands?" Grant asked.

"Let's just say that our government believes that trade with Asia will be huge in the years ahead."

"And that Japanese expansion could be a threat to our interests in the Orient?"

"Yes," Trask answered. "Mr. Sam tells me you have a friend in the Japanese consulate."

"That is true."

"Please visit me at my office. Here is my card."

Grant devoted the rest of the evening to Selena. She emphasized her dislike of Rudy Tang and related, "I have spoken to my father about you. He feels that we are from two different worlds and my relationship with you can only lead to misery. But I have his consent to date you."

Grant drove home, believing that this was the most incredible day of his life. His nemesis, Tang, was in jail. Selena made a breakthrough with her father. Soon the two would meet and he would offer a proposal.

"Whoopee," he yelled to the night sky as he raced his car along Kalakaua Avenue. He began to sing, paraphrasing the war song. *"Selena, your sweet face fills my dreams. My Selena of the lamplight. My Selena that I love."* He screeched to a stop in the family driveway, overwhelmed by the evening's events. He skipped into the house. A note lay on the entry table. "Call Asing any time of the night."

Grant rang the detective. "Kingsley," he said when Asing answered.

"Tang bailed out on the attempted murder charge."

"What about the two murders?"

"Not enough evidence. Shark knives are clean of blood. So is the dagger. He has alibis for the times the deaths occurred. As to the arson motive, the fire happened too long ago. No jury would believe he waited this long to execute a death plan against missionaries. Maybe we should pursue the Filipino angle. Come see me in the morning."

Grant hung up, the beauty of the evening shattered by the news that Tang is free.

CHAPTER 20

AS HE WAITED for Asing, an article in the morning paper intrigued him. The headline said, "**Sacrificial Temple May Get Makeover**." The story line related that a Hawaiian group known as "*Hui o ka aina*" had approached the Bishop Museum for the purpose of restoring the last heiau consecrated by Kamehameha the Great to his war god. The leader of the club asserted, "The heiau was originally dedicated to Lono, a god of peace and fertility. Kamehameha changed it to a luakini temple so he could make sacrifices to Ku before his fleet sailed to attack Kaua'i. We want to restore it and re-dedicate the temple to a kinder, more loving god." Abner Nolan, trustee of the Museum and the scion of an old missionary family responded to the request, "It would be a travesty to re-build a pagan temple. My ancestors overthrew the false gods and we should keep them gone and buried forever."

Asing marched out of his office, cigarette smoke fuming from his mouth. "Grant, what you reading?"

"Interesting article about a temple over in Makaha, it's a Ku temple, but Hawaiians want to turn the clock back and re-dedicate it to Lono."

"It is strange that with two sacrificial murders, Hawaiians want to dig up old temples."

"Maybe it's just a coincidence. Nothing will happen. This guy Abner Nolan, who used to be a partner with my grandfather in the sugar business, is on a warpath. He says he will do all in his power to stop this travesty."

"If you're ready, we have a meeting with the Filipino Resident Labor Commissioner."

"Why do you want me along?"

"You're the only one who has seen and heard the killer."

***

"I tell you, gentlemen, the union leader is a criminal. He becomes president of the labor unions, then, like a parasite, sucks up the honest laborers into his cause of dishonesty."

"Those are strong words Mr. Curzon. I thought as Resident Labor Commissioner, appointed by the Territory, you would be for the unions," Asing said.

"Since coming to Hawai'i to help solve labor troubles, I have met with the people from the HSPA. They are honorable men inclined to improve working conditions of the field hands. But the humble Filipino worker has been fooled by agitators from my country. These labor leaders are gamblers, criminals, and rascals, the worst of them is Santos."

"Is he the president of the labor unions?" Grant interrupted.

Curzon sucked in his breath then exhaled it like a bursting balloon. "Yes, he claims to be the head of the "Filipino Fair Wages Union" which gives him control of all Philippine laborers in the Hawaiian Islands."

"Powerful guy," Asing said. "But we didn't come to talk about labor and management. We are investigating two murders which have a connection to the HSPA and the sugar industry. There is the possibility that the killings are the work of a Filipino assassin."

"I knew it," Curzon said smacking his palm on his desk. "Santos hates the HSPA. Interrogate him, and you will find your killer."

"Why so sure?"

"One of the killings is Judge Wright. Is that not so?"

"Yes."

"On the evening of his death, the judge was at a sumo wrestling match in Kaimuki?"

"That is true."

"Santos was there, spying on Judge Wright making a deal to import Chinese laborers to break the Filipino union."

"You're suggesting that Santos killed the judge to prevent the deal from becoming finalized." Grant interrupted.

"I have no more to say," Curzon answered.

"Ok. Where do we find this Santos?" Asing asked.

"Office is across the street from this palace. It's a green and white plantation style bungalow."

Asing grabbed Grant's arm, "Let's go."

Curzon called after them, "You might ask him if the HSPA ever paid him for ending the strike."

They left 'Iolani Palace, Asing saying, "This building was designed by King Kalakaua, copying Louis XIV's palace at Versailles."

"I visited the Sun King's home while in France. It is bigger than this small place."

"Hawai'i didn't have the money that the French king had. Aha, here is the plantation style house."

"What do you want me to do?" Grant said as he and the detective stepped to the porch of the cottage. A shabby sign proclaiming it a 'Union Building' hung above the front door.

"Just look and listen. Study carefully whomever we meet. Listen to their voices. Remember you're our prime suspect until we find another."

"Thanks for your confidence in my innocence."

Asing smiled and opened the door.

The usual living room-kitchen of plantation cottages had been converted into a spacious reception area. Two men in white undershirts sat at a well-scarred table playing a card game. Warm breezes blew through screened windows stirring the smoke of lit cigarettes smoldering in coconut ash trays. One of the players looked up from his cards, his sweaty shirt pocked with burn holes. "What you want?"

Asing's face wreathed into a broad smile, "Are you Mr. Santos?"

"Who's asking?"

"Honolulu police."

"You got badge?"

"I ask you one last time, you Santos?"

"I know you," the second card player said. "You detective Asing. Put me in jail for gambling. We no want trouble. We not Santos. He back there."

"You one smart guy, how you say it in Filipino 'no be stupid.'"

"*Hindi estupido.*"

Asing looked at Grant, who shook his head.

"I thought it was "*hindi gago estupido.*" Asing asked.

"*Gago* and *estupido* is same thing. Both are Tagalong words for stupid. When you use them together means stupid fool"

"We're wasting time. Tell Mr. Santos we are here to see him."

One of the men gave a defiant look, but the other shuffled to a closed door, knocked, and yelled, "Two da kine police want see you."

"Police? What the hell they want? Keep them out," a voice growled from beyond the door.

"Detective Asing, we're coming in," the policeman said, pushing past the man at the door.

Unlike the reception area, the room they entered was dark, shades covered the windows. Two fans whirled air around the room. On a couch, set to the side of the room, a man stood up buttoning his pants. Another dim figure huddled in the cushions.

"You guys can't wait. Come, we talk outside."

"Sorry to interrupt," Asing said as he and Grant left the room.

Once outside, Santos said, "What you want?"

"We are investigating two murders. The first is Sheila Grant. The second is someone you know, Judge Wright."

Santos eyes narrowed, "You trying to pin something on me?"

"No, just following up on every lead we get. Are you going to cooperate or do I take you down to the station?"

"Every time something happens, you blame it on the Filipinos. You folks are in with the HSPA. You attacked us during the strike, made our life miserable with false arrests. Why should I help you?"

"I didn't make any arrests during the strike. I left your people alone. I know what a hard time Filipinos have in Hawai'i."

"America is bad for the Philippines. Defeated Spain and instead of freedom, you colonized us. Two million people were killed in the fighting to suppress our rebellion. With peace, we come to work in Hawai'i. What happens, plantations make promises, but all lies. No homes, no food, lousy pay, long work hours, law in Hawai'i against us."

"Then why not leave?"

"How can? Wages so poor no can pay for transportation. Besides, the plantations make us buy from the company stores. They rob us of every penny we make."

"You don't like the sugar plantations?"

"No."

"You don't like the HSPA?"

"What you leading up to?"

"You knew Judge Wright was one of the leaders of the HSPA?"

"So?"

"That he was one of the big movers in breaking up the labor strike this year?"

"Yeah, but we pulled out and settled. The Japanese kept on striking for months."

"I heard your union started the strike and to show solidarity with the Filipinos the Japanese went out too."

"What you getting at?"

"Your union got nothing from the settlement, right?"

"We were locked out. Japanese, Filipino workers got kicked out of their homes. HSPA brought in strike breakers, the National Guard."

"Your union got nothing. You betrayed the Japanese, all because Judge Wright promised you money to end the strike."

"Lie. Lie!"

"But Judge Wright never paid you, right?"

Santos did not answer, instead he looked at his two underlings who were shaking their heads, and spoke to them in Filipino. A heated exchange of words followed between the three men.

"Stop this jabbering or I will take you all to jail,"

"I think you hit these guys right between the eyes. Santos double-crossed the Japanese for money, but didn't pay off these two union leaders," Grant said.

"But maybe this is what happened," Asing thrust his face within inches of Santos, "Wright didn't pay you. He reneged on the deal."

"*Oo, oo*," two of the Filipinos said.

"*Tahimik ka*," Santos yelled.

"You can't stop your men from saying 'yes, yes'," Asing said. He seized the union leader by the shirt collar and thrust his eyes even with those of Santos, "and you or your hired assassin killed Wright."

"Bull-shit."

"You were there in Kaimuki, at the sumo wrestling the night Wright was killed."

"*Hindi.*"

"Don't deny the truth. I have an eyewitness that swears you were there."

"Man is a liar."

"You were at the wrestling matches because Wright continued to double cross you by making a deal with Choy to import Chinese laborers. It's *'gago estupido'* to deny it."

"You damn policeman, I'm not *gago estupido.*"

Asing looked at Grant who gave a slight nod. "Santos, you are under arrest."

"For what?"

"Murder."

CHAPTER 21

JOSHUA PROPPED HIS black shoes onto the desk. He pushed back deeper into the plush red seat saying, "I want you to start work doing legal complaints for my clients. You understand issue pleading, of course?"

"Yes," Grant answered, chagrined that his first legal duty was the drudgery of drafting documents.

"Good. You should also join the Hawai'i Bar and take the examination."

"Will do, anything else you have in mind?"

"Have you resolved the issues with your father?"

Grant sighed. He looked out the window of Joshua's second-floor office. He listened to autos honk and streetcars zip along the roadway, the overhead cables they grasped with slender rubberized fingers hummed with electricity. "No. He keeps avoiding it. The law says I am his son, but I think he has doubts."

Joshua sat upright and removed his feet from the desk. "That your mother and John Tana coupled and you are the love child."

Stung by the blunt words, Grant paused a moment before answering. "That's what Sheila Grant believed and I don't know, maybe my father too. You knew this man Tana?"

"I told you he was a client." Joshua paused for a moment as if uncertain what to say next.

"You're holding something back. What is it? Tell me."

"He has a daughter on Kaua'i, Nani Still, and several grandchildren. Your mother helped the family for years."

"She never said anything about this to my father. How did she do it?" Grant stared at the old attorney. "You were the go-between."

Joshua nodded.

"Why?"

"The explanation is a long one. The person you know as Malia raised your mother. John Tana moved in with his Aunt Malia when the last of his family died. The two young people believed they were cousins. They were not. Your grandfather, Robert Grant, had impregnated a young Hawaiian girl then abandoned her. The woman died in childbirth and Malia kept the baby, concealing the father's identity. The child was your mother. It was many years later that your grandfather acknowledged the truth."

"So that is how I got my Hawaiian blood," Grant said. Agitated, he stood and stepped to the open window, breathing in the warm morning air. He stared at the teeming life of the Territorial capitol baking in a late June sun. Lightly clothed pedestrians marched along Hotel Street. Some waited at the corner of its intersection with Fort. A police officer stood in a kiosk set in the middle of the roadways directing traffic, an open umbrella above his head. "What happened? Why did mother marry Dad and not this Tana guy?"

"Your father fell in love with her. He was rich. Your grandfather saw an opportunity to make money. He made certain that John Tana was kept away. With Malia's help, he convinced Leinani to marry James Kingsley. She was a virgin when she did. John Tana had protected her from evil men during the time he lived with Malia. On her engagement, John left for Kaua'i, married, and had a family. Yet they still loved each other."

Grant rubbed his hands over his hair, fingered the stubble on his chin and said, "Then during the revolution against the Republic Tana returned to Honolulu and made love with my mother?"

"That I do not know. Malia might."

"Why wasn't I told about all this?"

"Families do not advertise scandals. Why did your mother help the Still family? Maybe it was because of her past friendship with John Tana. If you want to find out the truth, Nani Still could hold the answer to who is your father."

Startled by the suggestion, Grant returned from the window to Joshua's desk. His fists clenched, he glared at the older man, angered by the possibility that James Kingsley might not be his dad. "How?"

"Blood typing, I could arrange it with Nani. We need your father's blood and yours."

Grant closed his eyes, agonizing over the suggestion. To know or not to know, why not continue on without the answer? As if nothing had happened. Could his dad disinherit him? He was born during marriage. It was irrefutable proof that James Kingsley was his father. But, did he want to live a lie? Was Selena entitled to know the truth? Why was it up to him to find out? Let others who might gain from his disgrace pursue the answer. His eyes came open. He clenched his teeth, imprisoning his tongue. He shook his head, forced himself to relax and said, "When Dad returns from Maui we will take the test."

"Good. If Nani needs to come to Honolulu to do it, I'll advance the money. Don't protest. You can take care of expenses later. You should know that blood comparisons are not for certain, but it could prove that James Kingsley is not your father."

Grant shrugged. "So be it. I have a lunch date with Selena. I won't be back until tomorrow."

"Where are you going?"

"To see a kahuna in Kaneohe."

"Why do you want to do that? You have a suspect to the murders in custody. Let the law take its course."

"The evidence against Santos is flimsy. He may have had a motive to kill Judge Wright, but why kill Sheila Grant? Plus the only connection between the killer and Santos are two words in Filipino that I could have misheard or, worse, I am a suspect also and considered biased."

"Your friend Hitchcock hasn't beaten the truth out of him?"

"No. He isn't trying to. He believes I'm guilty, that's why I need to keep working on the case, see the kahuna get more information about the rituals."

CHAPTER 22

WIND BLEW AROUND the long black car, whipping strands of Selena's hair into Grant's face. He throttled the powerful engine of his Big Six Studebaker. The inclined cylinders worked faster, thrusting the automobile up the steep grade of Nu'uanu highway toward the lookout point of the Pali. On both sides of the road mountain walls disappeared into the clouds. Hala, koa, ohia trees, and a myriad of green shrubs lined the pathway that led to the slim plateau where Kamehameha the Great had fought the army of O'ahu.

Charging upward like a black hound racing for a ball, the sleek phaeton sped past the white fencing bordering the dangerous cliffs that spelt the doom of a thousand warriors. Grant throttled down the Studebaker as he motored into a sharp curve. A solid rock wall loomed in the mist on his right. In front, the road lay covered in white clouds. He double-clutched, gearing down his auto. It was slow to stop. He jammed the brakes, forcing the vehicle into a slide that ended just short of a low, white concrete wall.

"Very exciting," Selena said as she stepped from the passenger door and walked to the stone fence. Above her, the peaks of the Ko'olau Mountains thrust though the heavy clouds like spears poking through a sheet.

"The wind is building. In a few moments, the clouds will blow away, and we can see Kaneohe and Kailua."

"Look, the mists are lifting. It is like a movie curtain rising to start the show. But instead of black and white it is a scene filled with the colors of the rainbow. How beautiful it is." Selena clapped her hands and danced along the concrete barrier, the wind whipping her hair, her polka dot skirt swirling around her shapely legs and lifting provocatively about her hips. Overwhelmed by the panorama of dark rocks, moss covered cliffs, orange hills, and green leafed fields, Selena ended her impromptu waltz, leaned onto the top edge of the barrier, and began to chant.

Grant came to her, admiring the even cadence of her voice. Her tone was emphatic when she sang the names "Pele" and then "Kamapua'a"

When she finished her prayer, he asked, "What are you singing?"

"I'm asking the goddess Pele to grant us a safe journey over the mountain. You must know the story. She was in love with Kamapua'a, a god of Kaneohe. He was an unnatural god, half human and half pig. Like all men, he dallied with another woman. In a rage Pele threatened harm to anyone who drives over the Pali with pork in their car."

"Then we don't have a problem with Pele. There is no pork in our car."

"What did you eat for lunch?"

"In the car, please." Grant said.

Selena laughed, entered the auto, and they drove down the winding road. When they reached Kailua, Selena smiled. "See, Pele didn't harm us. My prayer worked."

***

It was mid-afternoon when Grant parked near the sea. They hiked toward the mountains along an earthen bridge separating a series of rice fields from a taro patch. Grant veered away from the banana grove at the edge of the water, remembering the still that was hidden within it. Little children playing by a grass shack watched them pass. Two Hawaiian men, loincloths wrapped around their thighs, tended to a large fire heating a mass of round rocks. A suckling pig, shaved and cleaned, lay by the reddening stones. Another man kneeled nearby, swinging a pestle into a dish-shaped wooden trough filled with tubers of taro that he mashed like potatoes into a purple paste.

"In ancient Hawai'i, the men did all the food preparation, cooking, serving, and cleaning up. You are a traditional Hawaiian, aren't you?" Selena teased.

"In my family, the women do everything, sewing, cooking, cleaning, and minding the children. A man is expected to make money. When he returns from work his wife must have everything in order for his enjoyment," Grant answered a sly smile on his face.

Selena leaped on a big rock, switched his shoulder with a hala leaf, and said in an imperious tone, "You will starve in my house."

"Then I will make enough money to hire servants to cook," Grant said as he moved to take her in his arms. Selena jumped away. She crouched behind the boulder, her eyes wary, waiting for him to make his move.

"Playing at cat and mouse is fun. But we need to talk to the kahuna before sunset. I think her shack is over there, near the waterfall that is spilling down the mountain."

Selena stepped around the boulder. She straightened her dress, brushed away loose debris that clung to it, and smoothed her hair, reinserting her combs that kept stray strands in place. Grant took her hand and they strode toward the waterfall. They passed an old Hawaiian man sewing a net, one end attached to the wall of an unpainted shanty. His belly protruded over a thin loincloth. He stood barelegged and shoeless in the dirt, his toes inserted into the mesh applying pressure where needed on the cords of the net.

"These people live in the traditional way," Grant said. "Take fish from the sea, food and fiber from the land. They have nothing except what nature gives them. With their hands they make whatever they need." He pointed ahead. "There is the kahuna lady we came to see."

Outside a grass shack, an old woman sat on a rock slab. Her eyes fixed on the leaf basket that she weaved. A black garment covered her body from throat to feet. Her hair flowed in waves onto her back. Behind her, the entranceway to her home was open, its interior dark and ominous.

"Hello, Auntie," Grant said as his feet scuffed up leaves littering the ground, dropped by lauhala trees bending over the shack and its owner. "May we talk?"

"You bring *maka'ni*?"

"Yes."

"Come inside."

The old woman darted through the dim opening, but Selena wouldn't follow. "It's dark, scary inside."

"Nothing will eat you. Auntie will blow up the fire, and you will be able to see." Then Grant turned serious. "You know Rudy Tang much better than anyone I know. I think he is the kahuna nui. I need your help to discover the truth. That's why you came."

"Then tell Auntie or the kahuna lady or whatever she is to raise the light, so I can avoid the cobwebs, the poison spiders, and whatever evil spirits may be inside the dark hole of her house."

As if in answer, orange light glowed within the hovel as the old woman threw dried leaves on a fire. "Come in," she said, her voice thin and high-pitched. "Rain outside."

Grant ducked through the threshold and reached his hand to Selena. Reluctantly, she bent low and came through the bamboo frame of the opening. Loose grass leaves at the entry brushed against her shoulders. She jumped in. Grant caught her before she tripped on rolled mats near the entryway.

"Sit," the old woman said. The glow of the re-kindled fire cast flickering light on her face. The leaves she had thrown on the hot coals sent cascades of smoke spiraling to the shack's ceiling. Her high-necked garment and dark features gave her the appearance of a disembodied spirit hovering over the flames.

"Grant," Selena whispered. "Please do your business right now, and let's get out of here."

Sensing the fear of the young woman, the kahuna said, "Breathe in the smoke. Do not fight it. You will feel better. Good dreams will be yours tonight."

Grant saw Selena trying not to breathe. He took her hand and squeezed. He smelled the pungent air. He watched her inhale, her eyes widen as the smoke entered her lungs, and observed her relaxing, no longer frightened.

"You want awa juice?" the old woman asked.

"Squeezed from the root or chewed?" Grant answered.

"The best kine. Got my juices in it."

"No, thank you. The last time we talked about the sacrificial rituals to Ku, you explained that the mat of mixed seaweed and hala leaf is called an aha. It signifies the prayers of the kahuna nui, seeking omens from the god Ku, before the sacrifices begin."

The old woman nodded.

"The salt is from seawater cast over the victim to purify him. The slashes across the body are from a leiomano, a crescent-shaped piece of polished wood with shark's teeth sewn around it. The death dagger came from the bill of a swordfish. You explained that Hawaiians did not have iron to make knives. So they used what they found in nature to create weapons. These rituals we discussed in the past are the same in both killings. But with Judge Wright, there were additions."

Sticks were added to the fire, causing sparks to crackle from the hot coals. Selena reared back, startled by the staccato of exploding splinters of wood. The sudden increase in light revealed carved caricatures of gods set on a low altar behind the old woman. One stood out, its jaw wide with serrated white teeth poised to rip. The saucer-wide mother of pearl eyes of Ku stared at Selena. Grant saw her shiver and he placed his arm around her shoulder, drawing her to his chest. Selena did not resist.

"There are three things that are different in the Wright murder. Embedded in a tire of the judge's car was a star of iron, shaped like jacks that children play with. You said that Hawaiians didn't have metal, but did they have a bone or wooden star that had six prongs?"

The kahuna shook her head.

"At the heiau where Wright was sacrificed there was a pole stuck into the ground with a white cloth ball wrapped at the top. What does it mean?"

There was silence as the old woman rocked, her eyes closed. After a time she opened them and said, "In the old days you mark a kapu place, a forbidden place, with that kind of symbol. I think the kahuna nui is saying that the heiau is sacred to Ku."

"Maybe like the little wooden icon of Ku that was left at Sheila's home." Grant said.

"I didn't read about that in the newspapers," Selena said.

"Clarence, the butler, just found it on the mantelpiece of the fireplace. Asing told me that the investigators had missed it when they searched the den for clues, probably thinking it was a family artifact. Because of the icon and the wrapped ball it appears that the killer wants the murders identified with the war god."

"You said that there were three things different about Wright's murder. What was the third?" Selena asked.

Grant's brow furrowed. He looked at the kahuna and made certain she was awake. "The judge's killer wrapped a girdle of cloth braided with co-conut leaves around his privates. He drenched the garment with Wright's blood. What does it mean?"

The fire sparked higher as the old woman stirred the ash-covered coals with a stick. She dropped more pungent-smelling leaves onto the flames. She breathed the narcotic smoke, closed her eyes, and keened in a low voice.

Grant became impatient. "Do you know what the bloody girdle means?"

Her voice deep, as if she spoke from inside a cave, the old woman said, "After the first sacrifice to Ku, whether the ulua or a human, the high priest would wrap a bloody girdle of leaf-braided cloth around each of the main gods of the temple, Lono, Kanaloa, Kane, and Ku. Before each god the kahuna nui would recite a prayer, 'Gird on this *malo*, O god! War is declared.'" The old woman paused, rocking rapidly. Her brow furrowed.

"Is there any more meaning to this ritual other than a declaration of war" Grant said.

The old woman's eyes became narrow slits. They fixed upon him with an intensity that made Grant shiver. "What it means, I am not certain. Mrs. Grant did not have a malo. Women were never gods. The judge could represent a temple god. If so, there will be three maybe four others who will die. No more than that."

Selena interjected, "There were more than five missionaries who came to Christianize the Hawaiians. Why would the kahuna nui of the 'Cult of Ku' be satisfied with just four more victims?"

"Because Ku's downfall was not caused by the missionaries," the ka-huna answered.

Selena gasped, "Now I remember. A year before the Christians came, Queen Ka'ahumanu, Regent of Hawai'i, ended the taboos, ended human sacrifices, destroyed the idols and the ancient temples."

"How do you know this to be true?" Grant scoffed. "We just had a 'coming of the missionaries' centennial. It celebrated the deliverance of the Hawaiians from the pagan gods."

"That is just a popular myth," Selena said. "At the University, I learned the truth. The worship of Ku was ended by Ka'ahumanu and the reigning kahuna nui in 1819. If you need to find out the truth, go to the Bishop Museum and speak with its curator."

Grant jumped up. "This could mean that the murders are not related to avenging Ku. It could mean that Rudy Tang has a motive to kill business people who caused the Chinatown arson or Santos wanted to kill anyone related to the sugar industry. Come on, Selena. Let's get back to Honolulu." He handed the old woman the gift she had requested and pulled the young girl from the shack.

They raced along the earthen bank separating fields of rice and taro stalks thrusting above muddy water. The sun had set, dimming light from its afterglow slowly shading into night's ink. The Studebaker loomed ahead. Two figures rose from the brush. "Hey, where you guys going? Stop a minute," a man said.

"Selena, here are the keys. Get to the car and go. I'll hold them off."

"Look at the pretty girl. Moses, you get her I get the guy."

One thug stepped toward Grant, swinging a club. Moses circled between Selena and the car.

Grant danced on his feet, shifting his body left and right, seeking an opening where he could jab or punch. He worried about Selena. Somehow he needed to beat his opponent quickly and help her. But the man with the club was not giving him an opening.

"Oh," Moses gasped. "You kicked me."

Grant and his adversary paused, watching Selena smash Moses in the belly. The man's chin dropped. She kicked his jaw. He fell.

"Damn you!" yelled Grant's opponent, charging Selena.

Grant leaped to tackle the man, and sprawled to the ground, leaves and debris scattering around him. He watched the man raise his club. He knew Selena would be smashed. He could do nothing to stop the crushing blow.

"Hi yah!" Selena yelled, pivoting away from the descending club. She grasped the attacker's arm, inserted a foot at his ankle, and propelled him into the side of the Studebaker, his head crunching the dark metal. The thug slid to the ground, shaking. Like a ballet dancer, Selena pirouetted twice, and slammed her foot into his face. The man slumped against the car's fender.

Grant picked himself from the ground, brushing away dirt and leaves. He walked to the Studebaker and pulled the delirious thug from his car. He stared at Selena. "Where on earth did you learn that?"

"From a Buddhist monk, he taught me to use leverage and your opponent's clumsiness to defend myself. Speed and quickness can often defeat brute strength."

"Ah, ha," Grant said and smiled, "Selena, I promise that you won't have to cook, sew, or clean our house. Just defend it."

They laughed and drove back to Honolulu.

CHAPTER 23

ABNER NOLAN STEERED his auto along the precarious coastal road leading into Waianae. He turned to his companion in the seat beside him, "Jerold, I know that you're curator of the Bishop Museum and interested in artifacts, but this is the most dammed fool venture I have ever been on. I'm driving all the way to Makaha Valley to visit some long-forgotten heathen temple that is probably destroyed like all the others."

"As a museum, interested in the Pacific, its Polynesian people, and the gods they worshiped we can't overlook an intact temple. Besides, the Hawaiian I talked to said his organization would restore the heiau and make a large donation to our studies program. I can't overlook those promises."

From the back seat, Alistair McKenzie, University of Hawaii professor, said, "In my research of Hawaiian religious practices at the University I have been hampered by not having an intact heiau to examine. This will be a great opportunity to learn how they were constructed."

"Alistair, academics live in the past. We should forget the godless people who lived here years ago, and concentrate on making Hawai'i a fit place for Christians to live in. These Hawaiians are savages and we should not give any credence to their crazy beliefs."

"We are an institution devoted to the past," Roberts said. "It is our duty to learn everything we can of the ancient peoples, acquire what we can of their earlier life, display them in a meaningful way, and what we can't secure, try to preserve what is of value of the ancient culture."

"Heathen temples are not worth saving. But since you are getting money for this damn fool expedition I'll stop complaining."

"Yes, I've already received a tidy sum. Look that is the dirt road we need to turn onto." Roberts pointed to an earthen track leading into an emerald green valley.

After twenty minutes of driving, Nolan said, "Nothing but overgrown shrubs and kiawe trees. This is a wild goose chase. Let's turn back."

"Wait, I see an auto up ahead, next to that sign."

Nolan pulled his car to a stop by a black vehicle parked alongside the road. Nearby, stood a sign on it were crude letters, "Kaneaki Heiau". An arrow pointed to a narrow trail that disappeared into the jungle.

"Where's this Hawaiian priest we are to meet?" Nolan complained, stepping out of the car. McKenzie and Roberts followed him, both men stretching their arms and legs. Other than the cawing of birds and the rasping sound of leaves brushed together by a stiff wind, there was silence.

"Creepy place," Roberts said. "Why did Kamehameha choose this spot for his temple, its miles from the sea."

"He had beaten the Oahu armies by 1795," McKenzie answered. "Only Kaua'i remained unconquered. The ridge above us leads to Ka'ena Point, which aims like an arrow at that island, sixty miles away. From Makaha beach, Kamehameha decided to launch his invasion fleet. He needed to make sacrifices to Ku before he attacked. He didn't have time to build a proper luakini in this valley. That is why a temple dedicated to peace was turned into a temple for the war god where human sacrifices could be made to Ku."

"All that shedding of blood didn't do the man any good," Nolan said. "Storm destroyed his fleet and ended his invasion."

"Aloha, gentlemen," came a voice from the forest. "Please follow the trail. I am waiting for you."

The three men stared in the direction of the call, but the western sun blinded them. Responding to the request, they trudged up the hard-packed dirt path, bordered on all sides by wild shrubs and copses of kiawe and koa trees. Soon the dirt road and autos were hidden from view.

Within the forest, the silence became oppressive. Nolan in the lead stopped hiking, and yelled, "Where the hell are you?"

McAllister, in the van, fell to his knees howling, grabbing at a feathered barb in his neck. A dark-clothed man smashed an egg into Roberts' face. Exploding white powder covered his eyes. "I can't see," he screamed.

Nolan turned to meet the attacker and felt a rod striking into his stomach. Air blew from his lungs, and he fell onto the trail. I'm going to die, he thought as he tried to suck oxygen into his body. He heard thrashing in the bushes, a cry. He attempted to rise and help, but couldn't.

Someone stood over him slapping his face. Nolan tried to howl, without success. Slowly air seeped into his lungs. A rope wrapped around each arm, around his waist, and he was pulled to his feet. His eyes misty with pain, Nolan glimpsed an apparition shrouded in black. Along the path his two companions lay in awkward positions. He had no time to determine their condition. The wraith yanked the rope that bound him and he stumbled upward along the earthen trail.

"Who are you?" Nolan croaked. The effort to say the words hurt in every part of his chest. His captor said nothing, pulling harder on the binding rope. Bright light from the sun flashed through the trees into his eyes, expressing, he thought, the great orb's anger at surrendering its possession of half the world to the night.

With surprising suddenness, the trees and shrubs ended, and Nolan found himself in a clearing. In front rose walls reminiscent of the outer defenses of a medieval fort. Stone steps lay ahead, leading to a rock-filled plateau. Yanked, Nolan sprawled onto the steps, skinning his knees and bruising his hands.

Without pausing, the dark clothed killer pulled Nolan upright, and forced him into a courtyard covered with loose rocks and weeds growing out of cracks in the stone. He stumbled forward, impelled ahead by his tormentor. More steps loomed, leading to a second platform on which Nolan could see, in the fading light, a statute above a small alter.

"You're going to kill me in front of that thing. Why?" the trustee of the Bishop Museum croaked. He knew the effigy of Ku. Half the icon, a huge face, jaws agape, teeth large, supported by short, small, bent legs poised to leap and tear flesh from his body.

Drawn to the altar by the rope, a searing pain pulsed through his arm as a club struck it. Another hit broke his other arm. Worse came, when the weapon struck below his waist. Nolan fell onto the altar screaming.

The killer pulled Nolan's head to the edge of the sacrificial stone. His eyes caught sight of the orbs of the statute, its mother-of-pearl shells glinting in the gathering darkness. He gasped. A saw-like device shredded his chest. Again and again the cruel razor-sharp weapon cut into his body, tearing his blouse into tatters.

Salt water sprinkled over him, adding to his agony. Broken knees and legs sent shock waves through his spine, as his pants came off. "Kill me. Kill me." Nolan begged.

Quiet and methodical, the killer placed something over Nolan's chest soaking up his blood. Sharks teeth cut into his flesh at the lower belly, and drew upwards creating a furrow of torn skin and muscle. Tears clouded his eyes. "Enough, enough, stop," he cried and fainted.

Slaps forced him awake. Dying light from the sun flashed across the mountain and onto the altar, its sudden warmth adding to his pain. A long, thin weapon passed in front of his eyes. Metal with sharp points was thrust into his hand. Strange words came from the shrouded wraith standing above him. A bright light and it was over.

CHAPTER 24

GRANT PUSHED HIMSELF from the mat, fighting dizziness. He tried to focus his eyes, but he felt pressure in his ears. He yawned to clear them. His *'olohe*, David Kamaka, said, "Remember, when thrown, roll with the momentum of the fall like a tumbler. Rise, face your opponent. Do all in one motion. We practice the throw again until you master saving yourself."

The two men squared off, assuming a boxing stance. "Look at the feet," David said. "A good fighter will have a solid foundation to deliver his strikes. A skilled opponent will try to kick you first, before finishing you up close. But if you rush, like you did a moment ago, he will use your momentum and his body to throw you down. Make your move."

Grant jabbed with his left, and with his feet flat on the mat turned his hips and delivered a right hand punch. David slipped inside Grant's arm, grabbed his exercise robe, twisted, and flung Grant to the ground. This time, prepared for the throw, Grant rolled onto the mat, sprang up, and turned.

"Good. You must tumble and defend first before you learn to attack. What I teach is a combination of martial arts of the east and Hawaiian *lua*."

"That's why Joshua sent me to you. He praised your knowledge in the fighting arts. But lua? Isn't that forbidden?"

"There is no law against it. But since it involves bone breaking and was used in olden times as part of warrior training, the missionaries banned it as a pagan practice. They also banned surfing, the hula, and our Hawaiian language."

Grant glanced around the garage. Shelves of goods covered the side walls, but there were no windows and the doors were closed. A single overhead bulb lit the room, along the back wall stood a locked cabinet. He realized they did their training in secret. He shook his head. "Christian morality takes away the fun in life. Like the blue laws in Waikiki that force everybody to cover their bodies and punishes affection. Did the missionaries ever do anything good for Hawaiians?"

"Not much. They translated the Bible and gave us a written language. They started schools for the chiefs. They finally eliminated human sacrifices."

"I thought Queen Ka'ahumanu ended all that a year before the Christians arrived?"

"She got rid of taboos and idols. But old practices die hard. For hundreds of years, chiefs had ruled the people by fear. Break a taboo, you died. Sacrificing continued. It took missionary teachers traveling to the different islands to finally end this horror."

"Reverend Bingham came to Honolulu in May of 1820. Were human sacrifices still going on?"

"My great grandfather told me that for several years after he came, at Papa'ena'ena, a heiau below Diamond Head, chiefs were still killing men."

"Papa'ena'ena. Aunt Malia told me that is a Ku heiau. Do you know where it is?

"Yes, it is above the polo field at Kapi'olani Park."

"Will you show me how to find it?"

"Yes."

"Master, you know a lot about the past. Do you think a Hawaiian would kill missionaries?"

Kamaka paused, studying Grant, his brow creasing into deep furrows. He did not give a direct answer. "When the missionaries left New England, they signed a contract not to interfere in Hawaiian government or own land. But who runs the government today and who owns the land? Ninety percent of the wealth of the islands is controlled by less than two percent of the people. What does the Hawaiian have? He has nothing."

"True. I saw poverty in Kaneohe. Once there were fields of taro in Waikiki. Now there are only the homes of the wealthy. Hawaiians are restricted from 'whites only' areas. Could this be a reason for murder?"

Kamaka shrugged. "The common folk accept their lot in life whatever it may be. They would not seek revenge. But there could be descendants of the chiefs who resent the loss of their power or the takeover of the land by the sugar plantations. Whatever the case may be, it is time for you to go. Do your exercises every day and I will see you early tomorrow morning."

Shoving his Studebaker into drive, Grant headed for the law office, thinking through the last two days. He had been unable to see Asing to tell him the grim prophesy of the kahuna. He had found no new clues to the killer, though he was sure Rudy Tang was somehow involved. Tonight he would have dinner with Dan Choy to secure his permission to court his daughter. Tomorrow his father returned from Mau'i.

When Grant arrived at his office there was a message to contact Captain Trask, before he could do so, Asing strode in, his face stern. "Where were you two nights ago?" The detective demanded.

"Why do you ask," Grant said, made wary by the incriminating tone in Asing's voice.

"I ask the questions you give me the answers."

"Ok. I was in Kaneohe with Selena."

"What you doing there?"

"I was seeing the kahuna that helped me before. This time she said there would be three, maybe four more deaths."

"Can you prove you were in Kaneohe from four in the afternoon to eight o'clock?"

"Sure, Selena, the kahuna, a half dozen Hawaiians, and two thugs can vouch for me. So what's going on?"

"There are now three deaths in Honolulu all related to the sugar industry and maybe connected in some way to the missionary background of those who have been killed."

Grant whistled. "A third Ku death? Who is it?"

"Man by the name of Abner Nolan, missionary background, and connected..."

"To the sugar industry," Grant interrupted. "He partnered with my grandfather in a mill in Aiea. Where did he die?"

"Kaneaki heiau in Makaha, he was killed same way as Wright."

"That leaves me out. I haven't been to Makaha in years, and I don't even know where this heiau is."

"If you are not the killer of these three people, somehow you are involved in every sacrifice to Ku."

"What do you mean by that?"

"You threatened Sheila Grant before she died. The weapon that killed Judge Wright was found in your hand. And Abner Nolan on the altar at Kaneaki Heiau held this." Asing reached into his pocket and withdrew a ribbon with a Maltese cross attached to it.

"That's a *croix de guerre*. It looks like the one I was awarded."

"It is yours. Your name is on the back," Asing said turning the medal around to show Grant. "My question is: how did it get into the hand of Abner Nolan as he died?"

"I don't know. The killer must have stolen it and planted it on the dying man."

"Or as Nolan struggled while dying, he tore it from your shirt."

"Asing, I didn't kill anybody, and I'm not stupid enough to wear medals on my shirt so a victim can grab it."

The Chinese detective sighed. "Although Hitchcock wants your hide, I agree with you. For some reason the killer wants to throw suspicion on you and away from him."

"I still think Rudy Tang is involved in this thing, how about Santos?"

"We had to let him go. An attorney came up with a writ of habeas corpus, our evidence is flimsy, and Santos had the best alibi of all, he was in custody when Abner Nolan died."

"We are back where we were two weeks ago, no leads and no suspect."

"Except you," Asing said with a laugh and added, "Seriously, I have three murders and two people in the hospital. The governor demands a solution to these crimes right now. Everyone in the department is working to solve the cases, but, if the kahuna is right we have three more deaths to come. What do we do? Put every missionary and sugar planter in protective custody? Impossible."

"I'd keep an eye on Tang and Santos. In the meantime, I'll try to figure out who stole my medal."

"I know you don't like Rudy. But I don't think he is involved. Since you're friends with Selena Choy, why don't you ask her father to give up his protection of the man? Then I bust him for you."

"Dan Choy protects him from the law," Grant said, startled by this admission of bureaucratic corruption and chilled by the realization that he would be seeing the crime boss tonight. Maybe that is why they were meeting in a secluded tea house in Manoa Valley far away from Chinatown and the waterfront.

"Let us just say that I have my instructions on what I can and cannot do," Asing answered. "About the murders, we tried to figure out how the killer got into Sheila Grant's home without a key, breaking a window, or using a ladder. There is a tree next to the house, with a limb overhanging the roof. A possibility he used it to get inside. As to the iron star in the judge's tire nothing like that exists in the islands. We are checking on foreign origins of the object. You have news for me?"

"The kahuna says the bloody girdle around Wright signifies the covering of a primary god of the heiau. There are three more primary gods beside Ku. That is why she predicted three murders for sure and maybe a fourth to propitiate a lesser god."

"Does your priest accept the motive of the kahuna nui in killing descendants of missionaries because they ended sacrifices to Ku?"

"The kahuna says that the idols and temples were destroyed, and human sacrifices ended, before the missionaries came. But my 'olohe says that sacrifices continued after they arrived and that the practice of death was finally terminated by the Christians."

"Your teacher believes that there are Hawaiians behind the murders?"

"He didn't say. Do you think the kahuna is right and there will be more murders?"

"If there are, you better have airtight alibis. Hitchcock wants you charged with all the homicides."

"Yeah, the guy can't see beyond his nose. But you don't believe I killed Sheila, Wright, or Nolan do you?"

Asing hesitated. He removed his hat and rubbed the band inside. Then he grasped the brim, pointing the panama at Grant. "You got good alibis for all three, a motive for only one, so maybe not. But stay away from crime scenes and keep me informed. Aloha." Asing moved out the door, his whip coiled at his waist, his panama hat squared onto his head. Grant was thankful that the detective hadn't smoked during the interview. He liked the crafty policeman, but didn't appreciate his persistent vice.

Grant worked through the day on court papers, dreading the evening meeting with Dan Choy. More distressing would be the confrontation with his father in the morning. Sue Watanabe took all family messages, each one curt and to the point. One message said that his dad was returning from Maui to tend to the estate of Sheila Grant and the Robert Grant Trust.

He finished work, called Trask, set an appointment for the next day, and headed home to retrieve the box where he kept his medals. Despite a thorough search, he did not find it. Maybe someone at the house had stolen his awards. But who? Puzzled he dressed and headed for Manoa Valley.

CHAPTER 25

DARKNESS CAME, AND Grant had not discovered the Japanese tea house. He thought to turn around, but his headlights shone on a hard-packed dirt driveway and within a jungle of trees stood a building. Faint golden light filtered through the bamboo-framed white shoji windows of the structure.

Loose rocks crunched on his tires as Grant drove up to two wooden pillars that supported a large beam serving as a portal into the restaurant. The vestibule entryway had a pond in its center. A dark iron, temple-shaped ornament, rose from a rock island in the middle. Red, yellow, and multi-colored carp swam in the water, disappearing under a raised porch leading directly into the eating area of the restaurant.

A squat heavy-set Oriental stepped from the interior of the building past rows of shoes, tatami sandals, and straw clogs. He said, "You Mr. Kingsley?"

Grant nodded.

"Mr. Choy is waiting for you. Take off your shoes, please."

They passed several rooms where patrons squatted on the floor using chopsticks to pick at food bowls set onto rectangular, black, teak tables. "Very hard on the knees," the guide said. He led Grant to a dark brown bamboo walkway overlooking a gully that sloped onto a grass plain half the size of a football field. Male peacocks strutted about, their iridescent tails of blue-green feathers fanned out in the mating ritual. In the dim light, Grant could see scores of golden eyes on the feather quills of the birds.

At the end of the bamboo walkway, the Oriental opened a rice paper door and waved Grant into a room unlike all the others. It had rich tan-colored teak walls, a side window overlooking the gully and the forest beyond. In the center stood a large teak table, simply set with chopsticks, porcelain spoons, and tea cups. On it was a rotating tray of food. Facing Grant sat a bulky Chinese that he knew must be Dan Choy. The man pointed to a chair opposite him. Grant sat, curious as to why they would talk alone.

A Japanese woman, in kimono and white socks, her lustrous dark hair wrapping around her head like a warrior's helmet, entered with a flask. She offered saki from a brown urn, left it, and departed. Sipping the rice wine, Dan Choy said, "You may wonder why I invited you to this remote restaurant deep in the valley?"

"I hope it's because of the good food and not because it might be a convenient place to cause me to depart this earth permanently," Grant said, uttering a half-hearted laugh.

"My daughter would be angry with me, if I eliminated you. We are here to avoid prying eyes and ears of those who may want to know our business. We meet because Selena tells me that you wish to court her and may seek to become part of our family. I have resisted this until now, but she insists. If I will not consent, she will leave home. Very disobedient, but young people are headstrong these days, and I have chosen to please her. I know much of the Kingsley family. It has an illustrious reputation. I'm sure you want to know about mine?"

It seemed an innocent question, but Grant thought it filled with hidden meaning. Should he hide the truth? Surely Choy had read the news articles about the murders. The media had only hinted at a family scandal. They had not written of his mother's adultery or he a possible bastard. How much of this should he tell? Was Selena worth the price of these admissions?

Dan Choy picked food from the tray. He shoveled steaming white rice between his lips. He sipped wine. He looked at Grant. "Try some of this fish marinated in soy sauce, scallions, and ginger. Delicious."

Grant knew he must say something. "Tell me of your family."

Choy put down his wine cup and chop sticks. "My father came from Shantung province, China. He was the youngest of six. Hawai'i was an opportunity for him. But sugar plantation work was hard, twelve-hour days, six days a week, living conditions brutal. When he finished his contract he left the plantation. The sugar people were angry. They passed laws against the Chinese leaving agricultural labor or buying land. My father was not afraid. He leased property. He grew rice in Waikiki. He made enough money to open an import/export business in Chinatown. He purchased a picture bride from the homeland. My mother had four of us. I married a woman from China and had two sons."

"Selena is not your daughter?"

"She is." Choy looked out the paned window into the darkness. He wiped a hand over his eyes. "The Chinese who continued to work in the sugar fields threatened strikes. The sugar people ended importation of Chinese and brought in foreigners, Portuguese, Japanese, other nationalities. The intent of the business people was to divide and conquer. When they could not stop us from seeking freedom, they set Chinatown afire. It destroyed all we had. It killed my mother and my wife." Choy stopped speaking, the edges of his mouth turned down in bitterness. He closed his eyes.

Grant's heart went out to the distraught man. "I am sorry to hear of your loss. Was it after the catastrophe that you remarried and had Selena?"

Choy relaxed a little and opened his eyes, saying, "She was a beautiful Portuguese woman. She died of the Spanish flu."

"Just like my mother. Did Rudy Tang lose family in the great Chinatown fire?"

"Yes, his father died trying to save his sister."

"Is Rudy angry with the government for the arson of Chinatown?"

Choy sucked in his breath. "You think Tang is the murderer of your grandmother and the judge?"

"Maybe, he has a couple of those shark knives and I saw what looked like a swordfish dagger in his office."

"There are others beside the Chinese who might want revenge against the business community."

"You mean like the Hawaiians who are angry with the missionaries for getting rid of Ku or the Filipinos who didn't get paid for calling off their strike?"

"That is all possible, but the Japanese also have good reasons. They struck for higher wages and better living conditions in January. The plantations locked them out of their homes. Thirteen thousand people living on the streets, a third were children. The plantations starved them. The flu killed hundreds. They had to settle the strike."

"And the Filipinos double-crossed them. Judge Wright was the deal maker for the HSPA, the sugar planters," Grant interrupted.

"Yes, and the night he died he brokered a deal with me to import Chinese workers in case the Japanese or Filipinos went on strike again."

"I get it, divide and rule. But didn't the business people pass laws stopping the importation of Chinese because your people caused trouble for the plantations?"

"Yes, but that was long ago. Now, to control the new races that are brought in, the sugar owners want to hire cheap Chinese laborers as strike breakers."

Grant rose from his seat, gesturing. "And you're the broker for importing these new workers."

Choy's eyes narrowed to slits. "Yes, and Rudy Tang works with me on this project. Judge Wright's murder is bad for our business. You should look somewhere else for your killer. It may be a person close to you who knows your habits."

"That is limited to a handful. But I came here to speak of courting your daughter. What do you want to know of my family?"

Dan Choy's wolfish look eased. He shook his head and said, "I do not believe that you killed your step-grandmother. I believe you are honorable. I believe you are interested in my daughter's welfare. That is sufficient."

"I know at one time, Rudy Tang was your choice for Selena. Does that create a problem for you?"

Choy smiled. "I do not make choices for Selena. She chooses for herself. She wants you for a companion. I will not say no. But Rudy Tang serves me well. He has a powerful Tong behind him. I will not stop him from competing for Selena's affection."

"Thank you for your consent. I promise not to dishonor your daughter."

"I accept your promise. But even though you are welcome to my house, I cannot protect you from Rudy Tang."

CHAPTER 26

GRANT WATCHED THE inter-island steamship steering for Pier Seven. He shuddered as the boat approached. His father controlled the Trust and Sheila Grant's estate, would he reject Grant as his son and disinherit him? Losing his inheritance was not important, but he would grieve if his father rejected him. For some moments his mind wandered to the conversation of the previous day. Who could have stolen his medal and committed Nolan's murder? None of the women he knew could have done it, not strong enough. Joshua was too old. Maybe his teacher, David Kamaka? He didn't like missionaries and knew the rituals of the ancient gods. What did he hide in his locked cabinet?

In the street, Charles sat in the family car waiting for his father. Grant remembered the chauffeur had taken him to see Sheila. He received the message that became invisible. Charles lived in a room attached to the family house. He could have stolen his medal. Maybe he is the kahuna nui.

The gangplank trundled up to the ship as it pulled into the dock. His father stepped onto it striding to the pier. Grant waved and received a curt nod. They walked in silence to the car and Charles drove them home. Not a word passed between them.

At Waikiki, Kingsley dismissed the chauffeur, asked Sue Watanabe to mix cool drinks, and guided his son to the outdoor lanai overlooking the sea. A strong wind flung crashing waves onto the sand. Only the best of the beach boys surfed in the powerful sea. The few tourists were satisfied to sit beneath parasols along the beach sipping exotic drinks.

Grant's father unwound his tie and said, "What have you been doing since I left?"

"I work with Joshua Kanakoa, Mother's attorney. I've been investigating the murders with my lady friend, Selena, and done some surfing."

"Who is this lady and who is her father?"

Grant thought for a moment, wondering how honest he should be in his answers. He knew that a wide gap existed between the Occidental and the Oriental. But covering up the truth would lead to too many lies. "Her name is Selena Choy. Her father's name is Dan and he runs an import/export business."

"You are seeing the Chinese daughter of one of the most notorious men in Hawai'i." Grant's father exploded in anger. "The rumors I heard of your activities are confirmed by your own tongue. It is best that you no longer traffic with the woman or her father."

Grant winced, shocked by the virulent demand. He chose his words and answered without delay. "Sir, she is intelligent, helpful to me, and as wonderful a person as you will ever meet. Surely you should see Selena."

"Her father is involved in every vice known to man, gambling, prostitution, opium trading. The wrong-doing in the family goes way back. When Dan Choy's father left the plantation he started an illegal lottery business. His machinations helped bring down the old Queen. The son is the same, crooked as they come. He might even be the murderer of Sheila and Wright,"

His father's anger forced Grant into an agony of indecision. Last night he wondered if Selena was worth revealing his past. Now his father demanded that he give her up. For his entire life, he had been raised to obey his parents. But his heart ached when he thought of casting aside the beautiful Eurasian. If he disobeyed, would his father terminate their relationship?

CHAPTER 27

GRANT EASED HIS Studebaker into the slot that the Marine guard pointed to. Construction workers swarmed around the budding naval facility at Pearl Harbor. He noticed the newly completed dry dock as he stopped his car. He smiled as he remembered the news stories. It had taken ten years to complete. Construction had been hampered by the project undergoing a series of collapses. Hawaiians blamed the failures on the anger of the shark god, who lived in caves beneath the site. But finally the engineers had figured out a way to avoid the effect of seismic quakes that had knocked down the construction, and the dry dock had been completed.

He pushed open his auto door, struggling to gain control of his emotions. An airplane droned overhead. He ducked, recalling Fokker bi-planes strafing the trenches. Grant looked to the sky and saw a two-winged aircraft flying overhead, American insignia on its fuselage. The military activity reminded him of his days as a non-commissioned officer. On the battlefield he made decisions for himself and his men. You adapted, changed, or you died. There were no inflexible rules.

But he had not challenged his father. A lifetime of parental obedience had stilled his tongue. Instead he had left home mumbling about an appointment with a naval captain. He avoided giving a direct answer to his parent's demand. As he stepped into the naval administration building, he vowed that such obedience would end.

A male clerk took his name, buzzed the captain, and ushered Grant into a sparse office overlooking the lakes of Pearl Harbor. Trask rose from his desk, offered his hand and said, "Thanks for coming." He glanced around his office and with a wry smile said, "Congress is a little tight with the money, but we have spared no expense in making this a first-rate naval base."

"I've lived in worse conditions. Try wet trenches, floored with duck boards that squish mud all over you wherever you walked."

"Yeah, you fought in the war. I didn't see action, got stuck in Washington doing naval intelligence. You know why I asked for this meeting?"

"You wanted to find out how a Japanese consulate got established in Hawai'i. My partner Joshua told me that in 1881 King David Kalakaua traveled to Japan and proposed a marriage between his niece, Princess Kaiulani, and Prince Konatsu. It was some kind of an 'Oceanic Empire' proposal. The Emperor refused his offer. To justify the expense of his trip, he worked out a deal to send Japanese workers to Hawai'i. The contract workers arrived with a Japanese consul named Nakamura. He established a consular office to assist Japanese living in the islands. Other than the United States, he was the only diplomatic representative ever posted to the Hawaiian monarchy."

"So that's how they got rooted here. We couldn't get rid of them with annexation to America. You're a former army officer and a war hero to boot. I think I can speak plainly. At the start of the war, Japan seized all German possessions in China and the Pacific. After the armistice, President Wilson thought that the Japanese would give back to the native people the islands they acquired and return to China what they took. But Japan has refused to do so. Our current naval thinking is to have a two-ocean fleet. That's why you see this naval base under full construction. We believe that our next war will be with Japan."

"And you think that the consulate is full of spies."

"We don't know. From what you say, it didn't start out that way. You can help us find out. You've got a friend there. Check things out. Report back to us. On July 4 there will be a parade down Kalakaua Avenue ending in the park. There will be horse racing, a big polo match, and important people. Get me the names of the consulate officers who should attend. I'll send them invitations."

"Will do, I did see a telescope in my friend Sato's office trained on the entrance to Pearl Harbor. I also learned a Japanese battle cruiser is due in Honolulu Harbor in late July. Is that the kind of information you want?"

"Yes."

***

Grant and Kamaka worked through several lua moves and strikes. "I know you are tired of repeating. But to learn, there is no substitute for repetition."

"Sound advice," Grant said, his eyes fixed on the unlocked cabinet. He paid for his inattention by being slammed to the mat.

"You were distracted. Interested in what I hide in my cabinet? Come see." Kamaka opened the door of the container. In it were a trove of weapons, shark-toothed knives, swordfish bills, spears, tripping cords, slings and almond-shaped stones.

"Do you use them?" Grant asked, admiring the finish and pristine beauty of the ancient armaments.

"No. They are reminders of the past when hundreds of thousands lived in Hawai'i. Now we are only twenty thousand. These are desperate times for my people. The end of the Hawaiians may be coming. It is all because of the foreigners who came and contaminated our land," Kamaka said, bitterness in his voice. He reached into the cabinet and withdrew a sling. "You should learn this weapon. It is easily carried and deadly."

Grant nodded, feeling a sudden pleasure at the notion that he might have a concealed weapon that could not be detected. "There will be July Fourth celebrations at Kapi'olani Park, below Diamond Head. You said there is a Ku temple between them. Will you come as my guest to the special events and show me the heiau's location?"

Kamaka paced the garage. His face that a moment before had been friendly had turned sullen. Shaken by this sudden change of mood, Grant said, "Did I say something to offend you?"

His 'olohe stopped his walk, "You have Hawaiian blood but do not know your history. Our Queen, Lili'uokalani, was overthrown by U.S. Marines and a Committee of Public Safety composed of thirteen Caucasian businessmen. The committee sought annexation to the United States, but Congress refused. Why? Because President Grover Cleveland said the taking of our nation by the Marines was illegal. What did these businessmen do? They declared the Republic of Hawai'i and seized all the lands of the monarchy. Do you know when this occurred?"

Kamaka paused in his tirade and glared at Grant as if he were the enemy who had seized Hawaiian lands, "on July 4th 1894. The fourth of July is not a time for Hawaiians to celebrate, but a time to mourn the loss of our land that the Republic gave to America on Annexation."

Until this moment Grant had not realized the depth of emotion that his teacher and other Hawaiians must feel over the end of the Hawaiian Kingdom. The history books had been written by the winners of the nineteenth-century struggle for power in the Pacific. The pain that the native people suffered over the loss of their sovereignty had been hidden. There seemed to be reason, however warped it might be, for Hawaiians to seek revenge against the missionaries. The Cult of Ku might be a rallying point for dissident Hawaiians fostered by some misguided man. Hesitant, but determined to find out, Grant asked, "Do you know of Hawaiians who would want to kill missionaries or their families?"

"No. I will draw a map where you can find the Ku temple. Then we go outside and practice with the sling."

CHAPTER 28

IT WAS NIGHT when Grant returned to Waikiki. Though he dreaded the evening talk he was determined to take a stand, no matter the consequences. When he entered, his father was already at supper. He looked up from the dinner table, his silver hair shining in the glittering light of an iridescent lamp. His eyes focused on Grant. He said in a modulated voice, "You are late. Sue, bring supper for Mr. Kingsley." His mood turned frosty as he added, "You ran out without giving me an answer."

Grant did not waver in his determination to make decisions for himself whatever the consequences. "Sir, you surprised me by your demands. I think you should meet Selena. You should judge her on her merits and not by your perception of her father's character. I intend to see her tomorrow. I would be pleased to introduce her to you." He steeled himself for his father's explosion and banishment from home.

"I see. You are determined to thwart my wish."

"That is not so. I respect your opinion, but I believe it to be wrong to tar a child with the deeds of a father." He noticed his dad rear back, startled by his words. Desperately he hoped that the man he admired and loved could understand the pain he felt for something that was not of his making. But if his belligerence caused their relationship to end, then he was prepared to leave.

James Kingsley's blue eyes fastened on his son. For the first time since Grant had returned to Honolulu, the steely look in them softened. "I see. You are saying don't judge a book by its cover. But the woman is Chinese."

"She is half Portuguese. Mother was half-Hawaiian and you married her."

"Well, that was different. When will you introduce us?"

"If it is convenient, sir, tomorrow evening. Selena and I are exploring at Diamond Head and afterwards I'd like to have supper here."

"So you knew that I would consent to see her," Kingsley said, irritation in his voice.

"No, I did not. But if you refused, then I would still meet Selena tomorrow and prepare to leave home."

"You care for her that much?"

"She has been very helpful to me. I intend to court her."

Kingsley examined his fingers, and then turned his hand, searching his palm. He sighed, "I think I may need a fortune teller to advise me. Young people these days are so unpredictable. Yes, I will have supper with you tomorrow night and meet Selena."

Happy to have won his agreement, Grant did not press the issue of blood testing. Maybe time would heal the hurt that his father felt over his wife's infidelity.

***

"I can see by the rough rock outlines what might be a terraced heiau," Selena said as she paused in her climbing of Diamond Head to study dark black blocks of stone set into the mountain's side.

"This must be the spot that my 'olohe mapped for me. It's about four hundred yards above Kapi'olani's polo field. Judging by the traditional foundation stones that I can see, it has to be the Ku temple of Papa'ena'ena."

"What does the name mean?" Selena asked.

"I don't know, but I will find out. I don't see any dried blood on the rocks. The sacrifices must have ended a long time ago. Let's hike over to Fort Ruger. My friend Captain Trask has arranged for us to visit inside the crater and climb to the top where the military is building gun emplacements."

Selena took Grant's hand and they headed around Diamond Head Road to the military post. After a check with command, the guard let them pass. They started on the mile hike to the top of the dead volcano. "The Hawaiians called it Mount Le'ahi, the brow of a hill rising to the tail of a tuna fish," Grant said as they trudged up a steep trail aiming for steps chiseled into the inner wall of the crater.

"And a drunken British sailor called it Diamond Head because he found calcite crystals embedded in the rocks," Selena answered, wiping sweat from her brow that momentarily stung her eyes.

"Do you notice how round and perfectly symmetrical this volcano is?"

Selena nodded, gasping for breath as the climb became steeper. She stopped her hiking and asked, "Do you know why?"

"Geologists say that volcanic activity ended on this island two million years ago. Maybe a hundred-fifty-thousand years in the past, there was a sudden burst of eruptions on O'ahu. Within a few days of each other, Punchbowl, Koko Head, and Diamond Head exploded. For reasons un- known, the bursting stopped. It was like a giant threw three huge cannon balls into hot mud and the mud flew up and suddenly froze. We are near the top. Give me your hand."

Selena stretched her arm and Grant gripped it. He pulled her to the crest of the ridge, eight-hundred feet above Kapi'olani Park. He did not release his grip, but instead swung her into him. Selena's eyebrows arched, "Now, now, Mr. Kingsley. You told me I would be safe if I took this hike. You said you would protect me from any wild animals who sought to devour me."

With a rueful smile, Grant shrugged his shoulders, mumbling, "Yeah, I did say all that. Yeah, you are safe with me." He released his hold on her hand and they gazed out at the beautiful scene below. The western sun's rays added specks of gold to the spectacular colors of the earth and the foliage of the Waianae Mountains. From that range a great mantle of green spread over the hills into the valley of Nu'uanu where the last battle for Hawai'i had been fought. It stretched up and over Punchbowl volcano and into the stream-cut valley of Manoa. The vast cloak was colored with clumps of brilliant flowers and leaves. Below them, in the flat wet lands of Waikiki, thousands of slender green rice stalks waved in the wind.

Huge banks of cumulus clouds, dark and moisture-filled, drifted to- ward the island. Waves flecked with foam hurried toward the shore pushed by breezes that caught Selena's hair, whipped it around her face, and onto

Grant's shoulder. Columns of sunlight pierced the clouds, the filtered lighting extending like heavenly stairways into the sea. Like a refracting prism, the ocean shaded from purple to blue and then to blue-green as the water shallowed near shore. Riding on top of the white capped waves were outrigger canoes and surfers, all hurrying toward the sand beach of Waikiki.

The strong wind sweeping up the side of the volcano blew them together. "Beautiful," Selena sighed.

"Yes, you are beautiful," Grant agreed as his arm went around her waist and he pulled her body into his. He bent his face to hers. She did not fight his embrace.

"Ah, sir," a voice said. "I have to ask you to leave. You're in a restricted area."

A soldier dressed in khaki and wearing a doughboy helmet stood a few feet from them. A forty-five automatic holstered at his side.

"Sorry," Grant said, and he and Selena hurried down the trail heading for home.

They walked around the crater and strode onto Monsarrat Street. An open-topped sedan pulled to a stop ahead of them, and four men jumped out. One of the thugs said, "Get the girl." Three men charged Grant, the man in the lead swinging a meat cleaver. Grant stepped inside the attacker's descending arm, grasped his left hand, seized his shirt, pivoted on his left foot, and pulled his opponent over his hip, flattening him to the pavement. He did not stop, but leaped and executed a somersault, turning in time to see two other men stumbling onto the body of their fallen comrade.

He glanced at Selena. She defended herself with kicks and arm blocks but her opponent forced her to retreat. He could not help her. The two remaining thugs charged, one of them swinging a club. Grant sidestepped and tripped the club-wielder, sending him sprawling. The second man bulled into him. Grant rolled backward, his hands grasping the shirt of his opponent. He thrust his foot into the pit of the man's stomach and, using his backward momentum, threw the attacker over his head and onto his back. Grant did a forward flip onto his feet and charged Selena's opponent.

The man punched with his right hand. Grant stepped under the extended arm, slapping it at the elbow. At the same time he swung up his cupped right hand into the throat and Adam's apple. The man's left fist struck Grant's tightened stomach. He countered by jamming his knee into the scrotum of his opponent. The thug gasped and dropped to the ground.

Only the man with the club still stood. He looked in bewilderment at his three companions groaning on the street. "Where did you learn all those moves?" Selena said, admiration in her voice.

"I have a good teacher. I practiced *harai goshi*, the hip throw, for a week. I just learned *tomoe nage*, a foot in the stomach, roll backward, and let the man fly." Grant laughed.

"What about that Adam's apple punch and the knee between the thighs?"

A car came around the bend, its headlights picking up the men on the roadway. The thugs staggered back to their auto and sped away. Selena scowled as they fled. "Some of Rudy Tang's hoodlums, I'll tell my father."

"Don't bother. I think Rudy's men have learned their lesson."

"Maybe, but next time they'll come with guns."

***

At dinner, James Kingsley listened, fascinated with Selena's knowledge of botany. "We are having trouble on Mau'i improving our yields. The quality of our sugar is not as good as the competition. You say the University can help us in both areas?"

Selena nodded and then proceeded to enter into a discussion on proper nutrients for the soil, cultivation methods, and hybridization. His father asked questions about weed control and Selena had answers. On into the evening the two discussed physiology, horticulture, plant resistance to insects, diseases, and environmental stresses. By the time Charles drove Selena home, she and Grant's father were friends.

"That was a fine young lady," Jim Kingsley said at breakfast the next day.

"I knew you would like her," Grant answered. "She is beautiful, very intelligent, and a terrific fighter."

"I hope that is one talent this family will not need. I have to return to Mau'i after the Independence Day celebrations. Competition is fierce and we need help. I might put some of your lady friend's suggestions to good use. Maybe even hire her to help us."

"Great. Selena would love that. I bet you could also use agriculture information that the University has accumulated."

Kingsley looked away, drumming his fingers on the table. Grant realized that his father could not admit that he and his brother couldn't solve all the problems of running a sugar plantation. Until last night, pride would not have allowed them to seek outside help. Maybe Selena had made a breakthrough in the rigidity of their thinking. His father interrupted his thoughts. "While I am away on Mau'i, I need someone reliable to be in charge of the Kingsley office in Honolulu. We have interests in Aiea, O'ahu and Kilauea, Kaua'i, which need tending to. I want you to take care of things after I leave."

This surprised Grant. Yesterday he was prepared to leave home. This morning he was being offered a position in the family enterprises. "I'm grateful for the opportunity," Grant answered, "but I am starting a law practice with Joshua Kanakoa."

Kingsley fixed his eyes on his son. "Do both, I need someone I can trust taking care of our business in Honolulu."

Grant stroked his chin. He played his fingers over his brow, ran his palm across his hair smoothing out stray stands. Was this what he wanted? Tied to the family's sugar interests? He would become part of the establishment. He would enjoy wealth and power. But would he like it? Wouldn't it be better to make it on his own? Develop a law practice. Fight for those in need, like the Hawaiians. But maybe he could do both. If he helped his father maybe it would heal past wounds. "Okay, I'll do it."

"Good. The first order of business is to be introduced to important people. July Fourth is a big day for the business community. Lots of events at Kapi'olani Park, horse racing, a polo match. Meet me after the parade. I'll introduce you to my friends."

"I'm having breakfast with some navy officers and the Japanese consul. After that, we will take in the parade. I'll come to the park by noon."

Grant walked to the Moana Hotel and met Trask, a second navy captain, Japanese Consul General Hideo Matsu, and Sato. The morning meal at the Moana Hotel turned into a lively affair. The two navy captains questioned Matsu on the presence and purpose of the consulate in Hawai'i.

"Forty percent of the population of Hawai'i is Japanese. There is great discrimination against our people. It is most important that we take care of citizens of Japan. Our consulate makes certain that they are treated fairly in the law courts. Land disputes are an important part of our business. Alien Asians cannot own land, but Japanese who are born here and thereby are citizens of America can. First generation, Issei, take property in the names of their children to avoid the Alien land law. This creates legal problems for the families. Mr. Sato is our expert. He is second generation, Nisei."

Grant looked at his friend dressed in khaki trousers, white shirt, tie, and a light jacket. "You're an American citizen? I thought you came from Iga province in Japan?"

"I was born in Aiea, O'ahu." Sato answered. "When I reached five, my mother took me to Japan to be educated."

"And you returned to Hawai'i in January?" Grant asked.

"Yes, but Japan is my home," Sato answered. He gave a curt nod to the consul general.

"Does the consulate involve itself in military matters, foreign affairs?" Captain Trask interrupted.

"No. We take care of legal matters, deal with passport questions, the importation of picture brides, and issues involving the recent labor strike," Matsu answered. "I notice that your country is developing Pearl Harbor. Will battleships be berthed there?"

Trask paused for some moments before answering. "I cannot say for certain. It is the navy's intent to create a fleet in the Pacific to defend our commerce with Asia. I'm sure you are aware that the backbone of any navy is capital ships."

The consul general stroked his chin and smiled. "I do not trouble myself with military matters. I asked the question because there is talk of limiting battleship construction among the Great Nations, Britain, America, and Nippon. I naturally assumed that big gunned ships are very important."

"If someone were to start war in the Pacific, battleships would rule the seas," Trask said. "The British demonstrated that at Jutland. And you must know that when the Great War began, the battleship *Hizen* chased the German cruiser *Grier* and an armed raider into Pearl Harbor. They refused to fight the big guns of your country's warship. Since everyone is finished with breakfast, let's proceed to the grandstand and watch the parade. We have a fly-over by the newly arrived Fourth Observer Squadron."

***

"Let me introduce Donald Mills, a longtime friend of your grandfather and one of the most successful merchants in Honolulu," James Kingsley said.

Grant saw a tall, spare man, of sinewy build, his face golden tan, his hair white, with thick brows, the eyes beneath bright and penetrating. With his slightly hooked nose, Mills had the appearance of a bird of prey. Grant thought the man was accustomed to doing what he pleased and taking when he wanted.

"Good to meet you." Mills extended a hand wrinkled, but strong. "Your grandfather and I went to O'ahu College together. His dad and mine were the last of the one-hundred-and-fifty-three missionaries that the Board of Missions sent to Hawai'i to spread the Gospel to heathen lands."

"Why did the Board stop sending missionaries?" Grant asked.

"They claimed that Hawai'i was Christianized, but the truth is that they ran out of money. They cut off funding and forced the missionaries to go into business to make ends meet. My father went into merchandising and your great granddad into sugar planting."

"And the actions of the Board of Missions proved in the long run to be a godsend," James Kingsley added. "Freed of their contract not to own or possess land, the mission folk got the kings to give them property. They developed these islands into the agricultural powerhouse that it is today and made Honolulu the mercantile capitol of the Pacific."

Mills smiled. "Your grandfather and I worked well together. He had his sugar mills. I had my merchandising stores. Together we squeezed out the competition. It was a very synergistic relationship that benefited both of us. I miss Robert. We were a tough team to beat."

Grant heard the sound of a trumpet. "I think the horseracing is about to start. Dad says you play polo. Are you in the match today? What's your number?"

"Look for number one. Bet on our team. We will win."

CHAPTER 29

ONALD MILLS WAITED for the sixth and last chukker to begin. He looked over at the rail separating the ten-acre field from the spectators. He found the Eurasian woman that made his heart race. She was stunning. Grant introduced them during divot stomping at halftime. It was then that he resolved to wrest her from him.

He whispered, "I'm going to take your sweetheart, little boy, and fly her to the moon." He smiled when he remembered how Grant's face turned sullen. He knew he would win. He never lost.

The referee yelled, "Are both teams ready for the sixth and last chukker?" The captains nodded. Two teams, each of four mounted players, faced off. Eight ponies pawed the earth. Mills exulted. This is the ultimate game, he thought. A game created by the nobility of Persia. Played by the Maharajas of India and brought to Hawai'i by British lords. It's the game of kings.

The round white ball bounced onto the playing field. Mills charged. His offensive midfielder raced by his side. The red team hit the ball first, sending it in a line toward its eight-yard-wide goal. Horses swerved to follow the path of the speeding sphere that soared over the green turf at a hundred miles an hour. The defensive back of the white team intercepted the strike and smashed it hard across the field. A red player raced to the ball, but the pivot man of the white team rose in his saddle, extended his mallet and interfered with the swing of the red player. The white midfielder struck at the ball. The bamboo-shafted mallet made contact with the ground, flinging up a shower of turf. Its head smashed into the three-and-a-half-inch ball and it sped along the ground heading for the white goal.

Mills raced to the ball, following its line. A red player charged to intercept, shoving his horse into Mills' pony. "Hey, that's a foul," he yelled.

"Go to hell," his opponent answered, trying to push Mills away from the line of the hurtling ball.

"Asshole," Mills swore, angling his horse into his opponent. Rising in his saddle, he struck an off-side shot into the polo. The sphere sped for the goal. To his right, a red player charged. Timing his maneuver, Mills forced the nose of his horse into his opponent and back-handed a shot from the left side of his horse. "Watch this."

The shiny brown-coated mounts of the opposing players pounded against each other at full gallop, Mills' polished leather boot scraping the saddle of his opponent. "Oh, my God," swore the red player as the white ball raced through the goal posts. "You made the most difficult of all polo shots."

Mills raised his mallet. "I did it," he screamed. "We're ahead by a goal." The crowd roared its approval. Mills rode back to the face-off position, knowing that the sixth and last chukker was not over.

For the next two minutes, the teams galloped, tore into each other, and smashed the ball back and forth along the green turf. At one moment, the red team drove for a score, but the white defensive back knocked the ball away. Mills took it down the field racing for the goal. Red players converged on him and spoiled the final shot of the game.

Spectator cheers ended the match. Players walked their ponies back to the barn near the club house. Mills showered, changed, and took his place at the gaming tables as his team-mates congratulated him. Despite Prohibition, one of the contestants produced a bottle of Scotch and the gambling began in earnest.

By the time Donald Mills quit gaming, night had come. He staggered to his car parked by a small forest of kiawe trees. Opening the door, he fumbled for his keys mumbling, "Where is the damned ignition." He bent his head to the side to look. A cord settled around his neck and jerked back. He grasped his throat, trying to pull the thin rope away. He kicked, bruising his knees against the dashboard. Reaching behind, he sought to grab his attacker, but touched only the shoulders of a man in the backseat.

Despite the excruciating pain he forced his head forward. The cord bit into his throat, drawing blood. He felt it dripping over his shirt. The garrote tightened. Breathing stopped. White spots danced before Mill's eyes. He gave a shake of his head, and then nothing.

CHAPTER 30

WHAT A FABULOUS evening, Grant thought, enjoying his conversation with Selena. They sat at a corner table in the dining room of the Moana Hotel. A candle lamp bathed them in low light, its glow making the Eurasian woman more beautiful than ever. The moon silvered the sea, sending a shimmering path across the water toward the beach. Warm breezes rustled the coco leaves as the orchestra played a dance tune. Coyly Selena said, "You think Mr. Mills is competition for my affection and not Rudy Tang?"

"He said as much during half-time. And did you watch him when he made a goal? He pumped his mallet in your direction, raised himself in his saddle, and gave you a huge smile."

"Mr. Kingsley, are you jealous?"

"Whatever made you think so? Not a bone like that in my body. Besides, he's too old for you, almost sixty."

"That is a very good age. Older men have lots of experience in what women want," Selena answered, her eyebrows arching, her eyes sparkling with merriment as she reached her hand under the table to grasp his.

"Come on. Let's go and enjoy the moonlight," Grant said.

It was the Sabbath, and they were careful not to show affection, nor hold each other until they passed the white Grecian columns at the hotel entrance. They walked arm in arm along Kalakaua Avenue, staring at a moon hanging bright over Diamond Head. The night was still, except for the gentle swish of waves washing onto Waikiki Beach. Grant started to whistle.

"What's that song?" Selena asked. "It's stirring."

"'God Bless America.' Irving Berlin wrote it, very patriotic." Grant began singing.

Selena clapped her hands, saying, "It's wonderful music for the Fourth of July, but your loud voice is powerful enough to wake the dead." She laughed, twirling her body like a ballet dancer. Her skirts flounced high, revealing long, slender, legs.

The pale light of the moon glinted from her eyes as she pirouetted along the roadway. After a final twist, she stopped and faced him. Her outstretched arms gracefully descended. Her hands came together, forming a 'V' at her thighs.

Excited by her haughty posture, Grant ended his singing, rushed to her, and pulled Selena to him. Her soft curves, the perfume in her hair, raised an excitement that he could not suppress. He thought of his promise to Dan Choy, and fought to suppress his passion.

Selena pulled away, and skipped to the lighted steps of the Kingsley home. "Maybe someone can take me to Chinatown." She paused, pointing. "Look, there's a leaf-wrapped package on your stairs."

Grant came to the entry steps and retrieved the bundle. He unwound its bindings and opened the leaves. A doll, eyes wide, jaws gaping, hair smeared with red, rolled out. It fell with a thud, the paste reddening the white marble of the stairs. What remained in Grant's hands were matches, burnt coals, and a small dead red fish.

Selena gasped as she picked up the doll, her earlier joy gone from her face. She stared at the awful caricature, the damp mixture on the doll's hair covering her fingers like blood. "This is a symbol that something terrible will happen," she gasped.

"But who will be killed and where?" Grant said, shaking his head. "Into the house, let's find Charles. He's Hawaiian. He may know what the articles mean."

But none of the servants were in. Grant realized that this was Sunday and a holiday for them. He went to the phone and called his 'olohe, David Kamaka. The man's irritated wife said that his martial arts teacher was away.

"I will call Malia. She will know."

Lehua, the old woman's teenaged caretaker, answered the incessant ringing of the telephone. "Auntie asleep, I cannot wake her," the young girl complained.

"Get her up. Please!" Grant begged. "Someone is going to die. Maybe he is already dead. I don't know, but we have to find the place." He heard a thin voice complaining, "Eh, what going on. Too much noise."

"Auntie, it is Grant. Help me!"

"You some kind crazy kid. Wake people up. What you want?"

Grant apologized, and described the symbols he had found on his doorstep.

"What the leaf look like? Taro? Ti?"

"It is green and heart shaped like the taro, but not the same. The ends turn up, and it has white flecks over it. There are three ridged stems dividing the leaf."

"That is ape. Kahuna use it to find evil spirits. When you bind something in ape, it is like a death warning."

"What about the doll with its hair smeared in red? Inside the leaves are matches, burnt coals, and a small red fish?"

"Not sure what mean." Malia paused, then said, "Before sacrifices, high priest, he go around villages. Hair colored with *alaea*, red clay mixed with water."

"So the doll could be a warning that a sacrifice is about to begin. What about the dead fish?"

"Hard to say. Ku also god of fishermen. Sometime first sacrifices are fish, like the ulua or the red kumu."

"The matches? The burnt coals?"

"Don't know."

Selena interrupted. "Grant, remember when I asked you the meaning of Papa'ena'ena? Ask Malia to interpret the Hawaiian name of the heiau beneath Diamond Head."

Grant relayed the request. He listened for many moments, nodding his head. "Malia says it means 'burning with a red hot rage.'"

"That is it!" Selena said. "The matches, burnt coals, dead fish, doll, they mean that Ku is burning with rage and the high priest will sacrifice at Papa'ena'ena."

"It makes sense. Thank you, Auntie."

"Selena, call Asing, the police. Have them meet you at this house. Take them to Papa'ena'ena."

"Where are you going?" Selena asked as Grant rushed to a hall closet, retrieving a flashlight and a long stick.

"I'm heading to the heiau to stop a murder."

Grant ran into the street. The moon, hanging high over the dead volcano, shed faint light onto the roadway. Grant backed his Studebaker, gunned the automobile, and raced for the polo field at Kapi'olani Park.

***

Mills woke to excruciating pain, his hands bound behind him. A pole, thrust between the crooks of his elbows, had a rope wrapped around it and his chest. It stretched tight as a shrouded figure yanked him uphill. Whoever dragged him was oblivious to the pain he suffered as his body scraped and bumped along the jagged rocks. He tried yelling, but a gag around his mouth stifled his cry. Blood from his lacerated throat soaked his thin shirt, and the semi-circular cut of the strangling cord hurt as he struggled to suck in air. He tried to focus his eyes, but sweat and dizziness obscured his vision. Finally the brutal hauling stopped. He felt his body being pulled onto a flat rock. The pole between his arms came out.

With the momentary rest, Mills saw above him the tail of the tuna thrusting its point toward the moon. He knew that he was below Diamond Head. Could the soldiers in the gun emplacements built into the hill see his plight? Come to his rescue? He forced a yell, but nothing but coughing rattled in his throat.

Water sprinkled over his body, some falling into his gagged mouth. It tasted salty. He realized he was being purified with sea water. He tried rocking his body. A pole with a white ball slammed between his legs. He felt a cord wrap around his feet.

Mills wiggled, trying to free himself, but only succeeded in forcing his head and neck from the rocks on which he lay. Partially suspended, his eyes fixed upon the dark craters of the moon, its crest brightened white by the light of the sun. Above him he saw a cloth ball affixed to the pole thrust between his legs and he knew that he lay on sacred ground, a he-iau. Below him, an automobile slid on rocks.

***

Grant swerved into a parking area near the polo field. Pebbles flung up, thudding into the underside of his car. He brought his Studebaker to an abrupt stop. His headlamps shone on kiawe trees spread in a half crescent around the level ground. Twisted tree branches rose from the small wood into the darkness of Diamond Head. A car rested at the side of an unlit building with no one in it. He pounded on the polo cabin door. No one came. Grant checked the car. It was empty and he started up the trail that he had explored with Selena hours ago.

***

Teeth sharp as razors slashed across Mills' chest, slicing past his belly to his thigh. He saw above him a figure covered from head to hips in a dark shroud. The face of the man was hidden by a black kerchief around his nose and mouth. The shark teeth sliced again, cross-cutting across his body. Blood poured from the wounds, superficial cuts not deep enough to let his organs pour out.

Mills heard the sound of someone climbing the slopes. I'm not dead yet, he thought, if only the person could reach me before the fatal strike. "Help! Help!" he begged, his words muffled by the gag in his mouth.

***

Grant's torch shone onto the white cloth ball of the pahu pole. He saw feet shaking between it. He played his torch over a human body lying on the rocks of Papa'ena'ena heiau. Grant pushed up the rock path, leaping toward the sacrifice. Small stones dislodged and scudded down the slope. A cloud obscured the moon. He played his torch over the stone and shrubs of the ruins of the outdoor temple. A chain struck his arm, dislodging the light. A shrouded figure rose from the stones. An iron ball slammed into the side of his head, upsetting his balance. He fell backward, onto his buttocks, dazed by the blow.

Nestled between rocks, his torch picked up a leiomano. The weapon disappeared in the darkness. He did not hear a cry. He did not know if the shark knife had sliced into the victim. His head ached. His eyes were blurry. In the street below, sirens wailed. Someone said, "Die, missionary."

Grant struggled to his feet. A body near him jerked in death. He reached for a dark figure near the shuddering corpse. The pahu ball slammed into his chest. He fell backward. He heard the clanking of chains and realized an iron weapon descended upon him.

CHAPTER 31

SIRENS BLARED. VEHICLE lights flashed through the trees surrounding the temple. Instinctively, Grant rolled away from the descending sound of jangling metal. Iron struck rocks where his body had been, flinging out slivers of broken stone. He rolled downhill into a low bush. A dark figure moved past him.

"Hey, anybody, Ku priest is here."

The killer swung a mace-like weapon, its chain links jingled. Grant pushed into the shrubs, the sharp spines piercing his clothes, flesh. An iron ball smashed onto the branches. Its deadly force absorbed by the wood fibers. The wail of sirens came closer. The murderer rushed downhill.

Grant rose up, "The killer is heading for the park." He picked himself from the bush, rushed over to Mills. The man lay dead. Breath was absent, only blood oozed from a wound at his heart.

Grant slid down the slope of Diamond Head. Sirens blared. Revolving red lights whirled. An auto's engine cranked over. Grant stumbled toward headlights beaming through the trees.

The car chugged into life. Grant heard twigs breaking. He saw a Ford crashing through shrubs, turning around the polo cabin, and heading for the street. At the wheel drove the killer.

Grant ran onto the gravel of the parking area. He saw Asing in a police vehicle, Selena by his side. Another police car, siren whining, careened into the lot.

Grant raced to the detective's car. "The killer is escaping. Go." He leaped into the back seat of the four-door touring car. The Chinese policeman shifted gears, scattered gravel, and sped after the escaping murderer. As he drove by the officers in the second police car, Asing called, "Check the hill."

"Look for my torch beam," Grant yelled. "The body's near it."

"Who died?" Serena asked.

"Not sure, looked like Mills, but too dark. The guy ahead is the kahuna nui."

"We will catch him," Asing said, throttling his engine faster as they sped from Paki Road onto Monsarrat circling the silent race track at Kapi'olani Park. His siren blared, but the Ford vehicle slid onto Kalakaua Avenue, its tires screeching. The auto headed north. Late-night revelers at the Moana pointed at the racing cars as they sped past the hotel. A trolley loomed in front of the fleeing Ford. "He's going to crash," Selena yelled. But the killer swerved to the left and into the oncoming traffic lane.

Horns blared. Metal ground against metal. The left front fender of the Ford clipped the side of an approaching car, forcing it off the roadway into a coconut tree. The kahuna nui swung his vehicle back into the bus lane, barely avoiding a collision with the trolley. He gunned his engine and sped up Kalakaua Avenue.

Asing shoved his police car into second gear, slowing to avoid a crash. The trolley conductor rang its bell incessantly, warning everyone on the roadway of its presence. "What a racket. Enough noise to wake the dead." The detective said as his siren increased in pitch. He gunned the engine, clutched, shifted into third gear, and sped around the street car. Far ahead, the tail lights of the Ford flashed pinpoints of red.

"Nothing but swamp water to our right," Grant said. "There is ocean to our left. The guy must intend to head for King Street and get lost in the residential area."

"We'll catch him," Asing said. "This car is hot." The police car charged forward as Asing floored the accelerator. The gap between vehicles narrowed. The Ford careened onto King Street, knocking down a road sign. The Chinese detective geared down and followed, his tires screeching along the pavement. Smoke sprang up, as friction burnt rubber.

"Oh my God," Selena screamed as her head and body slid out the side door. Grant seized her. Cloth tore in his hands as her dress shredded. He gripped the bras at her chest and pulled.

Selena fell back into the car, her side door slamming shut. "You can let go of me now, thank you," she said, removing his hands from her breasts.

"Sorry. Only thing I could think of to save you."

"I appreciate that. But your grip is strong. I'll be bruised for a week."

"We're catching up," Asing said, elation in his voice. "He won't stop. But I will ram him. I have a reinforced steel bumper in front for chases like this."

"Too bad you don't carry a pistol. We could shoot out the tires," Grant said as Asing gunned his police car into the rear of the Ford. Metal shrieked. Bumpers locked. The killer braked hard and then accelerated. His actions released the hooked vehicles, and the Ford sped away.

Asing frowned, saying, "You're not escaping." He throttled the engine and slammed his front bumper into the rear wheel well of the Ford. The killer's car shimmied, hurtling into the oncoming lane of traffic. A vehicle, its horn screaming, braked, slid to the left, and clipped the right rear of the Ford. The fleeing murderer retained control of his erratically moving car and sped across the lane, slamming into shrubs lining the roadway. The Ford slowed to a stop in front of a fence.

"Hey," Grant yelled. "He's leaving his car and heading into the Ward Estate."

"Thirty acres of trees, shrubs, lagoons, and gardens, a guy could get lost in there." Asing said. "Let's go after him."

"The killer's dangerous," Grant said, rubbing his scalp. "He's got some kind of a weapon. It's like a mace."

"My whip has never failed me," Asing answered, leaping from his police car and heading across King Street. "Come on."

"Selena, this guy is big trouble. Stay in the car."

"You think I'm some kind of helpless female, Mr. Kingsley? I'm coming," Selena answered. She raced after Asing.

The detective followed the killer, who easily leaped over the wooden fencing bordering the roadway. The man disappeared into a copse of coco trees.

"I know this place," Asing said, climbing clumsily over the fence. "There's a big lagoon ahead. It stretches for a third of a mile."

Grant straddled the fence, hurried through the light woods, and burst onto a grass plain. Ahead lay an embankment lined by a string of coconut trees. The killer stood fifty yards away. His shrouded head flitted about like a trapped bird seeking an avenue of escape. "He's stymied by the lagoon," Grant called. "Let's get him." The hooded figure raced along the berm of the big pond heading toward downtown Honolulu.

"He's going for the ornamental bridge," Asing yelled. His hand reached to his whip, loosening it from his side. Selena ran past him. Grant yelled, "Slow down."

"Catch up," Selena called back.

The moon shone silver on the murk of the long narrow lagoon. Its light spread across the water and onto its earth shoulders. As they raced along the grass berm and the line of coco trees, Grant saw the killer glance at the sky. Huge clouds blew in from the sea, hiding the stars. He realized that the moonlight would soon be blotted out. "Go faster," he ordered.

"In this half-light, if we go faster, we fall," Asing gasped.

"The man ahead is uncanny," Selena said. "It's as if he could see in the dark."

The cloaked murderer raced for an ornately decorated bridge that arched over a stream flowing into the shallow lagoon. Beyond the bridge spread a green lawn that ended in a forest. To his right, Grant heard traffic from King Street and saw a light from a second-story window of the Ward mansion. The moon faded as dark clouds covered it. Rain pelted the lagoon, drumming the flat water into rippling waves. The murderer disappeared in the gloom.

"Slow down," Asing said. "Spread out. Look around. Maybe he went on the bridge, but the man could be anywhere."

Grant grabbed Selena's hand, saying, "Stay with me."

A shape rose from the cross-over, a cloaked arm reared back. "Down," Grant yelled, pulling Selena to the grass. Something whirred over their heads. He rolled upright and charged. Racing onto the wooden platform, he saw the hooded figure exiting on the other side. He ran after the killer, and into a trap, tripping over a low cord fixed between the bridge's railings. He sprawled headlong toward the cloaked murderer. The man's arm went high. An iron ball and chain attached to a rod in his hand whipped back. Grant felt a blow to his head. Then everything went dark.

CHAPTER 32

BRIGHT SUNLIGHT POURED between the lace curtains of the hospital room. Grant forced his eyes open. He felt his head and pulled his hand away as a shaft of pain shot through his skull and down the base of his neck. He propped himself up. Selena lay curled in an armchair in a corner of the room. Her disheveled hair flowed over her shoulders and onto the white hospital gown that covered her body.

Grant pulled the sheet covering away from him and twisted to get out of his hospital bed, its springs protested his movement. The discordant sounds woke Selena, and her eyes fixed onto him. "You're finally awake."

"How long have I been under?"

"About twelve hours. Doctor gave you a shot to put you to sleep. He told me to get him when you were up." Selena disappeared.

Grant slid from the bed, his feet unsteady. His head ached. He felt the back of his scalp. His fingers found a newly stitched cut, and he suspected he had been put to sleep while the doctor closed the wound shut. A door opened, and a man in a white smock strode in, saying, "You're up and about. Good. Let me check you."

After a series of tests, the doctor said, "All functions working fine. X-rays we took last night show no broken bones. All you have is a cut and mild concussion."

"Can I go?" Grant asked.

"Detective Asing wants to see him as soon as possible and so does his father," Selena said.

"You should stay for the day and night just to make sure, but if you want to go, I'll discharge you."

As they walked from the hospital, Selena said, "I know you're a little fuzzy about what happened at the bridge. The killer tried to split your skull with a strange weapon, a ball on a chain attached to a stick. Asing struck it with his whip. The lash wrapped around the murderer's arm and spoiled his aim. He kicked your head as you sprawled on the bridge. His shoe must have some kind of sharp metal on it. That's what cut you. The man ran off into the woods. We thought it best to take you to a doctor rather than chase him. You can guess the rest."

"Get a look at him?" Grant asked as they drove off.

"No. The guy wore black from head to toe. He was creepy. When he attacked you he looked like Death coming to take you to Hell."

"I'm glad you saved me." They drove in silence to the police parking lot. He rumbled the car into an open space and they hurried into the building. Asing stood at the entrance waiting for them.

"Hospital called that you were on your way. The murdered guy is Donald Mills."

Grant sucked in his breath. Selena gasped. "We just saw him win the polo match yesterday. Why kill him?"

"I heard the killer say, 'Die, missionary.' The high priest must be continuing this parade of death of those who came from New England to save the pagans," Grant said, then added, "There were a hundred-and-fifty-three who came. He can't mean to kill them all?"

Asing looked at Grant. "Maybe I should lock you up. You're always connected with the death scene. If you aren't there, then the killings will end."

"I wish you would smile when you say that. Right now, you're talking like Hitchcock. He doesn't want to look any further than his nose for the murderer. But you saw the guy escaping. You saw him run into the Ward Estate. You know I'm not the man that did the killings."

Asing sighed. "I agree. But all we have to go on are a vanishing note, pagan symbols, and glimpses of a black-clothed figure. I suspect the killer drew you to the crime scene so you'd be blamed for the murder."

"True. What's interesting is when I got there, I remember him saying the words, 'die missionary.' He wanted me to hear that. But maybe this whole 'Cult of Ku' thing is bogus? Some cooked-up concoction of ritualistic mumbo jumbo meant to confuse us as to who the killer is and the real reason for the murders?"

"I've thought of that angle, but I have no suspects except some black-clothed guy calling himself the 'kahuna nui.'" Asing's brow furrowed. He took out a cigarette, lit it, and tasted a long drag of smoke. "I have to find the killer. Wright, Nolan, and Mills were big men in this town. The mayor is angry. He wants the crimes solved before the Prince of Wales returns to Hawai'i in August."

"Were there any new clues at the death scene?"

"Only the killing itself. It was brutal. Someone took a sickle and hacked Mills to death."

"The man didn't have enough time to commit the murder pursuant to all the rituals. Your sirens were blaring. I was at the heiau so he had to finish the job quickly. He never expected that I would solve the clues he left as soon as I did. Do you have any important information from the two survivors at Kaneaki heiau?"

"I had to wait until the doctor released them from the hospital. Roberts, the curator was blinded by powder smashed into his face by a hollowed out egg. He saw only a blur of a figure in front of him before he was hit and passed out. He said he talked by telephone to someone that identified himself as a kahu, priest. The man claimed that his organization, *Hui o ka aina*, wanted to restore the heiau. He promised a large donation and specifically asked that Nolan come to Makaha with the curator. That's all Roberts could tell me."

"What about the other guy?"

"McKenzie got hit by a dart. Seemed it had some kind of drug on the tip. He passed out, never saw the killer."

"Did we recover the dart?"

"No."

"The kahuna nui has an interesting array of weapons, an egg filled with blinding powder, a poisoned dart, a ball and chain, definitely not Hawaiian. Those could be Chinese weapons, or Filipino, or..."

"Maybe Japanese."

Grant shook his head, "The killer could be anyone of those races or a Hawaiian who has knowledge of those weapons. It is time to go and seek out some answers."

Grant dropped Selena at Chinatown. He stopped at the main library and researched. After an hour, he headed home. Sue Watanabe worked in the kitchen. He decided to inspect Charles' room.

A lone window, curtained shut, made the chauffeur's chambers gloomy. Grant switched on the light. A devil's mask leered at him with wide jaws filled with sharp white teeth. Its mother-of-pearl eyes, with dark pebbles in the center, glared. In corners of the room stood poles crowned by white balls. Grant opened the closet, and found a dark suit, like a chauffeur would wear. He checked the dresser. A long feather wand and a metal neckpiece rested on its top. In the center of the medallion were crossed pahu sticks. The name Pa'oa stamped upon it. Grant searched the room for weapons and for his box of medals. He found nothing. He turned out the light and shut the door. What he saw had meaning, but not enough to make an accusation of murder.

His father returned home with a briefcase full of papers. He scowled when he saw Grant. "You should be in the hospital. When I saw you this morning, you looked sick."

"I'm fine, just a sting in the back of the head where they stitched a cut."

"Good. I have to leave for Mau'i. Come to the office tomorrow and get to work. There may be issues between us which we need to solve, but right now I need someone I can trust. We'll have lunch with some sugar planters. Big labor problems for all of us."

Time to deal with the question of paternity, Grant thought. "Sir, Joshua Kanakoa is in touch with Nani Still, the daughter of John Tana. He says blood typing might resolve the issue."

James Kingsley pursed his lips. He closed his eyes, turned away from Grant, and uttered a deep sigh. "It is something I have avoided dealing with. I cannot look at your mother's picture. She should have left the sordid past alone. Not knowing would be better than the turmoil she has created."

"Sir, she was a wonderful mother. While at the hospital everyone spoke of her as if she was a saint. They talked of her charity and good work with the sick. I know what she said on her deathbed must have brought you pain. We can solve one of the issues she raised, and that is whether I am your son."

James Kingsley's handsome face became haggard. He put his hand over his eyes and nodded his head. "I loved her very much."

Without another word, he walked upstairs to his room.

***

"You have a nasty cut on your head," David Kamaka said as the two men did arm thrusts and leg kicks. "Maybe you should have rested instead of coming here to practice?"

"I needed to talk to you about Pa'oa."

Kamaka stopped exercising. His teeth clenched together, then his lips parted and he said, "What about Pa'oa?"

"The history books say he was a Tahitian high priest who came to Hawai'i five hundred years ago. He brought with him the worship of the war god Ku and the practice of human sacrifice."

Kamaka nodded, his eyes narrowed.

"From what I read, this shaman developed a hereditary priesthood that worked with the kings to suppress the common people using fear of Ku to keep them in line. When the missionaries got here the idols were gone, but the history books don't speak of what happened to Ku's priests. I thought you might know the answer."

The teacher reflected for several moments before saying, "I see what you are driving at. If you can find descendants of the high priest, the kahuna nui, you think that you could solve the murders."

Grant nodded.

Kamaka looked at him, hostility in his eyes. "You're thinking that I am a descendant of Pa'oa and may be involved in the killings."

"I am clumsy. I apologize. No. I don't believe you are involved. I suspect someone else. I need to know how I might identify that person as a descendant of the high priest."

"I don't know if I can help. The original kahuna nui, Pa'oa, set up a two-level society. Priests and chiefs were on top with the common people on the bottom. When the idols were overthrown, the chiefs did not disappear, but the priests who had practiced death and idol worship became hunted men. To survive, the Ku kahunas went underground."

"Is there a way to trace them?"

"I know there are Hawaiians who still practice sorcery, but there is no way to identify a Ku priest."

"So you're telling me that I can't find out if this 'Cult of Ku' really exists?"

"I don't think it does. But you should seek Hawaiians practicing the old ways. Maybe you can find out from them."

CHAPTER 33

GRANT WALKED INTO Chinatown. He could smell the aroma of sweet *cha siu* pork, its honey glaze, mouth-watering. As he came closer to Maunakea Street dozens of white banners were stretched over the roadway, all covered with incomprehensible Chinese lettering that made no sense to him. He passed shops with crispy, red Peking ducks hanging on metal hooks. These were fowl full-grown in sixty days and fattened to roasting perfection in the last twenty days of their life. He passed an apothecary shop and almost gagged on the smell of herbs, leaves, and roots specially prepared for their medicinal value.

He looked forward to dinner at Dan Choy's. It was Selena's idea. Meet her family and learn about each other. It was the best way for East and West to come together, even though with his Hawaiian blood, he felt more akin to the Oriental than the Occidental.

He stopped at a stand selling dumplings to sample a white coconut confection made with sweet dough. From an alley, a hooded figure lunged, his knife thrusting for Grant's belly. Returning with change, the business proprietor stepped into the blade. He screamed. The attacker thrust again. Grant hurled a wooden stand into him, knocking his assailant to the pavement.

The assassin rolled up from the fall. Grant seized the legs of the stand, and shoved it into him. The attacker dropped his knife and grabbed an end, trying to wrest it from Grant. The two men fought for control of the bin until Grant heaved it to the side, spinning the attacker to the ground.

But, as if invulnerable to pain, the assassin leaped up, drew another knife, jabbing it at Grant in short quick stabs.

A mop head smashed into the hooded man. A woman wielding its handle like a club screamed in Chinese as she hammered her wet, greasy weapon into the face of the attacker. Another Chinese came at him with a broom and a third joined in wielding a baseball bat. Grant could not suppress his laughter as he saw the killer fleeing down the alley, leaping over a fence, and disappearing into the night.

He picked up the dropped knife. A forged iron blade, long, narrow, sharp, and set into an ivory handle. Embossed into it reared a red dragon, its raised paw pointing at a heavy butt of silver at the end of the knife. He slipped the blade into his belt and offered to help pay for the damages. The woman with the mop was more concerned with her husband who had fallen to the sidewalk in a pool of blood and dismissed his offer. Grant found a telephone and called Asing, leaving word of the attack and saying he would be at the home of Dan Choy.

He pressed a hundred dollars into the hands of a relative of the wounded man. He gave his name and left. The noise of the fighting had attracted a crowd. Grant slipped through the people that filled the street. He broke free of the mob and found himself confronted by two burly Chinese. He assumed a fighting stance.

One of the men said, "Are you Grant Kingsley? Selena sent us to find you."

***

"Try some of this pork hash with duck egg," Dan Choy said. "Delicious."

"No, thank you," Grant answered. "I can't handle those sixty-day-old eggs."

Selena laughed, "If you live in a Chinese house, you better get used to them."

Grant smiled. "If you insist on stink eggs, I'm going to have to walk around our home with a clothespin on my nose."

Selena rolled her eyes. "Big joke, who would want to live with you? I bet you snore like a warthog."

Dan Choy interrupted, "Selena, be nice to our guest. An assassin almost killed him this evening. Was he the same one you fought at the Ward Estate?"

Grant thought over the question, recalling all the memories of his confrontations with the man calling himself the kahuna nui. "It is possible," he answered. "The build of the guy in the alley and the hooded figure at Papa'ena'ena are similar, though it is hard to tell when someone is shrouded in dark clothes. The man who attacked me tonight dropped this knife." Grant withdrew an exquisite ivory-hilted dagger and laid it on the table. Wrapped around its handle was an embossed red dragon, its tiny sapphire eyes glinting in the scented candlelight that lit the table.

"A Tong symbol," Dan Choy said. "But it is not one of the local gangs in Chinatown. Its owner is from elsewhere, maybe San Francisco."

Selena sucked in her breath. "Gang Tongs in California are vicious. Dozens have been killed in the fights in San Francisco. Who would want such wild men in Hawai'i?"

"Your best friend and mine, the great Rudy Tang," Grant said sarcastically. Then asked Dan Choy, "Rudy's got some kind of protection from those high up in government. Are you the one who saves him?"

Selena interrupted, "I thought there was a criminal action against him for trying to murder you?"

Grant reached with his chopsticks for a piece of Peking duck. Dipping it in sweet plum sauce, he placed it on a dumpling, making a small sandwich with some cut scallions. With exasperation in her voice, Selena said, "Grant, answer me, isn't Rudy facing criminal charges? At the very least he should be in jail for his attempt to kill you."

Grant took a bite of his dumpling and said, "The city prosecutor refused to press charges. Rudy had too many witnesses who denied I was in his house. Asing told me that he could not get a warrant to search the building. There is no water entranceway, boulders cover it. So there it is. Like I said, Rudy's got protection from someone high up in government." Grant stared at Dan Choy.

Selena's father picked his teeth, folded his hands over his broad stomach, drummed his fingers on his belt, and said, "There is much labor unrest. Labor unions are forming among the Japanese, the Filipinos. The plantations need strikebreakers and someone like Rudy to organize them. He is useful at the moment. Who can say about tomorrow? But for now I would watch my back. The man who tried to kill you will try again."

CHAPTER 34

STREET NOISES BLARED through the second-story window of the business office in downtown Honolulu. James Kingsley smoothed a newspaper on his desk. Pointing to the editorial page, he said, "This article highlights our problem. The Organic Act of 1900 made Hawai'i a territory of the United States. We became subject to American law and could no longer have labor contracts binding people to work. Since then, we have had fifty labor strikes. The courts won't help us. It's a major problem at our West O'ahu plantation. I need your help."

Grant drummed his fingers on his father's massive brown desk. The office of Kingsley Enterprises was cool. The morning sunlight streaming through the open windows glowed on the polished walls of koa that paneled the room. He rubbed his hand over his hair. "I don't know much about labor unions or the law that applies to strikers."

"You went to Yale. You fought in the war. Led men into battle, became an officer because you used initiative and know-how. You've met the big boys from the HSPA at the Honolulu Downtown Club. You're a member now. You have all the tools needed to help me solve our problems."

"What do you want me to do?"

"Go to our plantation on the west side. Speak to the manager, the supervisors. Get the lay of the land. Use your connections at the Downtown Club. Go there often and socialize. Bring your navy friends. Congress is spending millions fixing up Pearl Harbor. The navy is leaving the Port of Honolulu. The business community needs to know what the military is up to and how much money they are spending. Talk to your friend Dan Choy.

He's a bad man, but can help us with strikebreakers. I'm leaving for Mau'i and putting you in charge of our Honolulu operations."

***

Grant pulled into the main parking lot of the West O'ahu plantation offices of Kingsley and Company. The neat whitewashed buildings stood in stark contrast to the iron-roofed mill and warehouses behind it. A black steam locomotive, its rail cars bulging with burnt stalks of sugar cane, chugged to an off-loading area.

When Grant exited his Studebaker, he inhaled the sweet aroma of cooked molasses, a syrupy smell so powerful he wanted to vomit. Trash lay everywhere, he knew the sugar mill ground cane because its brick stack belched reams of black smoke, spreading burnt leaves over the ground.

A man hoed weeds in a flower bed. Grant asked for directions to the manager's office. The Filipino stopped his work, took out a file and began to sharpen his iron tool. He squinted at Grant and shook his head. "Da guy. I no no."

Grant could not understand his pidgin. He stopped a Japanese in a neat shirt and overalls and said, "*Go-men na-sai. O-ne-gai shi-mas-u, luna?*"

The Japanese stared. "Are you looking for the office of the field supervisors?"

"No," Grant answered, relieved the man spoke English. "I'm looking for the manager's office."

"Come with me." The Japanese took him to the largest of the white buildings, pointed to a door and left. When Grant entered, a Caucasian clerk sniffed as if Grant had a foul smell. "What is it, *kanaka*?"

Grant recognized the hostility in the man's voice. He realized here in the countryside, his tan skin set him apart from the rest of the ruling minority. "My name is Kingsley. I have an appointment with the manager."

"You don't look like Mr. Kingsley to me. He's a white man. You're brown."

"I'm his son and I'll thank you to notify Mr. Duffy that I am here. Go and announce me, or I'll have your job."

Cowed by Grant's vehemence, the clerk went to the back of the building. He returned after a few moments, confirming the appointment. He ushered Grant into the manager's office and left. The plain room held a desk and four chairs. Robert Grant's portrait hung on the back wall.

A man with a bulldog face, bushy mutton chop sideburns, a thick mane of white hair, and a handsome beard to match it, looked up from his work. He pointed to a chair and offered a cigar, saying, "Name is Duffy. You're Kingsley."

Grant nodded, declined the stogie, and opened his briefcase. "From what I've read in the reports, this plantation has had multiple strikes with a major one this year. The HSPA just settled it. Why are we having such trouble?"

Duffy's face turned crimson. He puffed on his cigar. Tobacco saliva dripped from his lips onto his beard, staining the white whiskers brown. "It's those damn Japanese. They are cocky and unreasonable. Better in the old days when we had the masters and servants law and could force them to work or toss them in jail."

"You're saying because we became a Territory of the United States, which the sugar planters wanted, we have labor problems?"

Duffy drew on his cigar. He puffed out the smoke in a heavy wreath that wrapped around his head and spiraled to the low ceiling of his office. "Let's put it this way, before annexation we could keep the Japanese working. If they left the plantations to open businesses we would make them pay for leaving. The law was on our side."

"What do you mean 'make them pay for leaving'?"

The manager shifted in his chair. He removed the cigar from his lips, twirling it in his fingers like a drum major twists a baton. Ash scattered over the desk. Duffy brushed it away. "I think you should talk to Sven Larsen about that. He was your grandfather's right-hand man and did your Grandmother Sheila's bidding, if you know what I mean."

"No, I don't know. Where is this Larsen?"

"Somewhere in Honolulu, the man is a drunk. He caused us nothing but trouble. Your grandmother took care of him. Once she died, I fired him. I'm sure he will seek you out."

"Why?"

"Larsen needs money. Mrs. Grant was the only one who would give it to him. She insisted he be employed even though he was perfectly useless as a supervisor. The Japanese hated him. He was the cause of a lot of our labor troubles."

"That's what I'm here to talk about. The last strike cost the HSPA twenty million dollars. Another strike like that could topple the sugar industry. How do we solve the problem?"

"Look, you're a young kid, wet behind the ears. The Japanese are arrogant. They think they own the plantations because they're forty percent of the population. Divide and rule, that's how we won in the old days, and that's how we'll win again."

"You're saying the answer to labor problems is import more foreign laborers, Koreans, Puerto Ricans, Filipinos?"

"Not Filipinos," Duffy interrupted, shooting a stream of tobacco juice into a pot in the corner of the room. "Those dang savages almost did the plantations in. They started the big strike when they walked out. That caused the Japanese to do the same." Duffy squirted out more tobacco juice. "But then we made a deal with their union boss, Santos. He called the Filipino strike off. It left the yellow men high and dry. We locked those scallywags out. We kicked them out of their homes. We brought in strike breakers."

"Despite all you say, the plantations had to cave in. The strike cost too much money. That's why I'm here, to prevent another walkout."

Duffy pulled out another cigar. Clipped the ends, lit it and inhaled the smoke until the tip glowed red. "You're young and idealistic. The only way plantations can survive is to have cheap labor and men who don't talk back or ask questions. What Isoru Nakamura or Yamashita or Miura or any Buddha-head needs to know is that they either work or starve. That's what I would tell your father and the men of the HSPA."

Grant mulled the manager's comments over as he left his office. The clerk at the front desk did not answer his cheerful goodbye. His eyes remained fixed onto his desk. Grant was troubled by his hostility. The racism of the manager and his willingness to use force to suppress disagreement surprised him. It was a plantation mentality he had been aware of as he grew up. The wealth of his family and its social connections with the ruling elite had separated him from the multi-ethnic peoples who had been imported to work the sugar plantations.

Engaging the gears of his car, he realized what was troubling him. The use of brutality to suppress others did not solve problems. He had learned that from his experiences in France. For centuries, divide and rule had been the tactic used in Europe to allow one nation to dominate others. Germany had tried this with its policy of alliances. But the result had been a horrible war and a desire to punish her for starting it. Today, the defeated country was paying an enormous price for its policies in loss of land, people, and money.

The same tactic is being used in Hawai'i, Grant thought. Import different races to work in the sugar fields and play one off against the other to maintain control. But the plantations had made a mistake, the Japanese workers brought with them wives and families. By 1920 they had become a formidable ethnic group difficult to control with the divide and rule tactic.

Driving toward Pearl Harbor, Grant thought of another racial issue. His mother was half-native and half-white. During his growing up years everyone thought he was a quarter-Hawaiian. Despite some brown blood, he was acceptable within the ruling society. But what if his real father was pure Hawaiian? Would he lose his place among the Hawai'i elite? Certainly his step-grandmother indicated it. The clerk at the plantation office demonstrated it. Would excessive brown blood separate him from the small Caucasian strata of society that controlled the islands?

Grant parked and entered the naval office of Captain Trask. He didn't care what the ruling class thought. The Hawaiian beach boys are great. Selena is desirable. He had empathy for the plight of the imported laborers. But his father seemed conflicted by the issue of race. Grant felt a pain in his heart. He did not want to lose the love of the man he most admired.

"Thanks for stopping by," Captain Trask said, grasping his hand with a firmness that Grant liked. Too many had flimsy handshakes. They acted as if touching brown skin would contaminate them with what they perceived as the laziness and bad habits of the Hawaiians.

"A pleasure to visit with you," Grant said. Then he pressed on, not wanting to delay their meeting with small talk. "What is it that you wanted to discuss?"

Trask drummed his fingers on his desk. He studied his nails for a moment, before saying, "I'm going to bore you with history. But you need some background to understand why I am asking for your help. At the start of World War I, our navy was in shambles. Not enough ships, bad morale, and conflicted between President Wilson's desire for strict neutrality and the menace of Germany and Japan. Our fleet was like an eagle deteriorating in a cage."

"You said the menace of Japan," Grant interrupted. "What do you mean?"

"For thirty years, the Japanese Empire has seized territory in Asia, Korea, Southern Manchuria, parts of China. When the war began, they took all the German islands in the Pacific and all German territory on the Asian Continent.

"The sinking of the *Lusitania* in 1915 swung Wilson over to appreciating the threats to America from German submarines and Japanese aggression in Asia and the Pacific. Wilson got Congress to pass a building program of a hundred and fifty-six ships, a number of them battlewagons."

"You also told me about Congress providing funds to improve Pearl Harbor and the navy's desire to have a two-ocean fleet."

"Good, that means you can appreciate the problem. Once the war ended, Congress turned isolationist. They refused to join the League of Nations, President Wilson's pet project. They failed to push the naval program that they had authorized. Worse, Japan announced an Asiatic Monroe Doctrine, with Japan in charge. They took advantage of the Bolshevik Revolution and invaded Siberia."

"What you're saying is that Japan has become the most powerful nation in the Pacific. By announcing a Monroe Doctrine, they intend to control all commerce in the Far East. Bottom line, we don't have a navy strong enough to challenge them. But what about the British, they have the biggest fleet in the world. Won't they stop Japan?"

"Few people know that Britain and Japan have been allies since 1902. At the present time, the president believes we are on the eve of a severe commercial war. Our competitors are Britain and Japan. If we went to war with one, we would have to fight both of them. Because of this, Wilson has bought into the navy's belief that the best way to destroy a nation's commerce is by overwhelming sea power. For a decade, top officers have preached that the method to achieve an all-powerful fleet is an independent office of naval operations free of political control."

"But that would defy the constitution and citizen control of the military."

"Not if the president decides to permit it. Wilson has accepted our arguments. He realizes that Britain, and its fleet, controls the Atlantic. Their ally, Japan, controls the Pacific. Because we are threatened in both oceans, the president has established an independent office of naval operations and allowed the creation within it of a planning division. Our current chief of Naval Operations, Admiral Koontz, believes that Japan is our next foe and that a Pacific naval strategy is our highest priority."

"But you said if we fight Japan we must fight Britain? I'm confused by the politics and don't know how I fit in."

"Be patient. Let me complete the big picture. First the Anglo-Japanese Treaty is up for renewal in 1921. Second, to win, a navy must have battleships. But they need bases strategically placed. We are constructing them at Pearl Harbor, Guam, and the Philippines. What are the Japanese doing? Are they building naval installations in the islands they stole from Germany? How about battleships? What size are they, how many, and where are they based? If we can get that information, we can convince the British not to renew the treaty. If we give the same information to Congress we can get more funding for the navy."

"Hold it. This is a job for military intelligence. It is not something I can do."

"Grant, we are desperate, we have some money for construction, but none for..."

"Spies," Grant interrupted. "What you're asking is that I go beyond reporting to you what I observe. That I actively seek out secret information. Am I right?"

Trask nodded. "You are a civilian with solid Hawai'i credentials and a connection to the Japanese Consulate. You would not be suspected as an undercover agent. The navy is pushing to triple our battle fleet. To convince the politicians, we need more than just vague fears of a threat from the Far East. We need solid information that Japanese aggression is real." The captain chuckled. "We are getting unexpected help from West Coast business men. They fear the 'Yellow Peril from Asia' and are putting pressure on Congress to pay attention to Japan. Can I count on you to help your country?"

There it was, the patriotic appeal. The reason he had joined the army in 1917 angered by German aggression and the killing of innocent Americans on board the *Lusitania*. But should he add this new obligation to his existing plate of troubles? At the military academy they had a slogan, "Duty, Honor, and Country." He had done his duty and served his country with distinction in the Great War. But on returning to Hawai'i, he had been received with hate and prejudice. Grant felt like a juggler with too many balls in the air. If he dropped one, would they all fall? This new assignment would be known only by Trask. There would be no reward for doing a good job, only guilt for his betrayal of a friend.

Grant said, "I'll think on it." He left, hurried to his office, and made an appointment to meet with Sato and Counselor Matsu the next day.

CHAPTER 35

"**Y**OU MENTIONED THAT a Japanese battle cruiser is coming into Honolulu Harbor tomorrow," Grant Kingsley said. "Is it a peaceful visit, or does it forebode something more ominous?"

"Peaceful of course," Matsu answered. "We have been friends since King Kalakaua concluded a treaty with my country and arranged for laborers to immigrate to Hawai'i. The visit is to show the Japanese workers that the emperor is concerned for their welfare and to transport dignitaries to America."

Grant studied the photograph of the emperor of Japan posted behind Matsu's desk. The man stood in full military uniform with ribbons, medals, and a saber at his side. He appeared no different than pictures of the Kaiser, the Tsar, or King George of England, rulers who had thrust their countries into war.

Grant decided to avoid discussing politics, saying, "The labor situation is the reason I asked to meet with you and Sato. The HSPA, Hawaiian Sugar Planters Association, is vitally concerned about the worker unrest among the Japanese. There are too many strikes, costing the sugar industry lots of money. We must do something about it."

"It isn't just the Japanese who strike, it is the Chinese, and Filipinos as well," Sato interrupted. "You sugar people follow the Samuel Clemens philosophy, 'cheap, servile labor is necessary to make sugar plantations successful.' To accomplish this, divide and rule is the technique the HSPA uses. When one race makes demands, the business people bring in a new ethnic group to act as strikebreakers. Your people must give up on divide and rule. Instead, pay attention to the living conditions of the working man, correct disparities, and pay a decent wage. Until you do so, there will be labor unrest."

"We at the consular office have done all we could to help the sugar people," Matsu added. "We no longer issue passports for picture brides. At the recent strike I made a personal appeal in the name of the Emperor to ask the Japanese to return to work. But for our efforts, there is no reciprocation by the HSPA. During the strike, an assassination attempt was made on a Japanese newspaper editor. The police took advantage of this act and rounded up labor organizers and charged them with criminal conspiracy to obstruct the sugar plantations."

"The publisher of the *Pacific Gazette* has been a foe of the Japanese laborer for years," Sato said, his body shaking with anger. "He supports the sugar planters in whatever they do against my people. The paper's editorials call the workers 'cocky, unreasonable', and urges their discharge as an object lesson. He wrote in his newspaper that the union leaders of the Japanese Higher Wage Association are 'agitators and thugs.' I believe his editorials encourage a lynch mob mentality, for he says that anyone supporting the Japanese is a traitor. His vendetta against us includes supporting laws eliminating land ownership by the Japanese to prevent competition with white merchants, and exclusion of my people from America."

"Sato, you should control your hostility. It is not diplomatic," Matsu chided. Sighing, he said, "The Japanese are up against increasing hostility by America. Racial laws are enacted against us and when our diplomats introduced a racial equality clause into the Treaty of Versailles, the United States opposed it."

"But isn't it true that Japan has been aggressive? Your country seized the German islands and took over part of the Asiatic Continent," Grant said.

Matsu's usually impassive face broke into a slight smile. "Last year, the League of Nations confirmed our right to control the former German islands in the Pacific. The reason Japan is on the Asian continent is our alliance with Britain. They feared Russian expansion in Asia and when Germany went to war, they wanted to end German interests in China. We are only doing what our ally has requested. We do not threaten America in any way. Foreign Minister Uchida, Sato's mentor, has insisted that all Japan wants is peace. That is our intent."

"But aren't you building naval bases in the islands you control?"

"For defensive purposes only, but hold your questions. We are having a dinner tomorrow night for the officers of the Japanese battle cruiser. You are invited and will learn of our desire to be friends with America. Today, you should go with Sato to West O'ahu and meet with labor leaders, recently released from jail."

***

Sato was quiet during the trip to a Japanese labor camp a mile beyond the Kingsley sugar mill. The homes were shanties, huts, and grass shacks. A dry stream bordered the living structures, the smell was appalling. "No running water," Sato said. "Waste material no place to go. During the lockout, strike breakers did not bother to keep the place clean."

They entered one of the better-kept buildings where Grant was introduced to three men, one of them an attorney named Yuki Naga, the man who had formed the Japanese Higher Wage Association.

"Thank you for taking the time to hear our concerns," Naga said. "They are four-fold, inadequate housing, insufficient food, discriminatory wages, and excessive brutality."

Surprised, Grant said, "Brutality? You mean beatings?"

"Worse," Sato spat out. "There have been lynchings of Japanese who dared to leave the plantations and start competitive businesses with white merchants."

"It is like the Ku Klux Klan in America," Naga said. "The plantations have men like Sven Larsen who terrorize workers with the black whip and fear of the hangman's noose."

"Sven Larsen, I have heard of him. He was a henchman of my grandfather and his wife Sheila. Manager Duffy fired him."

"Thanks be to Buddha that he is no longer protected by the plantation," Naga said. "We don't know where he has gone, but I hope it is to the Christian hell."

"Duffy told me that he will show up at my office. The man is thirsty. He needs money for whiskey."

"I hope you don't give that scum anything." Naga answered, "But if he visits you, notify Sato. We need to find out about missing workers."

The men spent the rest of the afternoon discussing wage issues, sanitation problems, and inadequate housing. "The point," Naga said, "is that the HSPA must recognize the union as the bargaining agent for the Japanese laborers."

Grant left the meeting realizing the enormity of the problem he faced. The Japanese workmen deserved higher pay and better living conditions. But as long as the HSPA could import strike breakers, conditions in the plantations would not change.

***

Grant worked the next day on labor issues. In several meetings with members of the HSPA he came away from each conference discouraged that he could not make head way on the unionization question.

In the evening he met Selena at Ah Sam's Chinese restaurant. She was in a tight-fitting, red, sleeveless, silk gown that accentuated her figure. When he bent to kiss her, Selena shied away saying, "You will smudge my lipstick."

Gold leaf edged the ceiling of the elegant dining room reserved for the guests of the Japanese consulate. The long speakers' table included naval officers, the assistant mayor of Honolulu, and a prominent member of the HSPA. At a separate table, Grant sat with a young Japanese lieutenant commander on his left, dressed in fleet whites without ribbons or medals, with Selena to his right. A consular official and his wife, with another naval officer, completed the ensemble.

The lieutenant commander spoke excellent English, and Grant found him to be a witty and knowledgeable table companion. "Your first name is Isoroku, meaning fifty-six. Your school mates must have made your life miserable with a number for a name. Why did your parents call you that?"

"You Americans give a father's name to a child. For example, Peterson, the name comes from Peter's son. Why shouldn't my father call me Isoroku? He was fifty-six years old when I was born," the naval officer said. Then he winked. "In Japan, school children do not tease descendants of the samurai."

"If they do, then off with their heads?"

Isoroku laughed. "No. I'm just saying that Japanese children are respectful. They are not like your people. I have noticed at Harvard football games that American young men love to tease and challenge opponents."

"I played football at Yale. The heckling was ferocious. What are you studying at Harvard?"

"Foreign policy and economics I must learn about America. Your country is an industrial giant that is awakening because of the war. You are producing on a scale unheard of in history, manufacturing more than your people can consume. You must export your excess goods. It will mean serious competition throughout the world."

"Is that why Japan has invaded Asia and declared an Asiatic Monroe Doctrine?"

Isoroku scowled. "I do not agree with the army. All the military wants is to conquer land. What the politicians say about economic control of Asia, I am not concerned with. My country must have a powerful navy and widespread naval bases to protect our homeland."

"Is that what Japan is doing in the former German islands, building naval bases?"

"You seem overly inquisitive about our navy," Isoroku said with a grimace. "This dinner is a good-will gesture not meant to be a discussion of potential conflict between our countries."

"I apologize for being inquisitive. I have just returned to Hawai'i from service in the Great War. It seemed natural to talk to a navy man about political matters that could affect my home. But I will refrain from further questions on military subjects."

"You served in France?"

"Yes, just a common foot soldier, hiding in the trenches from the artillery fire."

"What did you think of the aero plane?"

"It is a good weapon, not an all-powerful one. But improvements continue. I believe that in the next war whoever rules the skies will win."

Isoroku compressed his lips and uttered a vehement, "*Hai*! Try to convince the army people of this. Impossible, I believe that someday we will have aircraft flying from ship carriers which will end the dominance of the battleship."

The table conversation descended into small talk of families and the sports rivalry between Princeton, Harvard, and Yale.

The good will speeches were completed and the dinner came to an end. Isoroku bowed, ready to take his leave, but when he learned that Selena came from Chinatown, he asked if she could guide him there along with several fellow officers who wanted to buy souvenirs.

"Nothing may be open at this hour," Selena said, "but I can show you where it is. You can go there tomorrow."

A group of four naval officers left to visit Chinatown with Grant and Selena. As they walked on King Street, Grant asked Isoroku, "With ships carrying airplanes, will Japan need naval bases in the Pacific?"

"Yes, we are building them in Saipan, Truk, Palau, and on out into the Pacific. We will have a ring of fortified islands sufficiently widespread to protect Japan. This is necessary until naval aviation becomes a reality."

The Chinatown shops were closed. With much bowing, the naval officers left for their ship. There was no one on the streets, only an occasional light shining from a second-story window. It was a moonless night. Grant took Selena's hand and pulled her body to his. "Party's over, you don't have to worry about smudging your lipstick."

Selena wrestled away. "Chinatown is dangerous for you. Rudy has men everywhere."

"I don't give a damn about Rudy." Grant reached for the beautiful woman.

"No, no, Mr. Kingsley," Selena said, eluding his grasp. "You can't ignore me all evening and then expect to have instant romance like flicking on a light switch in a dark room."

"But Selena, I was helping defend Hawai'i by learning Japanese intentions in the Pacific. Surely you can understand its importance," Grant said, hurrying into the street to take her in his arms.

"Defense of Hawai'i," Selena said, pushing him away. "The war is over. It is peacetime. We are friends with the Japanese. Besides, it seems to me you could have involved me in your important conversation."

Grant didn't know what to say. He couldn't reveal to her the information Trask had shared with him. Nor could he tell her that tonight he had decided to become a spy for America. But her rejection flamed his desire for her. Would sharing his secrets lead to intimacy? Conflicted, Grant lamely said, "I'm sorry, I should have been more considerate."

"Good. You understand my feelings. Call me tomorrow," Selena said and rushed across the street to the gateway of her home.

Dejected, Grant walked into the darkness of Alakea Street, oblivious to danger within its alleys.

CHAPTER 36

ASING SAT IN Grant's office, surveying the pictures on the wall. "That's your father," he said, pointing to a portrait. "And that must be your mother. What a beautiful woman. She was one-half English, from your grandfather and one-half Hawaiian, from a princess of Hawai'i. Many people love her for her charity and good works."

"Thank you. My mother was wonderful, but, as you know, a cloud hangs over my head. My step-grandmother says I'm the bastard of a pure Hawaiian."

"And her murder made you the number one suspect in her death as well as three more killings. You always seemed to be connected with the scene of the crimes."

"I think the man who did the Wright, Nolan, and Mills murders used me as a decoy to draw attention away from finding him out."

"That appears to be true and that is why I am here. The missionary families are frightened. They have put a lot of pressure on the new mayor. He wants the killer caught."

"You are going to arrest me for the crimes?"

A wolfish smile broke apart Asing's lips. "No. You have too many alibi witnesses, including me. A jury would never convict."

"Then why are you here?"

"To capture suspects, you saw a tattoo on the right arm of the man who killed Mills, correct?"

Grant nodded.

"I also saw something on the killer's arm when he struck you down at the bridge. Across the street from your office is a gambling den. Tonight, a suspect plays dice there."

"How do I fit in to whatever plan you have?"

Asing walked to a window. He motioned Grant to come over. "You see the third-story set of windows? That's the place. At night, there's usually a guard or two at the entrance to the building. They check people coming in and alert their buddies on the third floor if there is trouble."

"You still haven't answered my question. Why am I involved in this?"

"Because you're the only man I can trust in this operation. We have leaks in my department. If I laid out my plan beforehand, the gamblers would be told and I wouldn't be able to catch them in the act. I need you as a lookout and a cohort in capturing the crooks."

"Why trust me?"

"Because you're the prime suspect in all the murders, and the guilty guy could be gambling upstairs tonight."

"I have a date with Selena. I need to see her. Can't your raid wait?"

"No, too many loose lips. I can't stop people from talking. Once the word is out of what I intend to do, we could lose our suspect. It's on for tonight."

***

"This is the most ridiculous date I have ever been on," Selena said. "I'm cooped up with three men from the sheriff's department."

"I'm sorry, but I couldn't risk breaking our date and having to explain why. After last night, I knew you would not accept 'I can't tell you why' as an explanation. This is the best thing I could think of. Besides, you saw the killer of Mills maybe you can identify him tonight."

Selena walked over to Grant who stood by a second-floor window. "Except for the fact that there are three police officers downstairs, I would have said you brought me here for a seduction. I'll accept what you say about capturing a suspect, but don't try anything funny." Selena paused, smiled and said, "Until after you buy me supper."

"I can't wait." He reached over and patted her hand. "I think you're beautiful."

Selena snatched it away, "Aren't you supposed to be watching the street for Asing?"

Grant sighed and withdrew to the office window. An occasional car chugged along the street. There were no pedestrians. A workman swept debris by the curbing. The third-floor windows of the building opposite him were hooded by awnings. The heavy red canvas shielded occupants from unwanted observation. Within a vestibule stood a dark figure, his presence only noticeable by the glow of a cigarette he smoked. The guard, Grant thought, ready to alert gamblers upstairs of trouble.

Selena sidled to him, her light perfume tantalizing. "What's going on?"

"Watch the street sweeper."

"He's disappeared around a corner."

"Keep an eye on the edge of the building."

They stood by the window, Selena close to his side, her breathing slow and warm. Their bodies touched. Grant felt an excitement hammering within him. His hand reached out to her. Selena gasped. "Look."

Inching up a side of the gambler's building climbed the street sweeper. His fingers clawed for handholds, his feet sought niches in the brick wall. "Asing," Grant said, regretfully releasing his hold on Selena's hand. "Go to the stairway door. Alert the officers that Asing is crawling up the building. When he gives the signal, I will relay it to you, and you relay it to them. They will charge the entranceway, take out the guard, and head upstairs."

"Why is the detective doing this? Why not just break down the door and grab the gamblers?"

"They are on the third floor. Alerted by the guard downstairs, they can cover up whatever they are doing and appear as innocent participants in a social meeting. Asing wants to peep through a window, see them gambling, and nab them in the act. If it's an innocent get-together he'll climb down and think of another way to arrest our suspect."

"He's going to go into that place alone? Does he have a gun?"

Grant smiled. "No, just a whip, but he knows how to use it."

"The man is insane to break in by himself. Do we help the officers?"

"No, we are back-up and stay put. Asing's climbed to the third story. Get to the stairway. Be ready to give the signal. He's clawing his way along the ledge. I think the guard below doesn't realize the detective is above him.

"Asing's at a window. He's uncoiled his whip. That's the signal. Tell the officers to go. Asing is breaking in."

Glass shattered. Shards showered the side of the building, splintering onto the sidewalk. The guard stepped from the vestibule, looked up, then scurried back into the shadows. Three police officers ran across the street, disappearing into the darkness. Grant heard swearing, scuffling. The guard staggered into the light and fell to his knees, holding his head.

The Chinese detective swung into the gamblers' den. A wild pandemonium of voices erupted. Asing's strident voice rang clear in the night. "You're under arrest."

At the entry way, splinters flew into the street like confetti as the police officers smashed the door with an axe. It toppled onto the sidewalk.

In the gamblers' den a whip crackled like a gunshot. "Somebody's trying to escape," Asing shouted.

"Is there a rear door?" Selena asked.

"There's a fire escape to an alley, backside of the building," Grant answered, racing for the stairs.

Selena yelled, "Wait for me."

"Stay," Grant said. He took the stairs two at a time, Selena running after him. Ignoring the disobedient woman, Grant ran onto the street heading for the back side of the three-story building.

Entering the dark, garbage-strewn alleyway, Grant heard shoes scraping metal. Above him, two men scurried down a fire escape. He searched the alley for a weapon and found a garbage can lid. Selena came up to his side, taking short quick breaths.

"You should have stayed in the office," Grant complained.

"I wanted to be with you, my darling, and enjoy the fun. Give me the lid." Selena snatched it from Grant's hand and smashed it onto the head of a man who had just dropped onto the alley. The gambler wobbled, and Selena kicked his feet out from under him.

"Get the next guy before he escapes," Selena yelled.

The second man jumped to the pavement. His eyes searched the alley. "Give it up," Grant said. The gambler aimed a kick. Grant danced to the side, countering with his own kick to the gambler's kneecap. The injured man howled and fell to the pavement.

A broad smile lit Selena's face. "You're not only handsome, but terrific with your feet. Teach me that trick sometime."

"Army smarts. Knock out the underpinning before you hit the structure. You're pretty handy with a tin can."

"Lots of gong practice for Chinese New Year."

***

They sat together, eating in a quiet corner of Ah Sam's. Only a few customers remained, finishing their dinners. From another room came the pleasant chimes of the *bianzhong* bells.

"Those musical sounds date back two thousand years to the time of the Warring States period in China," Selena said. "What you hear are specially cast brass bells. The frequency of the notes depends on the thickness of the metal. It takes an expert to forge one of them and lots of experience to play them."

"Music sounds good. But what's that weird wailing sound?"

"It's a flute. China had the first musical instruments eight thousand years ago. Though you do not read about us in the history books, we are an ancient and wise civilization."

"Yes, and being carved up right now by the Japanese. I knew I upset you the other night, but I had a special assignment."

"To spy for America?" Selena scoffed.

"Exactly, and what I do will help China. Another war is coming in the Pacific. The Japanese are seizing land in Asia. They are building armies and a first class navy. I know you think we are at peace with them, but, like Britain, they are empire builders. For them, the conquest of China and the oil of the East Indies are essential to be all-powerful in the world. "

"So you think this boogie man talk will make me care about you?"

"No, but I hope this will," Grant said, sliding to Selena, kissing her cheek, her neck, savoring the breath from her lips. The stiffness of her body relaxed as she responded to his embrace.

A servant's voice interrupted the moment. "Mr. Kingsley, Detective Asing on the telephone."

Grant left, returning in five minutes. "Sorry, I have to go. Wait for a call from Asing."

"Where are you going? Aren't you going to take me home?"

"No time. Wait for the call." Grant rushed off. He felt like a juggler who had just dropped one of his balls, fearful that if he bent to retrieve it, all the others would fall. He could not tell Selena that the next raid was about to occur on Rudy Tang's whorehouse.

***

"You took your time getting here," Asing complained.

"I had to run six blocks in the dark," Grant said.

"If I didn't need you to identify the assassin, I would have gone in by now. You said you got a look at him when the woman's mop hit his face?"

"It was a glance, but I would recognize him if I saw him again. We should also check for the tattoo on his right arm."

"Yes. That is our key piece for identifying the killer. If he is inside Rudy's building, we'll catch him. I've got men in place, two of them watching the back and a man in a rowboat in the water. Let's go."

Asing charged ahead of Grant, hurrying to the entranceway. Two big men, each outweighing the detective by more than thirty pounds, rose from hidden recesses. They blocked Asing's entry. Grant heard the detective say, "Honolulu Sheriff's Department."

"You got warrant?" one of the thugs said.

"No need. I see prostitution on second floor. Smell opium from windows. See illegal gambling. Illegal drinking of whiskey. Step aside."

Both men drew clubs. Before either could act, Asing's whip rose. The lash wrapped around an arm, slicing it. The detective pulled and the bully fell to the ground, blood spurting from his cuts. The other thug circled the detective, his club held close to his chest. Grant moved in to help but Asing motioned him away. The whip flicked. Blood flowed from the man's cheek. The lash struck again, ripping the bully's shirt, slicing into the man's shoulder. He howled, dropped his club and ran into the night.

Asing signaled. Three police officers converged on the door and broke in. Grant followed. Inside he saw a scene of pandemonium. Several scantily dressed females ran upstairs. Two more goons moved to intercept the officers, but backed off when they showed badges. The downstairs reeked of the sweet smell of opium, mixed with the unmistakable smell of spilled whiskey.

Grant, Asing, and a policeman rushed upstairs. Doors flew open, revealing women and men in various stages of undress. "You," Asing said, pointing to the officer, "round these people up and take them downstairs. Grant, let's hit Tang's office."

The door was locked. Asing yelled, "Open up. Police." No answer. Grant smashed the jamb lock and stumbled into the room, the detective following him. Under a window, on a low couch, lay Rudy Tang, unconscious. A nude woman next to him rose up and screamed. Out of a side room stalked a heavy-set Chinese, fastening his belt. Behind him came another man who whipped out a throwing dagger and hurled it. Grant pushed Asing down as the sharp blade buried itself into the wall where the detective had stood.

The first man rushed to the wall behind Tang's desk and unhooked the two leiomanos and the long swordfish dagger. He tossed a shark-toothed weapon to his companion. Asing scrambled from the floor, his uncoiled whip hanging loosely by his side. Grant retrieved the throwing dagger. The woman on the couch scurried out the door, her breasts jiggling like rubber balls trapped in skin. Tang slept. Grant judged that he was out and not a factor in the coming fight.

"The guy with the leiomano and the swordfish bill, he's the one that attacked me on Maunakea Street. Look at his forehead, still an angry scar on it where the mop iron tore his skin."

"Then he is the man we came to talk to."

The fighters shifted from side to side. Neither Oriental chose to attack. Asing's lash kept them at bay.

One man spoke to the other in Chinese.

"They are going to escape," Asing translated. "As long as we block the door, they will not get away."

The man with the swordbill made a sudden move forward, slicing with the leiomano and jabbing with the bill. Asing backed away and whipped. His lash wrapped around the shark-toothed knife and Asing pulled. The man released his weapon and stepped in with the swordbill, aiming a thrust at the detective's belly. Grant shoved a chair into the attacker, throwing him off balance. The other man yelled. Grant saw part of the back wall yawn open. Both Chinese broke off the fight and dove through the secret door.

"They are sliding into the cave, intending to escape out to sea," Grant yelled, running to the opened wall.

"Get outside quick. Call my man in the rowboat. Catch them before they get away. I'll clean up in here. Then come after you."

Grant rushed down the stairs past officers and prisoners being rounded up for transport to the jail. He took a quick look at the bedraggled patrons of Tang's varied businesses, and noted one highly-coiffured Japanese lady in a kimono, her hair lacquered jet black. He ran out the main door heading for the seawall and the entrance to the cave. Pulling out into the rushing stream that swept to the sea was a rowboat with two men. He yelled, "Police, prisoners escaping."

The two Chinese oared into the center of the stream, catching the current of the water flowing toward the harbor channel. Grant called again. A voice answered him. A rowboat bumped against the seawall. "Are you Asing's man?" Grant said.

"Yes."

"Prisoners are escaping. They could be heading for Sand Island or the Harbor Channel. Let's go." Leaping into the boat, Grant seized a set of oars. He let the boat drift for a moment as he searched for the enemy. He saw them in the dim light of a three-quarter moon. He ordered the officer to row, following his cadence.

They spun into the current, heading out to sea. Grant bent to the oars. His hours of paddling had bulked his shoulders into cords of solid muscle. He pulled with ease as his companion fought the oars. "Rest, you're slowing us down. Keep an eye on the enemy boat, give me directions."

The policeman nodded, shipped his oars, and faced ahead. After a moment, he said, "the other vessel has a lead on us, but not big. The two men inside seem to have trouble managing the boat. They are working against each other."

Grant pulled steadily on the oars, their boat skimming the water. "How are we doing?" he asked.

"Gaining. They're heading for Quarantine Island."

"That doesn't make sense. It's barely above water."

"I think they realize they're off course and are pulling for the harbor lights."

"Can you guide me so that we get on the land side of their boat? I suspect they want to get to the piers and escape into the city. If we can force them onto one of the tidal islands we can capture them."

"Then pull hard on the left, back off a little on the right. Good, you're heading on the inside track."

Grant put strength into his oaring. He felt the pull on his shoulders, the strain on his chest, he sculled the oars hard, propelling the rowboat through the protected waters inside of Sand Island. "Where are they?"

"You are between them and the island. The two guys are arguing. Turn into them. I think they have decided to fight us."

"Got weapons?"

"Sure, a four-pronged hook and rope, billy clubs, the oars."

"How far are we from Sand Island?"

"Can't you see it?"

Grant glanced. He saw the enemy boat thirty feet away. Sand Island loomed low in the moonlight. He pulled hard on the oars, yelling, "Get that grappling hook ready."

The first cast splashed into the water. Grant guessed the distance and position of the enemy and heaved on his oars. His rowboat leaped ahead at ramming speed into the hull of the enemy craft. The grappling hook crunched into wood. There was wild hollering. An oar swung down in front of him, barely missing his feet. He saw a Chinese lifting the oar. Grant pulled out the throwing knife, stabbed across the wale, nicking the side of his opponent. The man dropped his weapon.

The policeman used his oar like a lance thrusting it at the second man. They jousted with each other until the boats crunched onto the coral of the island. The jarring contact upset the Chinese who toppled overboard screaming, "I can't swim."

"Guy is in three feet of water," Grant said, "and he thinks he is drowning. Let's go after them."

The Chinese stumbled onto the shore. Grant unfastened the grappling hook and felt his way over submerged rocks onto dry land.

One man holding a leiomano, fenced with it, seeking to slice Grant's belly. The other thug fell onto the hard-packed coral. The policeman climbed out of the water nearby.

A lighthouse on the island beamed over the ground, catching Grant and his opponent in its brightness. In the glare, Grant recognized the man as the assassin who tried to kill him in Chinatown.

The beam turned away, its silvery shaft lighting the harbor and the sea beyond the island. As he had been taught in combat training, Grant watched his balance. He kept the soles of his feet planted onto the ground. His body faced his opponent, so he could twist or pivot from one side to the other. He knew his enemy had the advantage of a longer multi-toothed weapon, the leiomano, the wreath of shark's teeth.

Grant's opponent said, "This time you die like the shitface that you are."

A shaft of light struck the men, haloing their bodies in a ghostly glow. The Chinese lunged. Grant twisted to the side. Razor-sharp teeth grazed his skin. He knew from bayonet training that a cut three inches deep was fatal, but this was a scratch, a warning. The man was skilled with a knife.

He heard scrambling behind him, the sound of rock crushed by stomping feet. He dared not look back. His opponent slashed his weapon, ranting, "Your mother is a whore, your father a prick. You are scum."

Grant saw the lighthouse beam swing toward him. The eyes of the Chinese glinted. Grant knew the man planned to make his move. He danced to the left. His enemy turned, raising his weapon. The beam caught the Chinese in the face, blinding him for a moment. As his arm swept down, Grant swung his grappling hook between the assassin's legs.

CHAPTER 37

SVEN LARSEN STAGGERED, fell, grasping the woman in front of him, ripping her filmy dress. "Bastard, get away from me." The whore pushed Sven into another prisoner. Drunk, he could not control his fall, knocking into two more men. All four fell in a heap on the highly polished floor. A caricature of a Chinese warlord loomed above them. Metal cast figures of men on horseback pranced on each side of the gargantuan face.

"You drunken asshole," screamed one of the fallen men. He began to pummel Sven's chest and shoulders.

"Break it up," yelled a police officer. He enforced his command by swinging his club into the pile of bodies. Sven felt a blow to his back that blew the air from his lungs and he gasped with the pain that coursed through his ribs.

"Can't do this to me," he said, his words mush in his mouth. "Wait 'til Mrs. Grant hears about this. She'll fix you."

"Tell it to her gravestone," the officer said. "Now, move it!"

Wobbling, Sven picked himself up. He saw a Chinese man smiling at him. He had a panama hat on his head, cigarette in the corner of his mouth, and a whip at his side. "What you looking at, Chink?" he muttered. Give him the finger, he thought. Then decided he was hurting too much and didn't need more trouble. He shuffled out the door to the waiting trucks. The Chinese flipped his cigarette. Stamped it and headed into the night.

***

A dozen fanged teeth flashed in the twirling light. The leiomano shredded his shirt, slicing his skin. Grant's grappling iron swung between the legs of the Chinese, its metal hooks sinking into the man's buttocks, its flange smashing into his underbelly. The assassin dropped his weapon, clutching for the hooks biting into his flesh.

Blood smeared his side, dripping onto the white coral of the island. Grant yanked the cord attached to the metal ring of the device. The Chinese shrieked and staggered forward like a stubborn dog being pulled by a rope. Grant ducked under the man's flailing arms, stepped around him, and yanked the cord again.

"Aytah," the Chinese screamed. "No more."

"Surrender?"

"Yes."

Weakened by loss of blood, Grant felt the world spinning. He had to hold on, check on the other thug. A look told him his rear was secure, the police officer stood over a man sprawled on the ground.

"Up with your hands," Grant said.

"Can't, I hurt."

"Up with them," Grant said, mustering all the willpower he possessed to stay awake.

Two hands shot up. Grant wrapped the grappling rope around the man's arms, binding them to his head. He ignored the howls. Finished with his tying, Grant collapsed to the crushed rock of the island, blood smearing his body. "How's our boat?"

"Both vessels are staved in. You rammed real hard."

"Is there any chance of getting off the island?"

"Yes, I've been signaling. Help will come."

***

"Damn the police," muttered Sven. "The women are gone, men also, but they keep me in this stinking jail.

"Let me out. You got no right to hold me," the Swede yelled, rattling the iron bars of the Big Tank to emphasize his command.

"Shut up," an inmate said. "Guys want to sleep. You don't get out until a hearing before the judge."

"Who asked you to butt in, asshole? I want out," Sven yelled, kicking the cage.

"You want somebody to say 'please shut up'," another prisoner said, smashing his fist into the Swede's kidneys.

His back and head jackknifed. His knees buckled and he collapsed to the dirty floor of the cell. He tried to get up. A foot stomped into his stomach, again and again. He tried to suck in air, panicking when he could not inhale. He tried to speak, to stop the beating. Words would not come. This was not like the plantation, he thought, where workmen cowered when he spoke and men ran when he gave an order. He felt that he was drowning. Everything that he had eaten and drunk emptied onto the floor as his stomach heaved. The vomiting allowed air into his lungs.

The beating stopped. Sven heard the bully say, "Lie in your puke and shut up."

***

Morning sunlight beamed over the Ko'olau range, the sudden brightness momentarily blinding Grant Kingsley as he woke from a troubled sleep. Near him the officer stood, guarding their two prisoners. His eyes swept the ocean and he saw a police boat landing to pick them up. Once loaded, they headed for the harbor. Despite his injuries, the officer in charge insisted that Grant attend a morning lineup.

When he entered the lockup, Asing rose from his desk and came to him. "Thanks for coming. We need to check suspects captured in the raids. I can't hold them much longer. We must charge them, set bail, or release them."

"I understand. Let's go with whatever you got to do and then I need to see a doctor."

"We wait for Selena. She saw the killer, like you and I."

"It wasn't a long look. The man wore black clothes. It might be hard to pick him out."

"Maybe, but we saw his height, his size, there was a mark on his right arm. Ah, there comes the pretty woman. Good morning, Miss Choy."

Selena ignored Asing and came to Grant, saying, "They told me you were hurt in a big fight on Sand Island."

"Just little rips from shark's teeth. Not much to talk about."

"You had a rap on the head a few days ago with stitches. How many do you need this time?"

"Maybe a couple more, I'm sorry about last night. Asing needed me in the raid."

"You mean you couldn't tell me where you were going because I couldn't be trusted," Selena snapped, her body shaking with anger. .

"Honey, I trust you, but you got to understand, we were breaking into Rudy Tang's place."

"I understand perfectly. Your friend doesn't believe in me. He doesn't think I care enough about you to keep a secret. But when he wants something, he snaps his fingers and expects us to do his bidding. Listen, Mr. Big Shot Detective, just because you can threaten my man with crimes he did not commit, doesn't mean you can order either of us around. We are a team, Mr. Asing. Where he goes, I go. Got that?" Selena poked a finger into the wiry detective's shoulder.

Drawing back from her touch, Asing said, "Please understand, I am under a lot of pressure. The mayor is demanding resolution. The Prince of Wales is due in August. He's the future king of England. We can't have more killings while he is here. We make a deal, all three of us work together to get the killer." Asing reached out his hand. Grant took it and nodded to Selena. She added her hand and the Chinese detective clasped them tight, saying, "From now on we are a team. No more secrets between us."

Selena nodded.

Grant said, "What do you want us to do?"

"We have a lineup showing. There will be nine men. They are selected from those we arrested for gambling, violating prohibition, and smoking opium. We let everyone else go because the wrongdoing they were committing is unimportant. We must find the killer. We all saw the man at the Ward Estate. It is time for us to get him. Come with me."

Asing took them to a large room with a stage and glaring spotlights focused on it. Behind the platform stood a wall painted white with horizontal height lines across it. "There will be three coming out at a time. All shrouded in black. Look at them, see if anyone appears like our killer." Asing nodded to a policeman at the door. It opened and three men with black cloth draped over their heads and flowing over their shoulders stumbled across the platform.

The policeman ordered, "Stop. Face to the front." One man refused to comply, and the officer rapped his knee with a baton. "Face front, I said."

"Study them close. Each has a number on chest. See if one, two, or three is the same height and size as the man we saw several nights ago."

"Maybe number three," Grant said. "Have him show his right arm."

"Number three, raise your arms. Is that the man you saw at Pua'ena'ena or Old Plantation?"

"No."

"I agree. Do you?" Asing asked.

Selena nodded.

"Release them,"

Six more men were viewed in the same way. Two were detained, the others released. "We will study the remaining two, individually," Asing said.

Arms bare, shrouded in a black cloth, the first man shuffled through the side door and onto the stage. "He's got tattoos on both arms," Selena said.

"But they are images of nude women. Nothing like what I saw that night," Grant answered.

"Sometimes darkness can fool you," Asing said, then called to the man. "Take off your shroud. What's your name?"

"Screw you," growled the prisoner.

A nearby officer flipped off the shroud with his baton and in a voice filled with menace ordered, "Answer the man."

"Okay. Don't hit me with that thing. Name is Sven Larsen."

"Are you the Larsen that worked for Robert and Sheila Grant at the West O'ahu plantation?" Grant asked, surprise in his voice.

"What if I am? What's it to yah?"

"My name is Grant Kingsley. My father runs the plantation now. I'm interested in talking to Sven."

Asing whispered, "You can speak to him later. Is he the killer?"

Both Grant and Selena shook their heads.

"Let him go."

The last man leaned against the white wall. There was a tattoo on his right arm of a serpent. Both Selena and Grant thought he had the same build and size of the killer. Asing was not sure. But since he was the same man that tried to kill Grant in Chinatown and on Sand Island, the detective booked him for attempted murder.

"Was Rudy Tang one of the nine guys we looked at?" Grant asked.

"Yes, but neither of you identified him. I will charge him with running a gambling den, whorehouse, and breaking prohibition. He'll be in jail for a while until he can make bail. I'll work on him a little bit more and his hired assassin. Get some sleep, both of you. We have work to do."

CHAPTER 38

LARSEN STUMBLED FROM the jail house. "Damn them all," he muttered. He felt his pockets hoping he might have missed something, but they were empty. His belly and back ached where he had been kicked and punched. "No way to treat a white man. Savages, all of them savages, especially that squinty-eyed Chink. How dare he question me? I've bossed dozens of pigs like him. Damn stupid Chinaman."

Larsen staggered along the street, oblivious to the stares of others on the sidewalks. "Get to Sheila Grant's home. Get money. Find a place to stay. She owes me." He entered Nu'uanu, his feet crunching the hard gravel of the roadway. Vehicles swerved around him, horns blaring. He weaved his way to a set of iron gates. Beyond lay an imposing mansion ringed by beds of flowers and an emerald green lawn. He grasped the bars, trying to push them open. "Locked." He rattled the iron fence like a monkey in a cage. He hollered several times, "Open up."

The front door swung out. A man struggling into a dark coat stepped from the house, down the stairs, and came to the gate. "What is it, scum?"

"I want to see Sheila Grant."

"She is dead."

"Dead? She can't be. I need money. A place to live. She owes me."

"I'm just a servant, caretaking her home. Leave or I shall call the police."

Sven realized he could not get anything from the man by bluster. He fought to suppress his mounting anger. In a thin voice, he asked, "Is there someone I could talk to? Someone who is in charge of her affairs?"

"That would be Mr. Kingsley. His office is at Fort and Hotel Streets. Go away."

He released his hold on the gates and shuffled downtown. He turned over in his mind the name. Kingsley, he must have been the guy at the lineup. "He said he wanted to see me," Lars muttered. "About what, I don't know. Whatever he wants he must pay for it."

Pulling himself together, Larsen marched into town and found the Kingsley office. He entered and demanded to see the owner.

The clerk at the entry desk said, "He's on Mau'i."

"I'm an employee of Sheila Grant. Can you give me some money?" Larsen said, his tone desperate, a thirst for whiskey burning his innards.

"No, you're a stranger. Please leave."

His mind searched for a response. He couldn't leave without something. He thought to throttle the man, but a large counter stood between him and the clerk. Should he vault it and rob him? But that could end in disaster. He remembered the guy at the lineup and asked, "How about Mr. Grant Kingsley? I saw him today. He wanted to talk to me."

"He's out for the day. Back tomorrow."

"Tell him Larsen wants to see him."

Shadows spread like a blanket over the streets when he walked from the office. A stiff wind howled through the multi-storied buildings of downtown Honolulu. "Got to find some newspaper to wrap myself in. Seek out a kitchen. Beg for food, then bed down in an alley." The Swede shuffled down Fort Street, searching for a handout.

***

"We have made two raids. Arrested Chinese, Filipinos, Koreans, even a few Caucasians, but we have only one legitimate suspect," Asing said, striking his fist into his palm.

"You mean the guy who attacked me twice?" Grant said. "Has he told you anything?"

"He won't talk, but I'm sure he is from San Francisco. A hired killer and a member of the snake Tong."

"You know this from the dagger he dropped in Chinatown?"

"And the snake tattooed on his right arm."

"Isn't that enough evidence to charge him with the murders?"

"Don't think so. He claims he landed in Hawai'i after Sheila Grant was killed."

"Do you believe him? Maybe he came at night by rowboat, entered Honolulu through Rudy's cave in time to commit all the murders."

"Possible, but the tattoo I saw on the killer was on the side of the man's arm. This San Francisco Chinese has the mouth of a snake on the underside of his wrist and hand. Selena, what did you see?"

"It was dark. A lot of action was going on. I couldn't be sure."

Grant shrugged. "We are nowhere close to finding the killer. I think Rudy Tang's involved, but we can't prove it. Why did you call us to the police station?"

"A time ago you told me of your investigation of your chauffeur's room. You saw items there suggestive of ancient Hawaiian religious practices. I asked you to look at his room today while he is on holiday. What did you find?"

"All items were gone, including the effigy of Ku. Why do you ask?"

"Your chauffeur's name is Charles Maka. On a Hawaiian we caught in one of the raids was an invitation from Haku Maka to an *'Aha Hele Honua Na Kilu a AKUA.'* The location is *Ilina Hale O'Puuwaina.*"

"Sheila had an aha mat at her feet the night she was killed. The kahuna told me that it was an ancient symbol for a prayer ceremony before sacrifices were made. But what does the rest mean?" Grant asked.

"We know the invitation uses the word Ku in it," Selena said, "and I believe that the word haku means master. So master Maka is inviting selected Hawaiians to a prayer ceremony to Ku, but where and when?"

"The when is tonight," Asing said.

"We don't have much time if we are going to intrude on the ceremony. Let me use your telephone." Grant called Aunt Malia. He spoke to the aged woman for several minutes. He frowned as he hung up.

"What is it? What did she say?" Selena asked.

"*Hale* means house. *Ilina* is cemetery at Puuwaina, Hill of Sacrifice. But where is that?"

"I know," Asing answered. "Punchbowl Crater."

***

"This is a rocky hill to be climbing in the dark and without lights," Selena complained. "Why couldn't we do this raid in daylight?"

Asing laughed, "You can't expect criminals to meet when you want them to. You must catch them in the act."

"But what are we catching them doing?" Grant asked, then swore as he dislodged loose rocks that tumbled in a slight landslide down the side of the extinct volcano.

"You make too much noise. You will warn our prey of our coming. To answer your question, we will catch the participants in a Ku ceremony and by careful questioning find out if one of them is the kahuna nui who is committing these crimes."

"Why not just arrest Charles and question him?"

"On what charge, the possession of ancient artifacts? No, we must catch the practitioners in the act of worshiping Ku. Question the whole group and find our killer."

"Are we supposed to do it by ourselves?" Selena complained. "I'm already worn out hiking on this awful trail. Isn't there a better way?"

"So many questions. I have my whip. We have clubs. Is that not enough?"

"No," Selena answered. "We don't know how many people are in this house worshiping Ku."

"Then you can understand why we are using this trail, high on the crater's side. We look down upon the house where the ceremony is held. Find out what we are dealing with. If we need help, I blow this whistle, my men a half-mile below us will race up and help make the arrests."

"How did you know about this place?" Grant asked.

"After the war, the city organized a committee to discuss what to do with public land at Punchbowl volcano. I was part of the group. I learned that in ancient times, slaves and innocent people were killed on this slope, as gifts to pagan gods. That's why Hawaiians call the crater, Hill of Sacrifice. Until today I did not know its Hawaiian name."

"Your committee work, is that how you know about a house near a burial place?"

Asing nodded. "Look ahead, you can see faint light. Be quiet."

A wind whipped up, rustling the shrubs that peppered the slope. Carried with the breeze, came the rhythmic sounds of a pahu drum. A crescent moon above them fought vainly to pierce the clouds scudding over the Ko'olau range and into Kaneohe. As the trio moved closer to the house, they heard the sound of a flute wailing in time to the drum beat. There followed chanting by men and women, their words blunted by the wind.

"Must be a big celebration of some kind," Selena said.

"Yeah, let's get closer. I keep hearing something like 'ah Ku ah,' then another word, Lono, repeated over and over," Grant said.

"They must be done with their dancing - the drum and flute have stopped. Let's go over to that overhanging rock and look in," Asing said.

Five women and men were inside the house. All scantily clothed and seated opposite each other. In corners of the room Grant saw the taboo sticks wrapped with round white cloth that had been in Charles' room. Affixed on a back wall was the effigy from the chauffeur's apartment. A man yelled, *"Kilu kohe."* In the dim light, a coconut bowl whirled across the floor, striking an object at the knees of a woman. *"Ho'o kohana"* he yelled.

"A'ole, no," she answered, whirling the cup back across the floor.

"You missed," he screamed. "No," the woman said, "it wasn't you that I wanted tonight."

Charles Maka stood, a feather helmet on his head, making him tall and imposing. "Look at the tattoos on his arms," Selena gasped.

"You must pay the forfeit," Maka said, waving a long feather wand upon the shoulder of the female.

She dropped her head in submission. The victorious man stood and began to dance around her, removing her clothes as he did. When she stood nude, he caressed her body until she began to moan. He finished his dance and took her from the room.

Asing scowled. "This is just a sex party, nothing to do with the killings."

"Yes, but those tattoos on Charles' arms look like what I saw the night of Mills' murder," Grant said.

"I'll question him tomorrow," Asing said. "Find out what's going on and who else is at this ritual. Let's leave them to their game."

CHAPTER 39

"YAP ISLAND, WHO ever heard of it?" Grant said to his clerk standing by his desk. "The article in the paper describes this peculiar place where stone money is used. The natives quarry round rocks from some distant island and haul them by canoe hundreds of miles to Yap. It's crazy, but apparently the chief that has the biggest doughnut-shaped stone is considered the richest man on the island."

"It's all very interesting," the clerk said, "but..."

"What is interesting about this piece of news is that Yap could be the cause of war between the United States and Japan."

"How so?" the clerk asked, his face creasing into a frown.

"The Germans controlled the island before the war. They built a cable station there that established communications between the Far East, the Dutch East Indies and the rest of the world. The Japanese seized Yap in 1914."

"And own the cable station," the clerk added. "But why is it so important that it could cause war?"

"Communications and information control. A nation with the power of the telegraph and telephone can learn trade secrets, barter or sell at the best prices. If you're Japan fighting a war in China, you can distort the news or send out false information about what is going on. And if Japan has Pacific island naval bases, they can alert their forces of an overseas attack coming from America. It works the other way as well. The Japanese could create a total communications blackout in the Pacific and make a sneak attack on a naval base like Hawai'i. They did that to the Russians in

1904. Without a declaration of war, the Japanese navy made a torpedo attack on the Russian Far East Fleet in Port Arthur."

The clerk sighed. "It is far above my ability to figure out the politics of it all. What I came in to say is that you had a visitor yesterday, a Mr. Sven Larsen. He claimed he knew you."

"I only saw the fellow the other day. What did he want?"

"Money, he will be back this morning. Also, Captain Trask called and asked that you call him. Someone just came in. I'll tend to it."

The clerk left, and Grant began work on his labor proposal to the HSPA. His side ached from the knife wound and he mentally scolded himself for practicing martial arts when his injury had not healed. But he didn't want to miss workouts, especially learning to use the sling.

It was a pleasant morning. A light shower cleared the air of dust. Grant's mind wandered to the ocean, picturing the waves that were building up in roaring crescents of foam. He longed to be out there tangling with the surf, but his doctor had warned him to let his wounds heal first.

Grant heard footsteps stomping up the stairway. The door rattled. It swung open. An unshaven, dirty man swaggered in. "You, Kingsley."

Behind the intruder, the clerk rushed in. "I'm sorry, sir, I told Mr. Larsen to wait, but he just barged right past me and came up here."

"Need some money for food, a place to sleep. Your family owes me."

Irritated by the man's swagger, but interested in his claim, Grant waved his clerk away and said, "Please, have a seat."

Larsen sneered at the departing man. "See, I told you your boss would see me. After all the stuff I've done, he better or I'll talk." The obnoxious man fell into an easy chair. His bloodshot eyes roved the room, fastening on a picture of James Kingsley. "That supposed to be your father, boy? I saw the man a few times, out at the mill. Never spoke to him. You don't look like him. Look like somebody else I met long time ago. I can't recollect where. It'll come to me if we talk long enough. You got any whiskey?"

"No. What is it that you want?" Grant said, expressing his dislike by his sharp tone. He fixed a hostile stare on the miserable human seated in front of him with his feet splayed, his hands hanging limply at his side, and his mouth slack.

Larsen's eyes shifted from side to side. He straightened in his chair, hunched onto Grant's desk saying, "I got information that will destroy the reputation of your grandfather, your grandmother, and make the Federals investigate the HSPA."

There it is, the blackmail threat. Grant thought to kick the man out. Let him talk to whomever. No one would listen to such a tramp. But he remembered Naga's request for information about missing Japanese. Why did Larsen think he had met someone that looked like him a long time ago? It might be best to hear the man out. "Tell me what you know."

Larsen's face broke into a crafty smile. "How about a little something in advance? Some eating money."

Disgusted by the bargaining, Grant said, "Or whiskey money." But he fished out a silver piece and passed it over. He wondered if the man would just bolt out the door and find a gin mill somewhere.

The Swede took the heavy coin. Bit it. Nodded his head and said, "Jumped ship in Honolulu. Saw an advertisement for a field supervisor for your grandfather's West O'ahu plantation and took the job. I met the man in the first couple weeks. He liked my style of handling the Chinks and Hawaiians," Larsen smirked. "We talked for awhile. He sized me up real good. Your granddad offered me a job on two conditions that I obeyed his orders without question and I kept my mouth shut."

"What were you supposed to do?"

"Be his professional strikebreaker. Hire a team of guys and visit Grant plantations. Find the agitators, the organizers, rabble rousers, and stop them before they made trouble. My boys and I worked the different islands, Mau'i, Kaua'i. I took no nonsense from anybody. The law was always on our side." Larsen paused, his brow furrowing. "There was this one guy on Kaua'i back in the '80's. He was helping the Chinese leave the plantations. The more I look at you the more I remember. You are just like him, same brown face, dark hair, hard-looking eyes."

His words chilled Grant. His pulse pounded. For a moment he considered getting rid of the Swede, but he could not control his impulse, "Did the man have a name?"

"Yeah, I remember it now. He called himself John Tana."

Under his desk, Grant's hands balled into fists until his knuckles turned white. He fought to maintain his control. In a low voice, he said, "That must have been a long time ago when you met him. How do you remember his name? What he looked like after all these years?"

"Because he and I fought each other."

"Why?"

"Chinese having rights. Them Chinks are scum. Just like Hawaiians."

Grant could no longer listen to the man, the memories of the slights about his skin color and Hawaiian looks swirled in his head. It had started that first night at the Moana when he dined with Selena. They wouldn't serve him until someone recognized him as a Kingsley. The maitre d' questioned Selena because of her Eurasian looks. It wasn't just that time but other insults during the months since he had returned to Hawai'i.

Larsen kept babbling, oblivious to Grant's failure to respond. "Your granddad and his partner wanted to get this Japanese agitator. The guy was stirring up labor strife. One night we grabbed him after he attended a union meeting. We strung him up so all them slant-eyes could see what happens to those who cause trouble. We would have got away with it, but the damn guy's wife raised such a ruckus with the Japanese Embassy that they hired a private investigator. He uncovered the truth. The county attorney had to file charges. The *Pacific Gazette* was on our side. The editor thought white men shouldn't be prosecuted. We got convicted of manslaughter, but your grandfather and his partner pulled strings and charges went away. And true to my word, I never said a thing about who put us up to the killing."

The Swede talked on about beatings, breaking arms, whipping plantation workers, relishing his power over the hired servants. Grant remained deep in his thoughts, wondering what he should choose, the ruling class or the bottom scratchers, the immigrants and Hawaiians. But he might have no choice if he was the son of a Hawaiian and his father cast him out. "What's wrong with that?" Grant said. "I could do it."

"What did you say? You could break arms, lynch workers, and beat them like I did for Robert and Sheila Grant? You're not tough enough."

"Sorry for the outburst. I was thinking of something else. You mentioned my grandfather had a partner, what was his name."

"Abner Nolan, he's the guy that ordered the lynchings, especially of this Japanese labor agitator."

That's what Naga wants to know, Grant thought. "Tell me about it."

Larsen's face turned crafty. "You've heard enough. How about something to keep my mouth shut? Enough to eat and sleep on."

"How much?"

"Five hundred dollars."

"That's a fortune. I don't have that kind of money. I need to talk with my father."

"Call him."

"No. Come back tomorrow around five o'clock. I'll have an answer for you." Grant stood and directed the Swede out the door. He did not like the man and his bully boy attitude. But Naga needed to talk to him. And he wanted to find out more about this John Tana.

Larsen left.

Grant called Trask. He related his conversation with the Japanese lieutenant commander.

"So, they are building naval bases on the islands they grabbed from Germany. The president asked the Japanese to return what they took to the natives. But they have stalled and appealed to the League of Nations. You read in the paper about the Yap telegraph station?"

"Yes. Is that situation serious enough to cause war?"

"There are Japanese hardliners, a group called the Black Dragon Society, vicious men who are determined to hold on to the island. They call it the telephonic and radio nerve center of the Pacific. The president is trying to negotiate international control of Yap. Would you visit your friends in the Japanese Consulate? See what they have to say. Right now we do not have naval power in the Pacific and the British are not our friends."

"That sounds ominous. I'll see what I can find out." Grant hung up. He called Sato for an appointment, saying he needed to talk with Naga about meeting with Larsen. He completed work on his labor proposal that he would discuss with the Japanese, and left his office.

***

"You wish to help the Japanese workers," Consul General Matsu said, surprise in his voice. "Why only yesterday, the *Pacific Gazette* in an editorial said, 'Offer the plantation coolie a compromise and he thinks he is the master. There is one word which holds the lower classes of every nation in check and that is 'Authority.' The sugar people have only one philosophy: obedience or punishment for disagreement.'"

"You can't pay attention to the editor of the *Gazette*. He is conservative and believes that no mercy should be shown to immigrant laborers," Grant answered.

"I agree!" Sato said, his voice almost a shout. "He has preached violence and racial hatred against the Japanese since the days of the overthrow of the queen!"

Grant was startled by his friend's vehemence and noticed that even Matsu seemed perturbed by the outburst. Like a mother hen clucking to attract a wayward chick, he scolded, "Sato, it is not seemly for a diplomat to express such strong views even in a confidential conversation."

"Please excuse me, Excellency, but this man Thurmond has preached suppression of the worker and condoned lynching of the Japanese. It is difficult for me to restrain myself knowing what he has said in the past."

"He appears to be stirring up trouble between America and Japan. Did you read his article about Yap and his suggestion that your country return the Pacific Islands taken from Germany to native rule?" Grant asked, seizing an opportunity to gain vital information.

Matsu sighed, "Yes, I saw the story. But the man is wrong. Japan will aid the native people to have a better life. We are not a militaristic disturber of the peace as the editor would like the world to believe. We will accept whatever the League of Nations decides."

"But aren't you currently building bases and fortifying islands in the Pacific? With all that expense won't it be hard to give them up?"

"We are only acting in self-defense. We must protect our trade routes in Asia. Your country is the aggressor in the Pacific, constructing naval installations in Guam, Manila, and Pearl Harbor."

"Then we are in an arms race like the one that caused World War I."

"Not so," Sato interrupted. "But you did not come here to talk about world politics. You came to discuss the Japanese labor situation in Hawai'i."

"That is true. Your consulate has always been helpful in resolving labor disputes. I am here to tell you that the HSPA does not agree with editor Thurmond. Instead, their current position is to spend money and time on the welfare of the worker."

"That is surprising," Matsu said. "That has not been their attitude in the past. It has always been divide and rule, with fear, and force."

Grant nodded. "That is true, but I believe the leadership of the HSPA realizes from the last strike that hardball tactics are expensive. To show our good faith, brutal field supervisors like Sven Larsen have been fired from the plantations."

"Larsen," Sato interrupted. "The Japanese union has been looking for him."

"I spoke with him today. Your people couldn't find him since he has been living on the streets for some time. Tell Naga that Sven Larsen will be in my office late tomorrow afternoon."

The meeting concluded with Grant suggesting that the consulate work with the Japanese workers to organize a single labor union that the HSPA could recognize. He would propose to the sugar planters that a media-tion board be established to meet with union representatives to discuss and work out issues. The questions that could not be resolved would be submitted to binding arbitration.

Enthusiastic at the response of the Japanese officials, Grant left the consulate hoping that the HSPA would accept the proposal. But he real-ized he would have a difficult time convincing hard-headed businessmen to abandon their half-century policy of divide and rule. With these sober-ing thoughts, he headed for Pearl Harbor.

***

"The fortification by the Japanese of the Pacific Islands is vital information. Their actions clearly pose a threat to America and the British." Trask drew down a large map, affixed like a window shade to his office wall. He circled his hand around the Pacific. "Look at this, Japanese naval bases on islands within striking distance of Hawai'i. Military installations placed just a few hundred miles from Australia, the Dutch East Indies, Malaysia, and even India. The Japanese are in position to control all of the Central Pacific and the Oceans of Asia."

Grant studied the map. He frowned and said, "Isn't that an awful lot of sea to try to hold onto? How could you defend so much water?"

"It's a lot easier if you have bases to supply your ships and places for a fleet to assemble, ready to fight. With such a vast area, an attacker would be at a severe logistical disadvantage trying to penetrate the island defenses. I think your news will help convince the British not to renew their treaty with Japan. It will help convince Congress to increase naval spending, especially since Japan is negotiating with Mexico for a coaling station."

"That is a bold move. You mentioned the Black Dragon Society. Who are they?"

"They started as an espionage group of Japanese men organized by a man called Uchida. This criminal society has used all types of ninja-style tactics, sabotage, revolution, intimidation, assassinations. They killed the empress of Korea. By clandestine operations, they helped defeat the Russians in their war against Japan. They have abducted Japanese diplomats who express views favorable to peace. They are a militaristic bunch of zealots."

"Does this mean we are headed for war?"

Trask flipped up his map and returned to his desk. Retrieving a book from his drawer, he said, "This is secret information and you're not to reveal it to anyone. We do not have any battleships in the Pacific, and Japan has sixteen. Pearl Harbor is not yet ready to accommodate a war fleet. It will be several more years before it has that capability. The Japanese spend one-third of their annual budget on their navy. We may talk tough, but we do not have the power to confront the Empire. Congress still hasn't given us the money to build the twenty-six battle wagons needed to fight a two-ocean war. We must stall for time. Negotiate, get Britain on our side. Their treaty with Japan expires in July of 1921. The intelligence you have delivered will prove vital to convincing them to end it for all time. "

Grant shifted uncomfortably in his chair. He knew that he had been given information by the Japanese because they trusted him. He was breaching their confidence. Was it morally right to take advantage of friendships?

"You mentioned meeting a lieutenant commander who gave you a lot of information. What was his name?"

"Isoroku Yamamoto. He believes that in the next war, he who rules the skies will rule the seas."

Trask laughed. "Cracker box aero planes can't hurt a modern battleship. Besides, a country would need air bases all over the Pacific Islands to fight an attacking fleet. No country could afford that, and no military force could disperse its aircraft to a multitude of islands and hope to win. No, the navy with the biggest dreadnoughts will be victorious in the next war. Mark my words on it."

Grant thought about what the captain said and recalled watching airplanes that machine gunned and bombed trenches. There had been nothing the men on the ground could do to stop the air assaults. Yamamoto had suggested building naval carriers for planes. A sea force of floating air bases could go anywhere to attack an enemy. If such ships were feasible, then you would not need land air bases all over the Pacific to win. Hawai'i could be vulnerable to such an attack. Grant decided it was morally right to spy for his country. He said goodbye and headed for downtown Honolulu and Asing's office.

CHAPTER 40

THREE HOODED MEN stood in the glare of lamp lights. One man flinched, stepping away from the others. A police guard rapped him on his side, saying, "Get back into line." Grant took his eyes from the lineup to whisper to Asing, "Is one of the guys up there my chauffeur?"

Asing assumed a deadpan expression. "Pick anyone or no one on that stage. If you pick someone, it is because he resembles the killer we saw."

Selena nudged Grant. "You're not supposed to ask questions. Just decide if somebody in front of us is familiar to you."

"Anyone ever tell you that you have the most beautiful eyes? The softest skin I've ever touched?" Grant said, his palm stroking Selena's bare shoulder. Despite the warmth in the room and the business of identification, he felt an urge to be close to her, to make something happen between them.

"You will please pay attention to what we are doing," Asing said, exasperation in his voice. "You two can play a game of kilu later."

"Kilu, is that what we were watching the other night? It looked like a sexy version of spin the bottle. Selena, are you ready to try it?"

The young woman's lips parted, blowing a kiss she said, "Yes, just as long as Rudy Tang and a few of your beach boy friends play, too."

"Stop that," Asing scolded. "Do you recognize anyone on the stage?"

"Have them show their arms," Selena answered, moving away from Grant to the far wall of the rectangular room. She leaned her back against it, studying the three shrouded men.

Asing called an order. Three pairs of arms shot up, all with tattoos inked into brown skin.

"Hawaiians?" Grant asked.

"Recognize anyone?" the detective answered. "If no one is the right one we let them all go, except..." His voice trailed off.

"They all have tattoos, but I don't recognize anyone," Selena said, shaking her head. She turned away from the lineup, her eyes downcast, arms folded across her chest. "This is like fishing without any bait. We're catching nothing."

"Don't be discouraged, honey. We'll find the killer. You just wait," Grant said, reaching to take Selena's hand. He glanced at Asing and saw the detective whispering to the guard and pointing to a stout man in the lineup. The policeman sent him back through the door leading into the jail. The other two were ordered to exit through the opposite side.

Freedom for two, Grant thought, but not the other guy. He was curious but he decided not to ask the reason. Instead, he took Selena's arm, saying, "Let's have dinner and after that maybe we can take a ride in my car."

"Sorry," Asing said, but I want you to stay for the interview. I'll have a policeman take Miss Choy home."

"What interview? Why can't Selena stay?" Grant said, disappointed that Asing wanted him to remain, send Selena away, and spoil any chance for an intimate date.

"Too many questions. You will please leave, Miss Choy. Mr. Kingsley, come with me."

Grant knew it was useless to argue. He said goodnight and followed Asing into an interview room. At a round wooden table sat the family chauffeur, Charles Maka, and next to him, Lieutenant Hitchcock. There were two vacant chairs. Asing took one and motioned Grant to the other. He said, "I detained you because of the peculiar ritual that your employer and I observed. You call it kilu which is a game that appears to result in a sex orgy. But in your invitation to the event you use the terms aha and Ku. We know from the murder of Sheila Grant that aha is a prayer mat placed by a victim before sacrifices begin. Ku is the God of War. You will please explain."

Maka studied the invitation to the kilu that Asing passed to him. He said, "Aha has several meanings. It can mean a ceremony that people are invited to take part in. In this instance, a game of kilu honoring the akua, meaning the gods. On the occasion you witnessed, we honored Lono, the god of fertility."

"And your role in this ritual was what?" Hitchcock demanded.

"I am the haku, the master, since I am the only unmarried man among those who attend and I am of royal blood. It is my duty to extend the invitation and enforce the rules."

"Are you telling us that everyone who attended this kilu, except you, is married?" Grant asked.

"Yes, and those who participate agree not to object to husband or wife swapping. That is why you see the taboo poles in the room. It is interesting to observe whom a woman will choose to mate with. Often it is not her husband."

"And the house by the burial grounds?" Asing asked.

"It is a Hawaiian meeting place. Secluded and close enough to allow our people to tend to the graves of our ancestors."

"You say that you are not worshiping Ku in the house. But I could see an effigy to the war god on the back wall," Asing said.

"Ku is not the only Hawaiian god that has a gaping mouth and big teeth. We who practice kilu worship Lono, a peaceful god. I know that you want to unravel the mystery of the murders, but the killer is not Hawaiian."

"Why do you say that?" Hitchcock demanded.

"Human sacrifices were killed swiftly, not by this cutting and slashing with the leiomano. The idea is not to inflict lingering pain, but to deliver a swift death to the victim to gain favor with the god Ku. Also, a shark-toothed knife was used in battle, not at the altar of the war god."

Grant palmed his hair and massaged his temples with his fingers. He took a deep breath saying, "You're suggesting that someone is masquerading as the kahuna nui and his motive may not be revenge on the missionaries. But what reason does he have for killing four people and possibly murdering more?"

"Revenge is a reason," Asing said. "These are not random killings, but carefully selected victims. There is a thread tying Sheila Grant,

Judge Wright, Abner Nolan, and Donald Mills together that may not be missionary-related."

"Sheila Grant was not from missionary family, but my grandfather Robert Grant was. Judging from the hook in her mouth, Sheila was a substitute for him," Grant said.

"Then what is the thread that ties the four together?" Hitchcock demanded.

"I don't know, but whatever they did, causing someone to seek revenge, occurred before January of 1895," Grant said.

"Why that date?" Asing asked.

"My grandfather was killed by the friendly fire of his own men during the counter-revolution against the Republic of Hawai'i," Grant answered.

"All four helped in the overthrow of Queen Lili'uokalani," Charles Maka interjected, his voice shaking with anger. "If it wasn't for them and United States Marines, we would still have our monarchy."

"That is it. That is the motive," Hitchcock said. "Hawaiians were opposed to the overthrow. When the white businessmen failed to secure annexation to the United States, they formed a Republic. This was done despite the protests of thousands of Hawaiians who signed a petition objecting to U.S. annexation and seeking the return of Lili'uokalani to the throne. When the counter-revolution occurred in 1895 many Hawaiians took part in it." Hitchcock concluded his summing up of facts by pointing an accusatory finger at Charles Maka. "I believe that you signed the petition against annexation, that you took part in the counter-revolution. You waited until the Missionary Centennial to seek your revenge for the loss of Hawaiian independence."

Charles Maka, who up until that point had kept his composure, broke into tears. His sobbing wrenched Grant's heart. The man had always been a decent servant to the family. He had never exhibited bizarre behavior. Whether it was his Hawaiian blood or a desire for fairness to the accused man, Grant said, "Hitchcock, three of us could not pick him out as the killer. I just don't believe that Charles is the murderer."

"Shut up or I'll book you instead," Hitchcock said. "He's got tattoos on his arms just like the killer of Mills. We'll keep him in custody for a while. Ask some more questions. We'll smash the truth out of him." Hitchcock grabbed Maka's arm and hustled him from the room.

Grant said to Asing, "I know the sheriff's department is desperate to satisfy the mayor, but don't let Hitchcock railroad an innocent man like he tried to hang me."

The detective shrugged. "Not much I can do at the moment. He is running this show. It's only because of what happened at the Ward Estate that he isn't putting you under arrest, too. Right now I would not make waves."

Grant left the station and met with Joshua Kanakoa to arrange bail for the unfortunate chauffeur. He wanted to get him out of the hell hole before the beatings took their toll and Maka confessed to crimes that Grant believed he did not commit.

***

"The newspapers love sensational sex stories," Grant said as he sipped his coffee. "They are making a big deal of Charles' arrest and the kilu party on Punchbowl. It won't be long before the pulpit gets into the act and priests and ministers demand punishment for adultery and fornication. Were you able to get bail set?"

"It appears I have to go to a magistrate," Kanakoa answered. "The sheriff's department is playing this one close to the vest. Not revealing all their cards. They are holding Charles for suspicion and my guess is, with the hubbub in the papers over the kilu game, they will cook up some crime that involves sex."

"And as part of the circus atmosphere, the news media is resurrecting my past. They are sensationalizing the murder of Sheila Grant. A reporter is hounding me for an interview about my mother's death and the letter she left. He only wants a headline like, 'War Hero a Murdering Bastard.'" Grant pounded his fist onto the newspaper on his desk. He twisted his hand over the articles trying to erase the ugly press resulting from the arrest of Charles Maka.

Joshua sighed. "The media thrives on sensational news, especially the *Pacific Gazette*. The editor picks on what he calls 'the lesser races' for their failures. The kilu game is a golden opportunity for him to rant on the lack of morals of the Hawaiian. He's done that often in the past. Making us appear to be savages."

A street car's bell clanged in the crisp morning air. A growing breeze ruffled the newspaper on Grant's desk, flipping a page onto the floor. "Wind is building up. Feels like a big rain heading our way," Grant said, then added, "The editor is just like a rising storm. He builds evil images out of all proportion to the truth. He wants to frighten people by what he says. But he conveniently ignores the arrests of prominent people in houses of prostitution."

"Really," Joshua said, drawing his chair closer to Grant. "What are you talking about?"

"In Asing's raid on Rudy's vice den, he picked up several men from the business community in various stages of undress. There was an interesting woman among the prostitutes, a high class Japanese, imported to Hawai'i by the Consulate and used to entertain the most significant people in our community. Asing told me that there is a demand for her favors. He also said that she is the last person to see Wright alive."

"You think she slipped something into his tea to drug him before he died?" Joshua asked. "I understand that the geisha rituals always require the elaborate service of green tea before the excitement begins."

"No, autopsy showed there weren't any drugs in the judge's body. He died from a stab wound into the heart."

Joshua stood and glanced out the second-story window. "Wind is getting worse. I feel rain coming. Best I get moving and see if I can get bail set for Maka. If that doesn't happen, it might take a writ of habeas corpus to get him out. I should mention that I have communicated with Mrs. Still. She is cooperative and I think we could get a blood sample from her in a week."

Grant winced. "That long? I've already had my blood analyzed. My father hasn't done it. He's promised to do so after he gets back from Mau'i."

"Is your father pushing this testing? Do you really want to know the truth? If you leave it uncertain you can continue to live in an upper class society without the blemish of race affecting your opportunities for success. You have the irrefutable presumption in your favor."

Grant grasped the old attorney's shoulders, his brown eyes fixed onto his face. "You can't expect me to hide behind the law. I'll accept what the truth is and live with it."

Joshua left as the storm struck with sheeting rain that filled the streets with a deluge of water. Grant watched pedestrians dashing for cover, umbrellas useless in the raging wind. He wondered what new disasters might be coming his way, especially since he had added Larsen to the balls he juggled.

***

Drumming pounded his ears. He felt dampness at his side. He struggled to open his eyes. Swim his way out of the whirlpool whipping around him. With a start Sven came awake. The rain smashed in large drops onto the planking above his head, beating out a staccato of sound. The stream that flowed slowly when he fell asleep rushed towards the sea. The rising water, splashing against the rocks under the bridge, soaked his clothes, causing him to shiver.

Peering from under the wooden bridge, he saw a sky filled with black clouds rolling over the island. Rain pelted hard against the planking. He would be drenched if he ventured from his shelter. Sven needed to go somewhere, but couldn't remember where. Confused, he muttered, "Drank it all. Must find more." But the rain proved too heavy to challenge the storm. He sank back onto the rocks, watching the stream rise.

***

"Thank you for coming to my office in this thunderstorm. It must have been a nasty little trip from West O'ahu," Grant said, helping Naga shed his dripping rain jacket. He hung it in a small closet and grabbed a cloth, soaking up the water that puddled the floor.

"Very sorry," the Japanese lawyer said. "Let me clean it up."

"All done," Grant answered, tossing the soaking cloth aside. "Where did you get your legal training?"

"University of California at Berkeley."

"The school of the Golden Bear, your big rival is Stanford, the Indians. I went to Yale. Our chief sports nemesis is Harvard. Princeton is a close second."

"I had no time to enjoy sports. You wanted to help us? You found Mr. Larsen?"

"Yes to both questions. For me to help the Japanese worker, you will need to form one union of all the laborers, in all of the islands. It will be easier to deal with a single bargaining unit instead of multiples."

"Difficult to do, but we could try, and Mr. Larsen?"

"He came to see me wanting money. He is due back this afternoon."

The two men waited through the last of the day, discussing Grant's labor proposals and intercollegiate sports rivalries. The Swede did not show up. By evening, they decided to leave. Grant posted a note on his front door advising the man of a hotel room that he had booked for him. He requested a contact the next day. The two men exchanged information and split, Grant hurrying to meet Selena.

***

An aching in his back woke him. Sleeping on rocks for a night and part of a day had taken its toll on his body. The soft bed of the rental room had made the pain worse. Larsen fumbled for his jacket, pulling out the bottle that sat in a pocket. "A little bit of amber left," he mumbled as he swigged the whiskey into his throat. He shook the bottle into his palm, lapping up the last drops of the illegal liquid.

"Must get more," he said to the wall. Sven stumbled to a washbasin. He poured water over his face, rubbing his hands into the heavy stubble sprouting from his cheeks. He would shave and clean up when he got more money from the Kingsley kid. A permanent hotel room would be partial payment for what the family owed him.

He staggered out the door, passed the hotel clerk's desk, and walked onto the street. The sun was high in the sky, the weather clear and beautiful, but he paid scant attention to his surroundings, his compelling thirst driving him toward the Kingsley office. When he arrived, he barged in. Confronting the clerk, he demanded, "Where is Kingsley?"

"You're Mr. Larsen. My employer expected you yesterday and left a note last night to call. Did you get it?"

"Look, you, I want your boss."

"I'm sorry, he is at a meeting with the HSPA. I'll leave word that you are here."

Sven felt rumbles in his stomach. He decided to modify his belligerence. "I'm hungry. Do you have any spare money for food?"

The frightened clerk said, "I can give you a dollar from petty cash. That should be enough for a good-sized meal." He tossed a coin to Sven. "While you are gone I will call the people that want to meet you."

He grunted and left. At a small café nearby, he took his time eating, deciding to let the little Kingsley boy wait for him. After an hour and a half he paid his bill without leaving a tip and rushed back to the office. His thirst had built to a terrible desire for whiskey and he started to shake.

His hands wobbled as his pushed open the door. Not good, he thought, I've got to control myself. He paused at the threshold, waiting for the clerk to notice him. When they made eye contact, Sven said, "Kingsley in?"

"Upstairs. I'll announce you."

"Never mind, I know the way." He took the stairs two at a time. He came to the door, rattled it, and barged in. Two Orientals sat by the office desk. Grant rose, his face smiling, his hand extended.

"What are these gooks doing here?"

"They are here to talk with you, gain some information from the past. This is Mr. Naga, head of the Japanese Fair Wage Society, and this is his partner."

"I don't talk to yellow men. Get them out of here. Where's my money?"

Kingsley's smile vanished. He fixed a hard look onto the Swede. "You get nothing until you talk to these men and answer their questions."

"Yeah, well, that's not the way I deal," Larsen snarled, his voice pitched high with anger. "You'll be sorry when I tell all I know to the newspapers." Turning on his heel, he left the office, slamming the door. He hurried downstairs, saw the clerk and yelled, "Tell your boss he's a damn asshole, thinking I'll talk to a bunch of gooks."

Larsen stormed along the street, cussing and raving. Pedestrians jumped aside. A few vehicles swerved and honked as he jaywalked. After an hour of meandering, he calmed down. His hands shook again. He needed a drink. He reached into his pocket and found only a few pennies. He returned to Kingsley's office, but it was dark and the door locked. Head back to the hotel, he thought. Think this through. Maybe tomorrow, make another approach to the boy.

He walked into the lobby and the hotel clerk called to him, "Mr. Larsen, a message for you."

Lars unsealed the envelope which held a five dollar silver certificate with a note: "Buy whiskey at the address on the back of this card."

"That's more like it," Sven mumbled. He stalked out, heading for Chinatown.

***

They sat in their favorite place, sipping green tea, and sampling dumplings specially prepared for them by the chef at Ah Sam's Restaurant. From another room, guitars strummed and a voice sang, "*Ahi wela mai nei loko...*"

"What a beautiful Hawaiian melody," Selena said, her fingers tapping a pair of chopsticks on their dining table. "What does it mean?"

Grant grasped her waving fingers. The red lacquer polish on her fingernails glinted in the candlelight of the private room. He pressed her palm to his chest and said, "It means, I have a fire inside for you that drives me crazy."

Selena smiled, pulling her hand away. "You're just making that up."

"Not so. Ahi does mean fire and I know that the song expresses a man's desire for the love of the woman of his choice. And I choose you," Grant said, moving his chair closer to Selena, his eyes fixed on her face.

"Mr. Kingsley, this is a public place," Selena said, putting her hand against his heart, a smile curling her lips. "Besides, you invited me here to discuss the investigations, not fires burning inside you."

"I understand. It is privacy that you want. Would you accept an invitation to visit a hill named for a god and enjoy the spectacular nighttime views of Honolulu?"

"Most intriguing, and we would sit there chatting about murder suspects?"

"Yes, and Greek gods, and Honolulu city lights."

"Let's go," Selena said, taking his hand.

***

Sven stumbled along the street searching for an address. "Must be in this alley," he mumbled, noticing the sign painted on the wall of a corner building. The narrow opening was dark and he wondered if something evil lurked in the shadows. He dismissed the vague fears, his thirst for alcohol driving him forward. There was a low light marking a door. "Must be the place of the moonshiners."

He reached for the handle. Steps crunched on dirt behind him. Swenson turned. Blinding agony shot through his head as hands clapped his ears. He raised his fists to protect them as a stinging blow smashed into the back of his neck. His knees buckled and he sagged to the pavement. Fingers grasped his throat, squeezing. He tried to beat away the hand, but his mind swirled, and darkness came.

***

"You know this volcanic crater as Mount Tantalus," Grant said, the nighttime breeze ruffling Selena's hair as his Studebaker roared up the low grade of the valley. "I think Hawaiians called it Pu'uohi'a, crater of the ohi'a trees, but students from Punahou school, on a fern collecting expedition, named it Mount Tantalus after the mortal son of Zeus. They also named the next hill over there Mount Olympus."

Grant shifted gears, steering the car onto an unpaved trail that switched back and forth along the side of the cinder cone volcano. The headlights of the car dissipated into a forest of ferns and low shrubs. As they climbed, lantern light from cottages filtered through the trees, helping to guide them higher up the volcano's side. "Electricity hasn't made it to this mountain, but when it does, this place will be a Mecca for the rich. Right now, only a few have summer homes here, Castle, Bishop, and Isenberg."

"What's the attraction?"

"The higher you go, the mountain becomes a forest of Eden. It is cool and the views are spectacular. Rich people want to live here to escape the summer heat of Honolulu."

"It is dark, quiet, and mysterious. Evil things could happen and no one would know about it," Selena said, as Grant reached his hand to stroke her shoulder. The Studebaker lurched to the left, crunching into shrubs. "Mr. Kingsley, pay attention to your driving. Place both hands on the wheel please. Look, there's a crescent moon. It is shining onto Punchbowl. Isn't that the house where they played kilu?" Selena pointed.

***

A sudden braking jarred Swenson awake. He was gagged and his hands tied behind his back. A figure shrouded in black left the driver's side of the car. Lars kicked and stamped his unbound feet on the auto's floor. Though he felt groggy, he was determined to fight this wraith who had imprisoned him. His neck jerked as a noose tightened around it. Choking, trying to snatch breath through the gag in his mouth, Swenson moved his head forward to ease the squeezing of the rope.

The side door of the car opened. A figure yanked the noose, dragging Lars from the car. His breath shut off as the ring of fiber squeezed his neck. He fell, rolled onto the ground, and fainted.

A hand cuffed his face. Swenson gasped as the rope around his neck loosened. He looked up into a cloudless sky where a crescent moon shone, outlining the rim of a volcano. Something smashed into his side. He was yanked and forced to stumble up.

Eerie, the man doesn't utter a sound. There are no lights. No sounds. Where am I?

He twisted his body, catching a glimpse of Diamond Head far away. He knew he stood on the side of Punchbowl Crater.

Forced uphill, Lars tried to stumble to the side to pull his captor off balance, roll down the slope and escape. But a shark-toothed knife cut open his cheek. It sliced across his thigh, shredding his pants. Wounded, he stopped resisting. Like a beaten dog, he obeyed the dark figure drawing him up the hill, the only sound between them the loose rocks crunching under their feet.

***

"Tantalus was a mortal son of Zeus and the king of a city in Turkey," Grant said as he swerved the Studebaker off the trail and onto level ground. The wheels shredded low shrubs. Small stones and debris made pinging sounds on the fenders as he braked the auto to a halt.

Spread out below was an awesome view, Diamond Head in the far distance, lights from Waikiki winking in the night. Directly beneath the mountain lay the town of Honolulu with its seaport and harbor lights shining in the darkness. To the west they could see a glow from Pearl Harbor. Grant wondered if men worked overtime to get the base ready for war.

"It is magnificent," Selena said, "indescribable in its beauty. You mentioned the son of a Greek god for whom this mountain is named."

"Yes," Grant answered, realizing that Selena sought to keep the conversation light. "Tantalus was a favorite son of Zeus, who invited him to dine with the gods. Tantalus stole ambrosia and nectar from the heavenly table to share with his mortal friends."

"That must have caused trouble."

"Yes, Zeus cast him into Hades to live in eternity in that hellish place. His punishment is water up to his knees and a fruit tree over his head. Whenever Tantalus is thirsty and reaches down, the water vanishes. When he is hungry and he reaches up, the limbs of the fruit tree are blown from his grasp."

"And the man is punished for eternity by food and drink that he cannot reach," Selena added.

"Yes, and it is from Tantalus's name and his trials that we have the word, 'tantalize,' meaning something you want but is out of reach. Just like you." Grant moved toward Selena. She did not open her door to escape.

***

Forced down onto flat rocks lining the hill, Swenson saw below the outline of a house, above, the silhouette of his abductor. The man threw a rope around the limb of a tree. He pulled it tight, until it choked him.

Why? Lars thought. What had he done to anger this man? Then he remembered the many beatings he inflicted and the killings he committed.

But they were ordered by Robert Grant and Abner Nolan. None of it was his doing.

The shark knife slashed across his chest, slicing twice, marking his body with an "X". The knife cut again, its razor-sharp teeth slicing down to the hair at his thighs. Blood flowed over him. The pain felt horrible. He looked to the sky, stared at the moon. He cried, "Thor, god of the Norsemen, strike with your hammer. Kill this heathen."

But Swenson did not see a crimson clad giant plunging from the sky on a heavenly chariot. Instead, the awful knife sliced across his forehead, the blood stinging his eyes. Tears of pain welled in them, mixing with blood, blinding him.

The noose tightened. Swenson's body rose from the ground. His legs dragged on rocks and slid over the side of the hill. He dangled above an abyss, shoes scraping a cliff. He tried to move his feet, find a purchase in the rock side, but it only loosened stones that plunged into the darkness. His struggles made his breathing harder. He fought for air. His mind fell in and out of darkness.

***

A mile away, overlooking the volcanoes of Punchbowl and Diamond Head, Grant Kingsley took Selena into his arms. She did not object, instead responding with eagerness to his kisses.

CHAPTER 41

WATER DREW BACK from the reef, nearly laying the coral bare. A strong wind built the growing wave into a towering giant, the crest of the curving wall of sea crowned with white foam. Sunlight barely lit the ridges of the Ko'olau Range. Diamond Head glimmered in the pink glow of the dawn's light. Grant kicked, stroked, and pulled his eight foot board forward, gaining speed. The powerful wave thundered as its curve became almost circular in its drive into the reef. The mass of water lifted the wili-wili wood above the rock bottom. Standing, Grant shifted his weight, dipped his foot into the raging torrent, and steered his craft along the curving hill of sea that pushed it toward the sand shore of Waikiki.

A little to his left, the beach boys in an outrigger canoe paddled hard, catching the same wave. The mass of water hurled the balsa surfboard and koa canoe toward a stream emptying into the sea near the Moana Hotel. While Grant knew the outrigger had an advantage of four paddlers, he had a more maneuverable craft. He could find the parts of the long crescent of rushing water that had not turned to foam. "Beat you to the beach."

"You're on," Pahoa called back, resting for a moment on his paddle as the canoe rode the top of the big wave. He laughed as Grant wobbled in the wall of water.

Grant spread his arms out like a diver ready to jackknife into a pool. He steadied his quivering body, knees bent, head forward, and arms hanging at his side. With his feet, he guided his surfboard along the wave.

208

The prow of the canoe dashed ahead. Grant did not worry. He saw foam building under the outrigger. It began to lose headway. Pahoa yelled, "Pull, pull." His three companions flashed their leaf-shaped paddles into the sea, forcing the craft to stay on top of the wave.

Grant lowered a hand into the water, stroking the wave several times. The surfboard angled along the water wall. He passed the canoe engulfed in foam, and coasted onto the sand. The outrigger swept into the shore behind him. Pahoa got out laughing, "What a ride, you slid along that wave like a high chief. Are you going to join us in the canoe races for the Prince?"

"Races? Prince? What are you talking about?"

"The future King of England is due in Honolulu on the battle cruiser *Repulse*. Once he gets here, we are giving him a big water show including a canoe race between Honolulu Harbor and Ku'ilioloa heiau in West O'ahu."

"A Japanese cruiser might be back from San Francisco about the same time. How about holding a regatta for the two countries?" Grant said, wondering if this might be an opportunity to gain valuable information for Captain Trask at a gathering of the two allies.

"Maybe," Pahoa said.

He waved goodbye to the beach boys, stored his surfboard, changed, and headed for the office.

Driving on Kalakaua Road, Grant saw Punchbowl Crater and beyond it the rising slope of Mount Tantalus. What an evening it had been, the most romantic ever. He began to sing, *"Ahi wela mai nei loko."* Oblivious to the stares of pedestrians, he rolled into his parking stall, belting out the love song of a man calling to his lover to put out the fire burning in his heart. Entering his office, he was startled to see two burly Chinese men standing at the counter, one of them Selena's step-brother.

"Mr. Choy would like to see you."

"Right now, can't it wait?"

"No. Come with us."

Realizing it would be senseless to argue, Grant left with the men. They strode in silence to Maunakea and turned toward the waterfront. Within a block, Grant was invited to enter a two-story building and directed to climb an inside stair. He speculated that Dan Choy was furious.

He probably believed that Grant had broken his promise not to dishonor his daughter.

They got to the second floor and walked down a hallway to an office door. One of Grant's Chinese guardians knocked. They entered. Dan Choy sat at an oak desk, a female secretary writing in a note pad.

Grant found the room tastefully furnished with a large red rug bordered in emerald green. A black leather couch stood against one wall with several matching armchairs arrayed around the room. The oil paintings on the walls fascinated Grant. They were nautical art, one of the pictures depicted a violent scene of seamen in a longboat harpooning a sperm whale.

Choy dismissed the secretary, indicating that Grant take one of the leather armchairs. The two Chinese ranged themselves on each side. Grant felt squeezed. He weighed his chances of escaping and realized they were slim. He had to trust to Choy's sense of fair play, his love for his daughter. "Dan, if you brought me here about last night, I didn't break my promise."

The Chinese crime boss smiled. He waved his two men out and said, "I see you appreciate my art. I have always loved ships. The interesting places they sail to, the many ventures that they undertake. Modern iron boats do not have the same handsome look as wooden ships flying along the ocean under a full load of white canvas."

"I do admire the art, but…"

"Every picture you see tells a story. The wall on your left is a painting of ships in the port of Shanghai in 1852. Two hundred Chinese are crammed into the hold of the *Exeter* heading for the Land of Fragrant Wood. That is what we called Hawai'i, for it once had an abundance of sandalwood. The painting next to it is the *Exeter* in high seas. Chinese are below decks stacked in a room no bigger than this. All are hungry, thirsty, and sick, many are dying. The ship's captain did not care whether they lived or died. The third is the arrival of the *Exeter* at Quarantine Island, Honolulu. As you can see, it is a desolate pancake of sand and coral. When the tide is high it covers the island. Only a hundred and fifty-two men survived that trip from China to Hawai'i."

Grant stroked his chin, puzzled by the conversation. He knew from history that the first Chinese to come to Hawai'i were treated with unbelievable cruelty, forced to perform hard labor ten to twelve hours a day, six days a week. Today things are different, Hawai'i is part of America and the Constitution ended involuntary servitude.

"You see that picture on the far wall? That is the *Priscilla* arriving in Honolulu Harbor in 1878 with a hundred-seventy-five Portuguese from Madeira. Look how festive the scene is as they step off the boat. There was only one fatality in the sixty-day voyage, a baby."

"Mr. Choy, I don't quite get the point that you are making."

"Like all young men you are impatient, always rushing to get to a point. My reason for telling you this is simple. For twenty-six years the plantations imported cheap Chinese labor. When my people began to organize and make demands for fair wages, the sugar companies struck back with the divide and rule technique. They imported new nationalities to break down the complainers. The labor contractors who arranged for these new ethnic groups to be brought in made lots of money. The plantations made lots of money by using these ethnic groups as strikebreakers."

"I understand the strikebreaking aspect of divide and rule. I understand that money can be made in arranging to transport labor, but what are you driving at?"

"The Japanese were brought in to further the divide and rule technique, but the plantations made a big mistake, they brought in too many and allowed the men to bring wives and families. The work force became swollen with Japanese, more than forty percent today. These people are demanding higher wages, better living conditions. They want to form unions, and you are helping them to do so."

"But Mr. Choy, this is the right thing to do. There have been more than fifty labor strikes since the Japanese were brought in to work the sugar fields. All these work stoppages are expensive for the plantations."

"But the tried and true technique of divide and conquer is what your sugar planters believe in. You will never convince them to give it up. I told you that Judge Wright, after the settlement of the 1920 strike, contracted with me to bring in Chinese laborers as strikebreakers. This should tell you that the HSPA will not make labor deals through bargaining. The Japanese will never come together into one union. They come from different islands of Japan. Each island has its separate traditions, beliefs, and prejudices. There is no chance that these Japanese laborers can form one union able to speak for all of them."

"Is this what our meeting is about? You want to make money from the labor agreement you made with Judge Wright?"

"You are a brash young man without understanding," Dan Choy said, smacking his palm onto his desk for emphasis. "You think that Chinese are greedy, only want to make money from somebody's misfortune. You are wrong. I tell you all this so that you know that the man who acts as peacemaker is often bitten by both sides. I do not want to see my future son-in-law destroyed by labor fights."

Grant thought that Dan Choy had thrown down the marital gauntlet in a subtle way. Marry my daughter, make her an honest woman, or your life would be forfeit. He knew that he was in love with Selena, but he had so many unresolved issues that could affect their future together. "Dan, I care very much for your daughter. She is important to me."

"Good, then you will understand what I am going to say. I cannot permit Selena to go out at night, to a dark and dangerous place with a man who is unwilling to make a commitment to her. She has one precious gift to give, and I do not want it taken away from her by an insincere man."

There it was, the choice he must make. Marry Selena or end their relationship. The beautiful woman was Asian. Grant realized that in his society discrimination was rampant against those of Oriental blood. In the past, he never thought about it. The class divide only became apparent to him with his mother's confession of a love affair with a Hawaiian man. Grant knew that the stigmata of race could cast them out of the small group of Caucasians who ruled Hawai'i.

"You are strangely silent. You are toying with my daughter's affections, to gratify your lust."

Choy's harsh words angered Grant. "I love your daughter. I treat her as the most precious gift a man could ever have. But at the moment I do not know what I am or what future I have."

"Are you speaking of yourself as an accused murderer or, as hinted in the news media, an illegitimate son? No matter. If two people love each other, they will find a way to solve all difficulties."

"It is not that easy. Give me time to sort it out. I want to know who my father is before I ask Selena to be a part of my life forever."

"Who you are is not a concern for me. Nor is it a concern for Selena. Asians know how to survive in a hostile country where there is no one to offer a helping hand, where doors are closed at every turn. Why is being of white blood so important to you?"

"It is the difference between being somebody and nobody." Grant stood and left Dan Choy. When he returned to his office he found a message from Asing to report to the police station immediately.

***

Grant stared at the corpse, its face bloated purple from suffocation. Clothes had been stripped from it. Grant could see the jagged wounds crisscrossing the man's body where he had been sliced.

"You recognize the guy," Hitchcock said. "He had your business card in his pocket."

"Yes, his name is Sven Larsen. He used to be a foreman at my grandfather's plantation in West O'ahu. For the last couple of weeks he has been drifting."

"Strange killing," Asing said. "He died by hanging, but it was slow. When you hang someone, he drops through a scaffold with a jerk, breaking his neck. That's usually enough to kill a man right then. This death was lingering. The killer wanted to make Larsen suffer."

"You seem to think there is a connection with the other deaths. Why?" Grant asked.

"It's the way the body is cut open that ties this murder to the others." Hitchcock said. "The killer slashed him good with a shark-toothed knife."

"Was there a note left or any other evidence connecting Lars' death to the Cult of Ku?"

"Only that the man died above the house where we saw the kilu game."

"Lieutenant, I wouldn't waste my time killing this man. He was a scoundrel and a plantation bully. There are many who hate him. He did come to my office looking for money. He claimed to have secrets about my grandparents. I gave him a few dollars, and that is all."

"Got you. Your motive, kill Larsen before he could spill the dirt about your family. Case closed. I'm arresting you for his murder and I'll figure out something on the other cases. Pin them on you somehow," Hitchcock said, reaching to take Grant's arm.

"Just a moment," Selena interrupted. "Grant was with me all night. I'll vouch for him."

"How'd you get in here?" Hitchcock demanded.

"Easy, door open and I just walked in," Selena answered. Her hands placed on her hips, her face thrust out defiantly, inches from Hitchcock.

"I'll arrest you for obstructing justice."

"Calm down," Asing interjected. "Mr. Kingsley has solid alibis for all the murders. Miss Choy appears to be his alibi witness for this one too. We should not make accusations that will not hold up in court. Let Mr. Kingsley go."

Grumbling, Hitchcock released Grant's arm. Asing bent his head to the side, indicating that the two young people should leave. Grant grasped Selena's hand, pulling her out the door. Outside the police station, he asked, "What brought you here?"

"Asing called me. He explained that Hitchcock is running out of suspects. Charles Maka is still in jail. Rudy Tang and the man who tried to kill you are out on bail, but they have alibis. He told me of the latest murder and thought that Hitchcock would trap you. That's why he asked me to come here, to save you, my darling."

"You did, but where do we go from here?"

"That is a good question. My father insists that you make an honest woman of me or end our relationship. Last night you said you loved me. Did you say those words to get what you wanted?"

"What do you mean?"

"I'm saying, are you toying with me? Saying lies to take what you lust for?'"

"Selena, I have so many questions in my life. Whose son am I? In what level of society do I fit? Can I prove my innocence of five murders? I love you very much but I need answers to those questions before I could be worthy enough to marry you."

"You have a strange sense of honor. I do not care if you are Hawaiian and not a member of the ruling class. You are the man I love. As I see it, you have only one objection left, the discovery of the killer. We will do so by eliminating racial categories.

"We think the killer is Hawaiian because he uses Hawaiian rituals and has expressed hatred of missionaries as a reason to murder. My father has suggested that instead of talking to the kahuna we go to an expert in Hawaiian antiquities, the assistant curator of the Bishop Museum, Samuel Mitchell. He can help us determine if the murderer is or is not Hawaiian and what his true motive might be."

* * *

"Charles Reed Bishop was an enterprising man," Selena said as she and Grant walked from a parking area toward an imposing black stone structure two stories high. "He and a lawyer friend by the name of Lee left New York by sea for Oregon in 1846."

They climbed granite steps, entering the building through an open archway. It was cool inside and Selena shivered from the sudden change in temperature. "Coming around Cape Horn," their boat was damaged, forcing them to land in Honolulu for repairs. At the time, Hawai'i did not have talented people. Lee soon became Chief Justice of the Supreme Court and Bishop the head of the Customs department. He met a Hawaiian princess and, over the objection of her father, married the woman. Bishop went into banking and became one of the richest men in the country. His philanthropy has made the Bishop Museum the finest in the Pacific." Selena concluded her explanation as they arrived at the reception desk.

They asked for Samuel Mitchell and were directed to his office on the second floor. As they climbed the steps, Selena said, "My father investigated Mitchell. The man has catalogued every known Hawaiian temple. He has written books on its ancient civilization and religion. My father believes he can tell us what we need to know."

A tall, spare man stood in the second level hallway dressed in a white suit. The plain color highlighted his red hair and freckled face. He smiled when they made eye contact and said, "I'm Samuel Mitchell. The receptionist alerted me of your coming. Please enter my office."

The room was small and cluttered. Books were scattered on the floor. Artifacts stood on two office chairs. Mitchell removed them, placing the articles on his paper-covered desk. He pointed to the emptied seats and took a chair facing them. "What can I do to help you?"

"How is Mr. Roberts?" Grant asked.

"Not well, he is on extended leave. The powder he inhaled at Makaha hurt his lungs, and his eyes are still red from the sting. Whoever did the killing of Nolan and injured our senior curator and Professor McKenzie should be hung."

"That's why Selena and I are here. We are seeking the killer of five people," Grant said and went on to describe the murders and the rituals involved in each one. He dwelt on Sheila's death since it had the most bizarre aspects of all the killings. He concluded with Sven Larsen's hanging and the shark-toothed knife slashes on the bodies.

Mitchell sat silent after Grant finished. He drummed his fingers, staring out a window. After many moments he said, "All of the murders you describe have no relationship to the worship of Ku. Ordinary people like Larsen were often sacrificed, but a noose was never used nor the leiomano to mutilate a victim."

"That's what Charles, my chauffeur, said."

"Could the hanging be symbolic retaliation, maybe even revenge for prior criminal acts?" Selena interjected. "The man was well known for his cruelty to laborers."

"I have no opinion on that," Mitchell answered. "But the placement of a bloody cloth around the loins of victims makes no sense. Girdles were used to cover the privates of the many gods in the temple, never the person sacrificed. The instrument you described that the murderer used to strike you, the iron ball tethered by a chain to a pole, has no counterpart in Hawai'i."

Grant rubbed the top of his skull. "Any thoughts about where such a weapon came from?"

"It could be European or it might be Asian, I don't know for certain. But if I had to pick one area, I would say Asia. The traditional European ball and chain had spikes. Your brain would have been punctured by the hit."

"What about Judge Wright's death?"

"Several interesting things, the caltrop that you mention in the judge's tire is not a Hawaiian weapon. The ancients did not have iron. Human sacrifices would be slaves or common people, never someone as high in class as a judge. What is most interesting about all these murders is that Hawaiians were overjoyed when Ku was overthrown. His reign of terror had sent hundreds, if not thousands, to their death. I do not think any native person would want Ku back or even seek revenge for his overthrow."

"And Sheila Grant's death?" Grant asked.

"That is an unusual killing. First, the small *aha* mat was commonly used in prayer ceremonies. It was seldom used before a sacrifice. The seaweed woven into the leaves is rare and can only be acquired from a deep part of the ocean. Salt water was never sprinkled over the victim. It was flung onto the worshipers to purify them. As to the hook in Mrs. Grant's mouth, your notion is correct. She is representing her husband. But the *kahuna nui* would never sacrifice a woman. A female has menstrual periods, so women are considered unclean and not worthy to be given in death to Ku."

"Are you saying that the killer is not Hawaiian?" Selena asked.

"I am saying that someone has read a book on Hawaiian religious practices and has come up with rituals that are unexpected in traditional sacrifice."

"The killer is using the rituals to hide his racial identity," Selena said. "And he is using you, my darling, as a convenient scapegoat for his crimes."

"If the man is not Hawaiian, what race could he be?" Grant asked.

Mitchell cleared his throat. "There is a connection between Larsen, Robert Grant, and Abner Nolan. There may be a similar connection to Mills and Judge Wright. You said that Sven was not of missionary family."

"True," Grant answered, rising from his chair. "He came to Hawai'i sometime in the latter part of the nineteenth- century. He took a job with Robert Grant and Nolan after he arrived. Something happened involving them before my grandfather was killed during the counter-revolution."

"Then that is the avenue that you must pursue. Narrow your search to the five years before Robert Grant died. It may help you solve the crimes," Mitchell said.

CHAPTER 42

GRANT WALKED ALONG the waterfront heading for the commercial center of Hawai'i at Bishop and Queen Streets. He had a scheduled meeting with a representative of the Big Five, a group of companies that controlled the economy of the islands.

The port of Honolulu was busy. A dozen freighters were docked at its twenty-eight piers. Shipments of pineapple and sugar cane were being loaded onto vessels and heavy equipment off-loaded. Grant saw workmen staking out the perimeters of the planned Aloha Tower which would serve as a welcoming symbol to Honolulu Harbor. He thought of it as a visible landmark of Honolulu's growing prosperity. He was proud that his kamaaina family helped make Hawai'i wealthy.

Grant strode into the building that housed the offices of the HSPA and was directed to a spacious conference room. Elegantly furnished, the walls glowed of burnished koa. The chairs and large rectangular table in its center were of the same native wood. Imposing portraits of bearded men lined the walls. Grant recognized some of them.

"You're Mr. Kingsley, I presume," a soft voice said behind him. "I'm John Ritter of Davies and Company, acting for President Waterhouse who couldn't make this meeting. This is Isaiah Johnson of American Factors and a director of the HSPA."

The men shook hands, and Ritter opened the meeting. "You've sent over a plan which you call 'Ending the Labor Strife that Costs Millions.' In it, you're proposing that the Japanese organize themselves into one collective bargaining unit and that the HSPA set up a mediation group to work with the unit to settle labor issues. The issues that can't be resolved by mediation will go to binding arbitration."

"Yes, sir. The labor strike that recently ended cost the plantations twenty million dollars. The striking workers lost millions themselves. The plantations locked the families out of their homes and more than a hundred and fifty perished."

"The Spanish influenza killed them. It was not our shutting them out that did it. More to the point, your proposal smacks of Bolshevism and it plays right into the hands of the Japanese Empire. That nation would like nothing better than the Japanization of Hawai'i."

"What do you mean by that?" Grant asked, surprised by Ritter's vehemence and the suggestion that he was being duped by Communists.

"You don't read the newspapers. That's your problem. In early January of this year, the Department of Justice arrested five thousand union radicals in America intent on setting up an American Soviet Government. These anarchists sent nearly forty bomb packages to important men in our country like Justice Holmes and J.P. Morgan. At the same time, a Japanese union in Hawai'i called for a strike against the capitalists. That's Bolshevism, Mr. Kingsley."

Grant remembered Dan Choy's warning. He realized that in his enthusiasm to do what he thought was right, he had stepped into a quagmire. In a subdued voice, he said, "And what do you mean about Japanization?"

Ritter shook his head. "You really don't keep up with current events. You don't read the *Pacific Gazette* and their articles on the 'Japanese Conspiracy.' The *Gazette* points out that the Nipponese Empire has taken over Korea, Manchuria, German holdings in China, part of Mongolia, and recently invaded Siberia. America is demanding they get out, but they haven't. The newspaper says the Japanese are seizing islands in the Pacific. They are planning to swallow up Hawai'i. How? We are almost forty percent Japanese. They would use the same insidious policy to colonize us as they did the countries I mentioned."

"But we're an American territory," Grant protested. "Our government would never permit a Japanese takeover."

"That's where you are politically naïve. Citizens vote. We are a democracy, in a democracy the voting majority rules. Which race has potentially the largest percentage of voters in Hawai'i?"

"But what you are telling me is that your divide and rule technique is a failure. You keep looking for the ideal worker who is cheap and doesn't complain. First you bring in the Chinese. When they grumble about wages, you bring in the Portuguese. Then, to stifle their complaints, you bring in the Japanese. When they complain, you bring in another race. The cycle has to end sometime, and you need to face the reality of today's workplace."

Ritter put his palms on the table. His fingers appeared to glow on the burnished wood. "The reality of today's workplace is cheap laborers who work hard and do not complain. The HSPA refuses to engage in collective bargaining. We will bring in more races to dilute the work force, divide and rule. We will add a new element to our arsenal of strike prevention. U.S. Attorney General Palmer's right hand man is J. Edgar Hoover. He has been hired to find the radicals, anarchists, and assassins. He will rid Hawai'i of the Bolsheviks."

"Assassins, what are you talking about?"

"You, of all people, should know that. Don't you think that the murders are assassinations? All five people are connected with the sugar industry in some way. Within the last few days, the HSPA uncovered a plot to dynamite a plantation manager in his home. We are after the culprits. They'll be caught, tried and convicted, all fifteen of them. I will bet that one of the men is your mysterious kahuna nui."

Grant realized it was useless to argue. His grand plan for labor peace had been rejected. He thanked the HSPA representative for his candid comments and prepared to leave.

Ritter had one last thing to say. "Your family has two plantations left, one on Mau'i, and the other in West O'ahu. Times are tough for independents like you. Walk carefully or you will be swallowed up."

Grant left Queen and Bishop Streets understanding how the power game worked, play ball or be run over. He had no doubt that his father's difficulties at the Mau'i plantation were due to the power brokers of Hawai'i. He realized that if he continued to challenge them, his family would lose all they had.

***

Grant returned to his office to find Asing waiting for him. The Chinese detective stood and unrolled the newspaper. "For some reason, Mr. Kingsley, you love to make headlines. You're on the editorial page of the *Pacific Gazette* and Mr. Thurmond is accusing you of being downright un-American. In fact he says, 'Anyone who supports the Japanese is a traitor.' That we are in crisis time, 'whether Hawai'i will be controlled by Asians or Anglo-Saxons.'"

"I don't know what Thurmond is talking about."

"He mentions your proposal to unionize all the Japanese and have the HSPA engage in collective bargaining. Thurmond says that will mean the aliens will take control of the sugar industry and substitute in their 'pagan priesthood' to be in charge of the plantations. He claims it is all part of the Nipponese Empire's plan to colonize and seize the Hawaiian Islands."

Grant shrugged. "That is the same thing that the HSPA representatives told me. I guess I should have listened to Dan Choy. The peacemaker is the one who gets hurt."

"Yes, and maybe you had better watch your back. There are people in our territory who do not like those who traffic with the enemy."

"You didn't come here to talk about the editorial page?"

"Correct, I wanted to learn what you found out at the Bishop Museum."

"Mitchell is a nice guy. From what he said, the killer is not Hawaiian. He suggested that there is a tie-in between all the killings that is not related to missionaries."

"I agree. So I have been doing some checking through police files. We don't go far back, but Larsen was a mean character. He did his share of shady deals and crimes against laborers. Nothing specific, but the records mention Mills' name in connection with Swenson."

"And my dad told me that Mills was a friend of my grandfather."

"There you have it. Now if you can tie in Judge Wright to the three of them, we might figure out who is the next victim and solve the crimes."

"You think there is going to be another murder?"

"That is what your kahuna said. But maybe it was you who claimed that there would be six deaths. Maybe you are the one who wants to kill missionaries." Asing laughed. "Of course, I don't believe it."

Grant wasn't so sure. The Chinese detective had a subtle way of solving crimes, direct an accusation and watch the victim squirm and stammer.

Well, he would not give his canny friend any pleasure. "I didn't kill any-body and I thought we were working together as a team."

"Ah, that is so. You might want to check the library archives. They have newspapers going way back."

"Good, Selena is due from school late this afternoon. We will go to the main library and see what we can find."

***

"There are so many news articles, what are we looking for?" Selena asked.

"I think it is an event or events that took place before my grandfather was killed and it would be something that involved the five dead people," Grant said.

"You say we must search in a ten-year period, because Larsen came to Hawai'i in the mid-1890s and your grandfather was killed in '95. That's at least two-thousand-one-hundred-and-ninety newspapers. Isn't there any easier way to check it out? And what if the event that triggered the murders occurred after your grandfather died? Something Sheila Grant was involved in."

Grant shook his head. "I don't know for sure. But it's something that Larsen said to me, something that involved my grandfather and Nolan. I can't put my finger on it, but if I could remember, it would narrow the search."

"This is some kind of date you talked me into. Sitting here and reading musty old newsprint."

They worked together for several hours until closing time. Grant escorted Selena to his car. The empty parking lot was dark, quiet, and mysterious. They fumbled with the doors trying to find the latches. Finally, they got in and settled down. After several moments of silence, Selena said, "Aren't you going to start the car?"

"I will in a moment. I found out today that I don't like the ruling class. All they want is money and will stomp on anyone who gets in their way. I'm beginning to think that having brown blood is not such a bad thing."

Selena arched her eyebrows. "Then you can understand how a half white like me feels. I don't belong with either culture, but I am definitely an outcast to those who rule Hawai'i."

"So you have felt discrimination. When I think on it, my father demanded that I choose. It was only after he met you and saw how smart you are that he relented. But I still think he has reservations."

"That's because if we were to marry it would be a mating of brown and yellow. These are the races despised by the elite."

"I did get an earful today about the yellow peril of Japanization. There is tremendous bias in America against Asians."

"Right now it is against the Japanese because of their aggressive policies. But my father told me that forty years ago Hawai'i and America passed an Exclusion Act aimed to end Chinese immigration."

"That is very interesting. Your father has made a contract to provide fresh Chinese workers to the plantations."

"That is true. And the sugar people are demanding that Congress retract the exclusion law and let Chinese be imported to Hawai'i."

"I guess all that counts is money. To the plantations, workers are just machines to be used to make a few people rich. Once one batch is worn out, you just import more and replace them."

"Yes, and it could serve as a reason for an angry person or persons to act out and commit murders."

"Selena, you make it sound like we're wasting our time reading old newspapers."

"Maybe, but I understand that good detective work requires that you track down every possibility. Besides, you are kind of cute to be with."

"How about tying one on?"

"No sir, Mr. Kingsley. Not until you decide what side of the racial fence that you are on."

"I am on your side, Selena." Grant leaned over and kissed her. She did not resist. When he suggested they move into the backseat, she agreed.

As they settled into the cushions, Grant kicked something on the floor. He reached down and picked up a box. "My medals. How did they get here?"

"Don't you remember? When we were first dating, you brought the box to show me your military citations and awards for being a boxing and wrestling champion in college."

"Yeah, I did. After I showed them to you, I tossed the box in the back and forgot all about it. Somehow the kahuna nui got into my car and took my *Croix de Guerre*."

"That part is easy to do. You never close up your Studebaker. Let's figure out where you left your auto unattended over the last few weeks."

For the next hour they discussed the possibilities. Finally Selena said she had to go home. A frustrated Grant Kingsley drove her to Maunakea Street, dropped her off, and headed to Waikiki wondering who could have stolen the medal from his car.

CHAPTER 43

GRANT SPED TOWARD shore. Pahoa slid on the same wave. The two men angled their boards through the white foam, riding the full power of the surf onto the beach. "Great ride," Grant said.

"Yes. Where have you been?"

"In the library, I have been searching for clues in newspapers from the last thirty years."

"That's a long time. Find anything?"

Grant shook his head. "Selena and I have hit a blank wall."

"Give it up. The Crown Prince of England is in town. Be here for a couple of days, then on to the U.S."

"Are you going to give him a luau with Hawaiian food?" Grant asked.

"No way. In April, he said, 'this food is revolting.' We'll just have a meat and potatoes banquet at the Moana."

"Without raw fish or petrified octopus?" Grant asked, a smile crossing his face. "These blue bloods can't stand native food. Are you going to have a regatta for him and a canoe race?"

"Yes, and we want you to join us."

"Are you racing to that temple in West O'ahu, the...what's the name of it?"

"'Ku'ilioloa, it means, 'The Great Dog, the god of navigators.' The holy place was created a thousand years ago to aid sailors in trouble and to study astronomy. It was also a place of refuge for defeated warriors. It's one of the few heiau on the ocean."

"Then it wasn't a Ku temple practicing human sacrifices?"

"No human sacrifices, but it was a Ku temple. Remember that he was also the god of fishermen. Sharks swim near it. I wouldn't be surprised if they sacrificed people to feed them. We are racing to the heiau. If you're afraid of sharks, stay in the canoe, and don't put your hand in the water. If you're still alive after the race is over, you're invited to a banquet in honor of the prince."

***

His black tuxedo felt like a strait-jacket. Grant thrust his finger into the collar of his white shirt, easing the tightness of his bow tie. The orchestra in the Banyan Court of the Moana Hotel played tunes from Gilbert and Sullivan. Irritated, he said to Pahoa, "That's not our kind of music. Why aren't we hearing some Hawaiian melodies?"

"On his last visit, the prince expressed his dislike for the local food and music. He longed for some English tunes. That's why we are trying to please him on this trip."

"That's royalty, unhappy about anything that is different. Look, someone's coming from the Prince's party."

An equerry strode up to the two men and said, "You are the man called Pahoa? The prince would like to meet you." The officer escorted them to a group of men standing at the top of steps that led into the wide banquet area of the hotel. When Pahoa was presented, the Prince of Wales said, "I have heard good things about your swimming and surfing exploits in Australia. Wave sliding has become all the rage in the Commonwealth. May I present my cousin, Lord Louis Mountbatten. I'm sure you both know Stanford Thurmond, editor of the *Pacific Gazette*. He seems to think our allies, the Japanese, are intent on swallowing up Hawai'i. A rather fanciful idea, I would call it."

"Not so farfetched," Thurmond answered. "The Japanese cruiser *Izuma* has just pulled into Honolulu harbor. It means trouble."

"Interesting, but I am not here to talk politics." The prince turned to Pahoa saying, "I understand that while you were in Australia, a sixty-pound eel bit off part of your finger. Will the loss destroy your chances in the coming Olympics?"

Pahoa smiled. He pointed to his black patent leather shoes and said, "Haven't you heard of my flutter kick? These thirteen-inch feet push me through the water like propellers. With their size, who needs ten fingers?"

During the laughter of the royal group, Grant caught a glimpse of Consul General Matsu and his associate, Sato, entering the hotel followed by two Japanese naval officers. He excused himself and headed for them.

As he left, Thurmond whispered, "Going to see your yellow buddies, traitor?"

Grant brushed past the editor. He couldn't tell him that Captain Trask needed information. The Secretary of the Navy had issued a warning that "Japan is making preparations for war." Trask had asked, "Find out why the cruiser *Izumo* is in port."

Grant greeted Matsu and his companions and ushered them to the group. Pahoa and the prince were comparing their names - Edward Windsor had eight and Pahoa had only six. The future king said with a laugh, "I have more, but your Hawaiian names are long and unpronounceable." Spying Grant and the Japanese, he added, "Here are our allies. Good chaps. They cleared the Pacific and Indian Oceans of Germans during the war and saved our bacon in the Mediterranean."

Grant saw Thurmond scowling as the British and Japanese exchanged compliments. The prince and Lord Mountbatten engaged the two Japanese officers in conversation regarding submarine combat in the Mediterranean during World War I. Matsu stood aside as the men discussed fighting the U-Boats. Thurmond sidled up to him and said, "The cruiser that's in port. It's come to take away Japanese assassins after they dynamite our plantations."

The usually taciturn Matsu recoiled at Thurmond's blunt accusation. "What are you talking about? The ship is here to take on supplies, refuel, then head for Japan."

"Back in 1894, after a lynching of a Japanese agitator by good Christian men of West O'ahu, one of your people murdered a field supervisor. A cruiser showed up in port. The killer escaped and ran to the ship. Your current Fleet Admiral, Togo, was captain. He said his vessel was Japanese territory and the killer could not be arrested. The murderer left for Japan on Togo's warship. Right now, the Grand Jury is investigating a conspiracy by twenty union leaders to dynamite the homes of plantation managers. One such act has already occurred. I'm sure your plan is to have these men escape to Japan on the *Izumo*."

While the two men spoke, Grant saw Sato shaking. When Thurmond made his accusation, Sato clenched his fists, shook his head, and stalked out.

Matsu sighed as he saw his associate leave. In a firm tone of voice he said, "Mr. Thurmond, you are wrong. My country has no interest in abusing the hospitality of this territory and the goodwill of America."

"Then I don't know why one of your thick-headed union leaders said at a recent meeting, 'The Japanese navy will rescue us.' Deny that if you can."

"I know of no such thing. But if such a statement was made, I will deny that Japan has any intention of protecting the labor people from your justice system."

With Matsu's last denial, Thurmond turned on Grant. "Make sure that your friends don't try to seize this territory or help any criminals escape to Japan. I'll hold you responsible if they do." With that warning, the news editor left.

Grant was upset by Thurmond's vehemence. His caustic words had turned a promising evening into ugliness. Matsu stood beside him wringing his hands. "Let's take a stroll to the beach. A little walk and fresh air will be good for us," Grant said.

Matsu bowed his acceptance. As they walked, he said, "Your country has great animosity for Japan. There is an American and British conspiracy against us."

"Not so," Grant said.

"It is so," Matsu answered. "In 1917, America had negotiations with Britain. If the United States provided England with escort ships, Britain would help America in a war with Japan. At Versailles in 1919, we wanted a clause of racial equality in the peace treaty. England sided with America and voted it down. It is economics that puts countries together or tears them apart. In 1902, Britain needed our help to stop the Russians who were threatening India, the 'crown jewel' of the British Empire. They needed us in the Pacific to fight the Germans who had raiders attacking British shipping. When the United States entered the war, they did not have a navy to defend your interests in the Pacific. We provided a force of ships to patrol Hawai'i and the Pacific coast ports to protect America from naval attack. Once the war is over, we are no longer friends, but competitors in commerce and industry."

Grant thought about what Matsu said. He did not understand grand politics and what pushed nations into war. But the consular officer had made it clear conflicts were all about economic advantages. Japan was expanding outward to build a trade empire. Their aggressive competition is a threat to American economic interests in the Pacific. He stopped walking and looked at Matsu. The moon broke through the clouds, shining on the face of the diplomat. "You are saying that war between our two countries is inevitable."

Matsu blinked. Grant was not sure if it was the moonlight or the controversial statement he had just made. The Japanese pursed his lips. He wiped his hands across his brow, suddenly damp in the cool evening. "The naval officers of the *Izumo* told me that our current military thinking is that America will be our next enemy. They say our countries are on a collision course. Japan must build military bases in the Pacific islands to defend the trade empire that we are creating in Asia. Despite all this, I hope we can continue to be friends." He paused and said, in a friendly tone, "Sato and I enjoyed the canoe races today. We watched them from the vantage point of Ku'ilioloa heiau. It is unfortunate your team lost."

Grant thanked Matsu and rejoined Pahoa. He sat through a boring dinner and left before the speeches. He jogged home and called Trask. "I think that the Secretary of the Navy is right, there will be war with Japan. The Japanese consul confirmed this tonight."

"And the reason the *Izumo* is in port?"

"It is difficult to say. The news editor thinks the ship is here to help Japanese labor agitators escape to Japan. Matsu says they are only taking on supplies before leaving for Japan. Maybe they stopped here because the Prince of Wales is in town. The ship didn't offload any spies, if that is your concern."

"I'll pass on the information. My commander, Admiral Fletcher, is worried about the Japanese. He claims 'seaplanes brought by swift carriers could sweep down on Pearl Harbor and destroy the plant.' Even though he is my boss, it seems like a crazy notion to me."

"The lieutenant commander I met, Yamamoto, believes in naval aviation. Your admiral may understand the future of warfare in the Pacific better than you or I."

"I can't see airplanes sinking battleships. I'm recommending that we build a fleet of those big boats. Thanks for the information, and keep up the good work."

After hanging up, Grant called Selena. The young woman grumbled, "You've destroyed my sleep, what's so important?"

"We are going to narrow our news search to 1894 and the lynching of Japanese."

***

There was a loud knocking on his bedroom door. Sue Watanabe called, "Mr. Kingsley, your father is on the telephone."

Grant got up and headed downstairs. His father was abrupt. "Ritter called me yesterday, complaining about you. He talked about a report and recommendation that you made regarding collective bargaining. He says the HSPA is dead set against it. He issued a warning to back off. What's going on?"

Grant explained the work he had done with the Japanese, Dan Choy, and the results of his own independent investigation of the strikes against the plantations. He concluded by saying, "There are 230,000 people living in Hawai'i, forty percent are Japanese. You can't expect ninety thousand people to be happy on wages that wouldn't feed chickens. If the plantations don't do more than ignore the problem they can expect labor trouble."

"I understand, but we can't go against the Big Five on this. Back off. With a little patience I think we can convince the HSPA to take a more reasonable attitude towards the workers. Talk to Duffy at the West O'ahu mill. The word is that some Japanese there want to get a union recognized. It may be because of your report. Find out what's going on. Be careful, you might have stirred up a hornets' nest. I'll be back in Honolulu in a few days."

Grant hung up. He sensed that something was heating up in West O'ahu. He called Selena to tell her that he would be away on plantation business. He asked her to check 1894 newspapers for a lynching and the escape of a murderer to Japan.

"I will do that. Last night, my father said 'a peacemaker needs to watch his back.' I don't know what he means, but be careful."

"You're worried for me. Maybe you like me just a little."

"Silly boy, who could possibly care for a charming, handsome, intelligent guy like you?"

"*C'est moi?*"

"Make me a proposal and you will find out."

"Once we catch the killer."

"I have to wait that long?" Selena said with a sigh.

"Hitchcock wants to nail me to the cross. Even though you and I know that I didn't kill anybody, I can't embarrass you and our families with a murder trial. Let's pursue this latest angle. I'm sure it will lead us to a solution."

***

Duffy, manager of the West O'ahu plantation, was not pleased, "This plantation is an independent, not a member of the HSPA. But if we break the line with the other sugar companies we could be run over by them and put out of business. Your friend Naga came here making demands that I don't believe we should agree to."

"Is it because you don't have the approval of the HSPA to do so? As an independent we have to show some leadership in the labor arena. Maybe collective bargaining is dead, but we can do a lot about fair pay scales, improving living conditions, and getting rid of the after hour regulations."

"What do you mean by that?"

"End the rules of lights out at 8:30 p.m., no talking after hours, or socialization. The working men should be allowed to visit outside their camps and not be confined to quarters during the night. Don't treat the men like prisoners in a jail."

"What other paternalistic thoughts do you have, Mr. Kingsley?" Duffy said, his voice rising in anger.

"You are not receptive to my ideas of treating workers as human beings. Here is the paper I wrote to the HSPA giving the reasons for my recommendations to them. Read it over. My father will be back soon, and we can discuss it further. But I am confident that if we adopt some humanitarian rules, it will go a long way to end labor strife. This plantation can set an example for others to follow."

"Your grandfather set up all the rules and regulations that we follow. It has worked for thirty years and made money."

"Times are changing and we have to change with them. I'm going to visit with Naga and see if I can get the labor strife under control for you."

Grant got into his car and slowly motored past the sugar mill and a string of women hoeing in a cane field. One female had a baby strapped onto her back, her large straw hat shading them. He knew that they were grossly underpaid. At fifty-five cents a day, they received less than half the pay of a comparable male worker. But they were like women everywhere else in America, unable to vote, and ripe candidates for exploitation.

The rows of white tassel-filled bushes of sugar cane ended, and he saw a dozen workers in pineapple fields planting crowns between mile-long rows of mulch paper. When fully grown the golden fruit on top of its spiny green shrub would result in a colorful carpet stretching from the government road to the foothills of the Waianae Mountain Range.

Grant drove onto a dirt pathway searching for a green painted house with white trim and fish kites tethered to its gate. To the side of the dirt roadway was a shallow pond of water. Two men were bent over, thrusting stalks of rice into the mud. Beyond them, in another field, a man drove oxen yoked to a wooden plow through the damp earth.

It was mid-afternoon when he pulled to a stop by the green house with the kites. Naga welcomed Grant. Three other Japanese were with him, all involved in the labor movement. Grant advised that the HSPA had rejected any plan for collective bargaining.

Naga shrugged, saying, "It wouldn't have made any difference if they had agreed to such an idea. We can't get our people to come together as one. We have Japanese who believe that strikes are 'like the acts of unruly children'. They are dishonorable to the Emperor and not a good way to settle trouble."

"We should concentrate on making a living and improving working conditions for workers in West O'ahu," Grant said. "I promise nothing, but I would ask that while we are dealing with the issues, no more strikes. Agreed?"

"Yes," Naga answered.

For several hours, the five men discussed the complaints of the workers and solutions. Evening shadows were growing long when Grant left with a plan for plantation paternalism to present to the HSPA. As he steered his car off the dirt roadway and onto the government highway, an auto ahead pulled away from the shoulder and into his path. He slammed on his brakes. His tires slid hard on the pavement. His vehicle careened to the side of the road, avoiding a collision. As he backed up to get around the car, another vehicle slid to a stop behind him.

Hooded men jumped out of the two vehicles. Grant pushed open the passenger door, unwinding a sling from his waist. He raced onto an earth divider between two ponds of rice, a bag of almond-shaped lead balls banging against his side. He scrambled along the embankment a short distance, before facing the highway.

Four men dressed in black stood at the shoulder of the road. One held a garrote in his hand and swung the knotted noose from side to side like a metronome. The assassins appeared confused, uncertain as to whether to charge across the berm or plunge into the wet fields to attack him. Grant took out three lead balls from his sack. Inserting one into the sling's leather pouch, he whirled the sling once and flung his lead ball into the mass of men milling at the edge of the ponds.

In rapid succession he hurled the remaining missiles. A man fell into the mud, clutching his head. Another hobbled away from the water, yelling.

One of the killers drew a pistol and fired. The bullet whined past Grant's ear. The shooter took aim again. The rays of the setting sun flashed over the Waianae Mountains, struck full onto the gunman's face. Grant crouched, squeezing his body to the thin earth berm. The assassin fired.

Someone screamed. Shouts came from the rice fields. An ox bellowed, its wild cries reverberating in the night air. Grant straightened up, whirled his sling and sent a lead ball smashing into the shooter. The man dropped his gun, grasping his side. "To the cars," he yelled.

The hooded men staggered to their autos and fled, leaving the gun and hangman's rope on the side of the roadway. A wounded ox thrashed in the mud. Grant knelt on the berm, staunching the blood flowing from a slight wound to his shoulder. He wondered if he had just been attacked by four members of the Cult of Ku.

CHAPTER 44

HIS BODY FLATTENED onto the floor. Grant's hands struck the mat to ease the sting of his fall. He rolled to the side, pushing himself upright. His hand grasped and twisted by his 'olohe, Grant bent his head, tumbled, and pulled away from the wrist lock.

"Good moves," David Kamaka said as he assumed a fighting stance, legs spread, clenched fists at his side. "Throw a punch, I will show you pink nose techniques."

Grant swung a round-house right. Kamaka pushed his arm to the side and swung his open palm lightly into Grant's nose and eyes. "Now, try a straight punch," the teacher said. He ducked under Grant's fist, swinging his closed palm up and into the bridge of Grant's nose, halting the strike before it caused damage. "You are learning jujitsu and lua well. With more practice you will be a master of these throwing and immobilization techniques."

His shoulder pained him. Grant clamped his hand over the bullet wound to halt a flow of blood.

Kamaka said, "I hope I didn't cut you by the judo throw?"

"No, four hooded men attacked me last night. One guy had a pistol. He shot twice. A bullet grazed my shoulder and another hit an ox. I'm thankful you showed me the rapid-fire technique of flinging several lead balls at an enemy. It saved my life."

"Hooded men. They wore dark clothes from top to bottom, with cloth concealing their faces?"

"Yes, similar to the outfit that the killer wore at Pua'ene'ene the night Mills was knifed to death. I thought the four black-clothed men were murderers of the Cult of Ku."

"There is no Cult of Ku. It's a smoke-screen to hide the truth. You said earlier you were in West O'ahu to meet with Japanese over their labor problems. Ever heard of the ninja?"

"Yeah, Captain Trask mentioned them, espionage guys."

"They are trained assassins who do their evil work in the night wearing dark clothes. They use special weapons like darts, iron tacks, short swords, and all kinds of lethal devices."

"Would they have a weapon like a ball and chain?"

"Yes, called a *kusarigama*. It has a short blade on one end and on the other, a chain with an iron ball attached. It's very effective."

"I know. I got smashed by one," Grant said, rubbing his head. "How do I find out more about these guys?"

"Maybe the library or ask the curator, he might know. All I can tell you is that they are Japanese killers trained from childhood in espionage and assassination. Except for lua, they know all the martial arts techniques that I have trained you in."

"If those guys were ninja last night, they weren't very good. They couldn't figure out muddy ponds and the sling. Thanks for the lead balls and the lessons. See you tomorrow."

Grant drove to the police station, found Asing, and described the evening attack. He laid the pistol and the hangman's rope on the detective's desk. "Could you check out the ownership of the gun? Maybe make some inquiry at the local hospital to see if any wounded men showed up in emergency." Grant described the two cars involved and suggested that the neighborhood be checked for witnesses. He concluded with Kamaka's opinion that the assassin might be ninja.

Asing smacked his desk. "There is evidence for that. At the mansion, we found marks on the roof from a grappling hook. The killer lowered himself by a rope, and entered the Grant house. The tack that was in Wright's tire was of Asian manufacture. Kamaka told you that the weapon that hit you on the head is a ninja weapon. The killer is Japanese."

"Or maybe someone trained in the art of the ninja," Grant said. "It could be any Asian imported to work the sugar fields or even someone who knows martial arts."

"Like your teacher, Kamaka?"

"Or it could be assassins' intent on terrorizing the sugar planters. That's what Thurmond believes."

"Why is that a possibility?"

"Consider the times. There was a labor strike starting in January. Plantation owners kicked the Japanese out of their homes. Families of the strikers are homeless, hungry, dying of influenza. Starting in late April, we have the Centennial of the coming of the missionaries to Hawai'i. The missionaries are celebrating the overthrow of the pagan gods. These missionary families started the great sugar plantations we have today. The Cult of Ku is a convenient excuse for killers to use, to strike fear into the hearts of the sugar people. All those murdered were connected with the plantation business in some way."

"So you believe that it is Japanese militants who are behind the murders?"

"I don't know. The union people I have met would not commit murder. Nor would a man like my teacher be a killer. But it is someone who is Asian that is the criminal, the evidence points to that."

"You rule out Hawaiians then. It is someone who is Chinese, Filipino, or Japanese?"

"Yes. Find out who owns that gun. Check on injuries at emergency rooms. I hit three of those assassins real hard. I've got to leave and type my report to the HSPA."

***

Grant put the finishing touches on his recommendations. There were three main points: end the curfew rules, provide safe and sanitary housing for the workers, and give equal pay for equal work. He concluded his report saying, "A worker who is happy, living in pleasant, clean homes will be healthier and more productive." He made several copies on his Underwood typewriter, left one for his father and hurried out of the office to meet with John Ritter.

The HSPA representative was not cordial, but listened to what Grant had to say. When Grant finished, Ritter said, "You've moved away from collective bargaining and dealing with one union. That is good. Your proposals are not unreasonable. We are getting similar suggestions from our directors. Let me pass on what you recommend. You'll hear from me."

Grant left the Davies and Company office, uncertain if what he recommended would be accepted. He thought them reasonable. Above all, he hoped the murders had ended. Any more could sour all hope of a settlement for the plantation workers. He drove to the library and found Selena.

When she saw him, she blew him a kiss. "Where have you been, handsome man? I missed you."

"Busy with labor problems and assassins. Your father's warnings were correct. I got bushwhacked last night."

"Are you hurt, sweetheart?"

"Just a scratch, did you find anything interesting?"

"Yes, news article about a Japanese merchant who was lynched in 1894. He was involved in solving labor problems for his countrymen. I haven't had time to pursue all the stories on the case, but now that you are here we can work more quickly."

For the next three hours, they searched through the news reports of a lynching. The library was closing, and they left without finishing. They decided to head to Ah Sam's and discuss what they had found.

"I almost missed the hanging of a man named Agato. The *Pacific Gazette* barely mentioned it," Selena said. "I had to check other newspapers to find out what happened. This Japanese guy was one of the early importees to Hawai'i. He served out his labor contract and went into the merchandising business in West O'ahu. He was the first to do so."

"It had to make the other merchants in town unhappy. I know that there are a lot of complaints about Orientals undercutting other businessmen."

"That's what caught my eye about the lynching. Donald Mills had a merchandising store in West O'ahu and complained about the unfair competition by Agato. He even suggested that the man should be run out of town."

"I found an article where Agato helped the Japanese workers with issues involving unfair fines. He was coming home from a meeting at night.

It was the last time he was seen alive. The next day, he was swinging from a telephone pole."

"Yes, the *Pacific Gazette* called it a suicide," Selena said. "Even though Mills was reported to say, 'He won't sell any more goods.' The paper had no explanation for how Agato managed to get the rope over the telephone pole and hang himself."

"Thurmond's bluster might have covered up the crime, but I read that Agato had a wife. She complained to the Japanese Consulate and they began an investigation. I was just getting to the articles about what the investigator found out when the library closed down for the night."

"We will know more tomorrow. Time for dinner."

***

The next day, they reviewed numerous articles about the lynching. Grant even searched out Japanese language newspapers and had the writing interpreted for him by a librarian. It was afternoon when they met in the courtyard of the library.

"Mrs. Agato forced an investigation. She had emigrated from Japan with her husband and other Japanese families. She worked with him in the sugar fields, and when he went into business for himself, in the merchandising store. They had a son who was five at the time of the lynching."

"From what I read in an independent newspaper," Selena said, "your grandfather and his partner Abner Nolan were angry with Agato for giving advice to Japanese laborers. Whenever there was talk of wages, the workers always said, 'Talk to Mr. Agato'. It also appears that Mills was upset because Agato undercut him in selling merchandise. The investigation by the Japanese Consulate showed that four men waylaid the Japanese merchant as he returned from a labor meeting and strung him up on a telephone pole."

"The four were a Hawaiian, Sven Larsen, supervisor at the West O'ahu plantation, another supervisor by the name of Johnson, and Donald Mills. After months of delay, a trial started and from the beginning, Mr. Thurmond of the *Pacific Gazette* said, 'white men should not be faced with execution for the killing of Japanese.' And that's the way his paper treated the case throughout the trial and even afterwards."

"Your grandfather and Nolan were not among the defendants, though three of the accused worked for them, and they had a motive for lynching Agato, his union activities."

"And Mills wanted to get rid of him, too. He didn't like Japanese going into business in competition against him. He even testified at trial that the only place for the Japanese in Hawai'i was in the sugar fields. An all-white jury convicted the four men of manslaughter."

"Which is a bizarre result, the case was either first degree murder or not guilty. But the prosecutor asked the jury for a conviction of manslaughter!" Selena said. "From what I read, he was afraid of repercussions from the community."

"And editor Thurmond went on an immediate campaign to set the white men free. Judge Wright, head of the Legislature of the Republic of Hawai'i at the time, joined the editor's effort and secured executive clemency for the three white men."

"And the Hawaiian stayed in prison, where he eventually died. So how does what happened twenty-six years ago fit into your step-grandmother's death and four other murders in 1920, and what happened to Johnson?"

"That is the most interesting part of the story and maybe the answer to the puzzle of who killed Sheila, Wright, Nolan, Mills, and Larsen."

"You read something I must have missed. What is it?"

"I had to go to the Japanese language newspapers to find the truth," Grant answered. "The Agato family had a two-story building, a store on the bottom and an apartment on top. The wife and five-year-old son lived in the apartment. After the trial, someone set fire to the building. Mrs. Agato and her son barely escaped death. Right or wrong, she believed that Johnson was the arsonist and killed him."

"What happened to her?"

"She escaped from prison, got her son, and fled to a Japanese warship berthed in Honolulu Harbor. The Japanese naval captain gave her sanctuary and sailed for Tokyo."

Selena began to comb her hair, vigorously smoothing out her long dark tresses. Her feet tapped, her eyes narrowed in thought. "So the murdered people were in some way involved in the lynching trial. And I'm thinking that, somehow, Mrs. Agato is involved in their deaths. But the kahuna indicated there could be six murders. If she is right, who would be the last one?"

"I don't know. I have a hunch, but I want to talk with Asing first. Selena, go to the Japanese Consulate. Speak with Matsu or Sato. Find out about the widow and what happened to her. I'll head to the police station. Meet me at Ah Sam's."

***

Stanford Thurmond put the finishing touches on his speech to the businessmen of the Honolulu Downtown Club. He thought it time to put the Japanese in their place. He would repeat what he said in a news article, "A more obstreperous and unruly lot of men cannot be found anywhere else. The plantations should discharge all of them and replace the Japanese with newly imported laborers of another race."

Then he would shock the businessmen with the latest news. "Our territorial governor is back in Washington striving to secure statehood for Hawai'i. But he is losing the battle that he is waging. Why? It is because of the allegiance of the Japanese strikers to Japan. These men refuse to integrate into our community. Instead, they support fifteen Japanese language schools that preach obedience to the Emperor and subservience to a pagan priesthood. Make no mistake. We are threatened with a takeover from the Orient. Congress understands this better than we do. It is up to us to fight for democracy and save Hawai'i for the Anglo-Saxons."

Thurmond enjoyed stirring up trouble. For forty years, he had been writing articles and editorials that had shaped the politics of Hawai'i. He had caused the overthrow of the Queen, helped establish the Republic, and was in the forefront of the battle for annexation of the islands to America. He was determined to preserve all the wealth and power the missionary families had gained after one hundred years of involvement in the Hawaiian Islands.

He folded his notes and walked through the pressroom. News workers looked away as he passed by. Thurmond knew that they feared him for his biting sarcasm and high expectations. He did not want to be loved. You can only accomplish greatness, he thought, by pushing, prodding, and shoving the mass of people out of their complacency.

Thurmond climbed into his black four-door touring car. The felt top was up, shielding him from a slight drizzle. He started the car, listening to the auto's cylinders come alive. The surging power of the engine exhilarated him. He knew that this would be an exceptional evening.

***

Pebbles crunched as Selena walked along a pathway leading to an imposing two-story building. Cooled by breezes flowing through the lush forests of Nu'uanu Valley, the late afternoon heat slowly vanished. A rising wind rustled the trees and shrubs of the Consulate property. Selena shivered, her skin puckering with the sudden cold. A storm is brewing, she thought. Reflected light flashed brightly into her eyes from a golden disc fastened above the entryway into the offices of the Consulate of Japan. Flags hung around it, stark white with a red sun stamped into the center.

Inside a short, slender, pleasant woman met her. Selena asked for Consul General Matsu. The lady said that her husband was away but his associate Sato was available. Selena climbed to the second floor office, wondering why the only staff was the wife of the consul general.

Selena knocked and, on an invitation, entered the office, a man five-foot-ten-inches tall stood behind a desk. He was powerfully built, the sleeves of his black coat bulging from the muscles of his arms. Bushy eyebrows crested over keen brown eyes. Selena felt naked under his penetrating stare. Beneath a well-shaped nose a moustache crowned slender lips parted in a slight smile. "Ah, Miss Choy," Sato said. "You are a friend of Mr. Kingsley. He is a fine man. Please sit."

The cordial greeting slowed the thumping of Selena's heart. It had raced when she first saw him, struck by the hidden strength that flowed from the Japanese. A superb athlete, she thought, a man who would be a formidable opponent in a fight. She realized that Sato was waiting for her to speak, so she said, "Grant and I have been reading old newspapers about a lynching of a Japanese merchant in West O'ahu in 1894. The dead man left a widow and a child."

Selena saw Sato glance at a picture on his desk. He turned back to her, his eyes narrowed as he fixed them upon her. "Why do you believe I could help you on an event that happened so long ago?"

"The woman's home was set on fire. She killed the man who did it, then fled with her son on a Japanese cruiser. Grant and I were wondering if your consulate could identify the woman and her whereabouts. We think she may know something of the murders by the kahuna nui."

Sato became agitated. He stood up, flinging his hands into the air, the sleeves of his dark coat baring his arms to the elbow. "Why is it that the Japanese are blamed for everything that happens in Hawai'i? Thurmond hates us for demanding fair treatment for workers. You come here accusing a good *mama san* of conspiring in the killings of missionaries." He slammed his palms on his desk. The picture sitting on it fell, revealing the face of a pleasant woman of middle age, dressed in a kimono.

Frightened by Sato's vehemence, Selena bolted for the door. She hurried into the hallway, down the stairs, and out the entranceway. She stood in the pebble pathway fighting to control the heaving of her chest. As she regained her senses, she remembered the black smudge she had seen on Sato's upraised arm. It was vaguely familiar.

Selena hurried down the pathway, fear of the growing night hastening her steps. Coco trees cast long shadows on the ground. Their leaves rustled like wild things seeking to devour her. What had appeared innocent earlier in the day became dark and sinister. She reached the roadway and thought to hail a passing car, but considered it foolish, realizing that her fright might be unjustified. In Sato's defense, he was expressing the anger of a suppressed people, discriminated against at every turn by a culture that refused to be humane. Her rapid pulse slowed as she proceeded along the road. Her fright subsided the further she got away from the consulate.

She could see familiar territory down the street and she hurried her pace to make it to her home. At an alleyway, she heard a soft voice pleading, "Help me. Please help me." Selena slowed her steps and turned into the ill-lighted passageway between buildings. She could see a lump ahead. A piteous voice wailed for help. Selena came to the body. She bent down. A hand shot up, seizing her by the throat. She tried to pull back. Another hand smashed into her neck from behind. Selena descended into darkness.

***

Grant waited more than two hours for Asing to return from his latest series of escapades. But the Chinese detective had not come back to the police station. He asked for the use of a telephone and called Ah Sam's. Selena had not checked in. He called her home and received the same answer. Worried, he stood to go, but Lieutenant Hitchcock stopped him.

"We traced the gun," the sheriff said. "It belongs to Rudy Tang. At the emergency room of the hospital, a wounded Chinaman showed up. He had a stomach injury. I questioned him and got the whole story. The four guys were intent on hanging you. We checked the rope and noose with the rope that was wrapped around Larsen's neck. They are similar. We got the other two guys and all four Chinamen are under arrest for trying to kill you and for the murder of the Swede. Give me some time, and I'll beat the truth out of them and solve all the murders."

"Then I'm no longer a suspect?"

"I wouldn't leave town if I were you," Hitchcock said, chucking Grant on his shoulder.

Grant winced as pain from the bullet wound laced down his arm and up into his neck. The sheriff appeared oblivious and stalked away without an apology. Asing came into the station, a trio of men following him. He said to the desk sergeant, "Book these guys for gambling." He spied Grant and strode to him. "Hitchcock tell you we traced the gun to Rudy Tang? I think we have solved the murders."

Grant shook his head. "I don't think we have. It is not the four Chinese who have done the killings. It is someone seeking revenge for past crimes. I'm afraid that there is at least one more death to come. It may be happening right now."

"What is your evidence?" Asing said.

Grant explained the news articles he and Selena had researched. "Five murders, all five involved in some way with the lynching of Agato. There is still one more to be accounted for. It may be the editor of the *Pacific Gazette*."

"You think the next victim is Thurmond? And Sheila Grant - was she killed as a surrogate for her husband?"

"Probably, but she was also a principal in the operations of the West O'ahu Plantation along with my grandfather. He and Nolan may have ordered the lynching, but she could have been a party to it, or even have been behind the arson of the store and apartment of the Japanese family."

"But for someone to wait twenty-six years to seek revenge? That is difficult to believe."

Grant shrugged. "I understand your point. But the only way to know if I am right is if Thurmond is murdered. Do you dare take the chance?"

"But he could be killed because there are people who hate him. Not by some serial killer from the past."

"I think you should warn him of the possibility."

"Since you have raised the specter of homicide, then we had better find him. I'll call his office and find out where he is."

"Do it, and I'll try to contact Selena."

***

Stanford Thurmond swirled the rich red claret in his glass. The tannins clung to the sides of the gleaming crystal container. He tasted the fine Bordeaux wine, heated and strained through a bag of spices in the old-fashioned way. The bold taste and full-bodied flavor warmed him. He stood, emboldened by the alcohol, to receive the applause of the two dozen important men assembled to hear his speech.

He charged right into his central theme, the Japanese had refused to integrate with the community. They were like a nation unto themselves. They are stubborn men who must be taught a hard lesson. If they did not work as required, they would be replaced.

He finished with a flourish, claiming that the Japanese had destroyed all chance for statehood and saying, "Democracy in Hawai'i is at a cross-road. Will we be controlled by Asians or Anglo-Saxons? We must stop Japanese ambition before it is too late."

The applause was light. Thurmond stood for several moments seeking questions, but none came. There were more frowns than smiles among the business people in the audience. He stepped from the podium watching the crowd disappear out the doorway. "What went wrong?" he asked Ritter.

"I think the last strike has convinced the majority of plantation owners that fear and repression is not the answer to solve our labor problems."

"Why isn't it? It has worked before. Divide and rule has worked. Why abandon tried and true methods?"

"I think that times have changed. The last race we brought in, the Filipinos, are already unionized and making trouble. We are returning to the Chinese, but Congress must repeal the Chinese Exclusion Act. So far, they have not done so."

"All those things I know, but I say that we cannot let these Japanese control us."

Ritter said nothing and walked away. Disgusted, Thurmond followed him out the door. It was dark, the parking lot empty, save for his car. He walked to it muttering under his breath of the foolishness of businessmen who were worried only about their profits. He started his auto and headed for the roadway. Sharp steel pricked his throat. A voice said, "Drive to the dark spot ahead. Turn off your lights and shut down your engine."

CHAPTER 45

SOMETHING NIBBLED SELENA'S skin, its soft nose nudging and sniffing her foot. She opened her eyes. Darkness. She lay on dirt. Any movement blew dust over her face. She sneezed. The flesh of her breasts was squeezed by the rope that wrapped around her chest and fastened her wrists.

The rat scurried away, its feet scratching the earth. Its slight movements broke the silence of the room. Quiet returned to the darkness as the vermin left. Selena tested her bindings. She was trussed tight, a gag over her mouth. Why did she live? Was she to be the next sacrifice at a Ku temple? She prayed for Grant to come, to save her. But how could he find her?

An auto drove up. She heard a door open. Moonlight flowed into the room. Rough hands settled a rope around Selena's neck. She felt the bindings at her legs release. Her feet throbbed from the tightness. A bulky dark-clothed figure pulled on the rope, forcing her into a stumbling walk. She tried to speak, but only gurgled.

Yanked outside the building, she was shoved into the passenger seat of an auto. Behind her, lay a bound and gagged body. Her hooded captor started the car, his face hidden by a cloth mask. Gears meshed. The silent wraith drove through an alleyway, onto the roadway, and headed west.

***

Grant spun into the lot of the Honolulu Downtown Club. Ahead of him, Asing had parked and entered the building. Grant followed, but spied Ritter smoking outside. "We're looking for Stanford Thurmond."

"He left ten minutes ago," Ritter answered. He dragged from the cigarette until the tip glowed red, blew out a cloud of smoke and added, "I thought his departure odd."

"Why?"

"He got into his car, drove to the exit and stopped for a while. Instead of heading home, he turned left. His vehicle jerked several times as if he had trouble with the gears. He lurched down the road. Stopped and turned off his lights. After a few minutes the car started again and headed west. Is anything wrong?"

"Did you see anyone in the auto with him?"

"No, there wasn't much light. What's going on?"

Asing came out of the building and Grant related what Ritter said.

"Not good. Thurmond was supposed to be going home, not taking a joy ride in the night. Did you locate Selena?"

"No. I called her home and Ah Sam's. She was not there. I called the consulate and spoke with Mrs. Matsu. Selena came, saw Sato, and ran out the building. I called Waikiki to see if she left a message for me, nothing."

"I checked Thurmond's residence. He is expected. I told the servant to call me at the police station when he shows up."

"What are you going to do?" Grant said, his voice trembling. "I think something is happening. Maybe two more murders."

"Good God," Ritter said. "Murders!"

"Let's not panic," Asing said. "I'm sure that Selena and Thurmond will show up. Their disappearance is just a coincidence."

"No, it is not." Grant said. "They are connected in some way. I'm heading west," He left the two men, running for his car.

"Where are you going?" Asing shouted.

"To the temple of Ku'ilioloa, it is the heiau of the dog god. The killer doesn't know that. My hunch is that he believes it is a place dedicated to Ku and human sacrifice."

"I'll call the station, tell them to alert officers to look out for Thurmond's car. I'll follow as soon as I can."

Grant raced from the parking lot, heading for the highway. A bright moon filled a cloudless sky with faint light. Grant prayed that his hunch was wrong and Selena and Thurmond were safe. But his instincts told him they were the next victims of the kahuna nui.

***

Thurmond's big car slid off the highway and onto a dirt roadway, fields of sugar cane lined the path. In the pale moonlight, their white tassels waved like hundreds of magic wands. The man in the backseat coughed. Selena twisted her head. Her gag came loose. "You have to stop. Thurmond is choking."

"Die in back seat or die on the rocks. No difference to me."

"You plan to sacrifice him like you did the others. And kill me too. Why? I have done nothing to you."

The car hit a dip in the road. Selena bounced up, her head striking the canvas roof. The newspaper editor rolled off the seat and onto the back floor of the car. He groaned. The hooded driver swung the wheel as the auto lurched toward a ditch. He braked. Small rocks and debris smashed into the underside of the auto. Dust clouded the air like a light fog. The car slowed to a stop. Inches from the passenger side of the auto, water streamed through a plantation canal.

Re-engaging the gears, the killer sped the car onto the dirt road. His eyes gleaming above the mask that covered the lower half of his face, he said, "I must kill you. You know too much. I regret it, but there is no choice."

"Kingsley sent me to your consulate. He is sure to discover your identity."

"Possible, but I leave in the morning for Japan, on the *Izumo*. I will never return. Once you are dead, my identity will remain a mystery."

"Why did you murder? Why the kahuna nui and Cult of Ku? Why throw suspicion on Grant Kingsley?"

The auto swerved onto a roadway paralleling the sea. Moonlight reflected silver on a restless ocean. Waves crashed onto shoreline boulders, spewing spray into the air. Far out to sea, banks of clouds built high on the horizon.

"They died for the suffering they caused my family. As to your other questions, consider this: I trained for years learning the ninja art. I spent many more years in espionage to become a member of the Black Dragon Society. That status gave me the consular job and returned me to Hawai'i. With all this training, I couldn't be exposed before I completed my mission. I kept Kingsley alive so he could be blamed for the murders."

***

The Big Six Studebaker easily mastered the slight bumps and crevices of the dirt path that cut through the sugar cane fields of West O'ahu. The moon brightened the sky. To the south, heavy clouds bunched across the horizon, blown toward the island by a rising wind that bent the tassels of the sugar cane.

Grant passed acres of land choked with sharp, spiny leaves and bamboo-like stalks.

He scanned the way ahead, looking for lights. There were none. He thought to honk, but realized it served no purpose except to alert an enemy. Had he made the right decision to head for Ku'ilioloa? He guessed the disappearances of Thurmond and Selena were related. The news editor would be the sixth victim of the man posing as the kahuna nui. But why was Selena involved? Did it have anything to do with Matsu or Sato, who had witnessed the canoe race at the temple of the dog god?

Grant swerved the Studebaker onto a roadway bordering the sea. The heavy clouds to the south blew in. Soon the moon would be blanketed by them. In the gloom, he saw car lights far ahead, heading for a heiau composed of three levels of rock terraces centered on a thumb-shaped peninsula thrust into the sea. Grant throttled his car. The beat of the cylinders matched the thumps of his heart.

***

Low shrubs crunched under the wheels of the auto. Thurmond's car plunged off the roadway and onto the rough ground of the peninsula. The hooded driver braked before smashing into rocks blocking his path. Dark clouds covered the sky, hiding the moon. The killer opened the rear passenger door, dragging the news editor out. He untied his legs, used the same rope to lasso Thurmond's neck and pull him over the rocks toward a terrace.

Selena felt helpless. She could not stop the impending sacrifice. Her hands and feet were bound. She tried yelling, but the killer had tightened the gag in her mouth. She watched the two men in the glare of the car's headlights. Thurmond stumbled through the rocks like a stubborn donkey.

To the west, lights winked at Ka'ena Point. Ahead and to the right, lay the yellow sand beach of Pokai Bay. Selena realized the car rested at the neck of the peninsula upon which the heiau of Ku'ilioloa had been built. Her heart beat faster. Death was coming for Thurmond and for her. All the other victims had died in hellish pain, slashed to ribbons by sharks' teeth. She struggled to free herself. The ropes bit into her skin. Her flesh swelled with the friction of her thrashing. Selena fell back, resigned to what seemed an inevitable death.

***

Grant sped his car toward pinpoints of light. Its wheels screeched as he careened around curves at high speeds, braking just to avoid overturning. He thought that the lights came from an auto parked near the entryway to Ku'ilioloa heiau.

A dip in the roadway blotted out what lay ahead. He gunned the engine, climbing up the low grade. At the crest, Grant saw headlights beaming. "Please God, let Selena be alive." He swung the wheel, braked, and the Studebaker skidded sideways, smashing into the parked car.

***

The rope around his throat jerked. He stumbled. A second pull flung him into shrubs whose sharp twigs plunged into his body. Headlights flooded the ground, the beams stretching out to him. Thurmond felt sick. He wanted to retch, but the gag stopped the vomit. He choked on the acrid bile bursting from his stomach. He rolled onto the rock-strewn ground. The rope on his neck yanked tighter. His breath came in snorts through a mouth soured by the last of his dinner. His grim captor wrapped the end of the neck rope around his legs. Thurmond kicked.

The hooded man smashed a fist into his belly. From his stomach, air exploded against the gag in his mouth. Thurmond stopped fighting. He watched the dark figure withdraw an object from his clothes. His hand whipped forward, flinging something into the stream of car lights.

***

Grant yanked the passenger door open. "Selena, show me your hands."

She turned her body. Grant sawed at the bindings. Something sharp plunged into the open passenger door of the car. Grant glanced ahead. The headlight beams shone on a hooded man who whipped an object at him.

Grant pushed Selena down. A metal disk whizzed above his head, struck the canvas top, and shredded it like a whirling saw-blade.

Grant heard footsteps. He cut the last of Selena's hand bindings, gave her the knife, and stepped from the car. A leiomano cleaved the air. Sharks' teeth screeched across the metal of Thurmond's auto. The hooded attacker thrust out his foot. Grant fell back and the attacker spun and swung his leg at Grant's side.

Anticipating the blow, Grant twisted, avoiding the full force of the strike. The attacker's leg smashed his ribs. Tears came and Grant danced away. The killer whirled like a dervish, swinging his leg again. The blow missed. For a moment, the attacker stopped his kicks.

"Why are you doing this?" Grant said, seeking to distract the killer as he spied Selena cutting the last of her bindings.

Without a word, the murderer attacked, leaping with his left foot stretched out, his right foot angled under it. Grant dodged. The strike hit, knocking him to the ground. Without pausing, the hooded killer whirled, stabbing a foot into Selena. The blow shoved her back into the car and across its front seat.

Grant knew he faced a master of martial arts. Somehow he needed to stay alive. Hope that Asing would arrive in time to save them. He un-hooked the long club the detective had given him. Taking a lead ball from his pouch, he threw it. The missile hit the killer. Without a sound, the man left Selena. He rushed in short sliding steps toward Grant who danced from the car and into the beam of its headlights. The assassin followed, reached into his clothes, and whipped out a dart.

Grant turned sideways, felt a sting on his side, and knew the missile had buried into muscle. He fumbled for it as the murderer came at him. Grant backed away, watching the man's feet. Behind him, waves crashed into the rocks of the peninsula. From the sea, wind howled, thunderclaps from beyond the horizon jarred the night.

The killer kicked. Grant hit his foot with his club. The man twisted, sweeping his leg into Grant, who took the jarring blow on his back. Grant pulled the dart from his side and plunged it into the killer's calf.

The wounded man paused in his attack. He yanked the feathered missile from his leg.

Grant stumbled toward the roaring surf foaming onto the rocks of the peninsula. Grasping his club in both hands, Grant faced his enemy.

The assassin released a ball and chain from his waist. He limped toward Grant and whirled the *kusarigama*, its iron ball thumping the air. The murderer flung his chained missile down.

Grant escaped the strike. The iron ball crashed into a boulder, drawing sparks. The killer's arm rose. The tethering chain went back and the small bludgeon on its end whipped forward. Grant swung his club, striking the deadly missile away. The iron ball came again like a whirling windmill grinding wheat. It shattered Grant's stick. The terrible weapon scraped across his temple, thudding into his shoulder. Pain stabbed in his head. Grant slipped in and out of darkness like a light switch turned on and off. He sagged to his knees. The killer paused in his attack. He fixed his eyes upon the injured man. He raised the *kusarigama*. Grant knew he could not avoid the fatal strike.

***

Selena stumbled from the car. Thunder clapped her ears. She looked for Grant. Lightning flashed, its electric branches whitening the sky. At the water's edge, two men fought. Her heart pounded.

She ran, picking up stones as she charged. She saw the hand of the hooded assassin swinging down. She heard the clash of chains, the splintering of wood, and saw Grant sink to his knees. The hooded man paused, raising his hand. With a howl, Selena flung a stone at the killer, striking him. Grant fell sideways onto craggy rocks pounded by the heavy surf.

Selena could not help him. The killer faced her. The ball and chain rose. Selena slammed a rock into the man, followed by a kick to his stomach. She pirouetted and smashed a leg across the assassin's side.

The *kusarigama* clattered to the ground. With a twist of his body, the killer thrust the closed fingers of his hand into Selena's belly. She gasped as air bellowed from her lungs. The murderer's hand struck again, jarring Selena's neck, forcing her to the ground.

Twigs snapped. Bushes thrashed near the fighters. The killer stopped. Auto headlights shone on Thurmond, staggering through the brush, his hands bound, a rope dangling from his neck.

"*Bakatadi*," the killer swore. He left Selena, pursuing the escaping newspaper editor.

***

Grant lay on the rocks at the edge of the sea. Waves flung water high above the peninsula and onto him. He had taken a risk rolling to his side. The killer no longer attacked. Blood streamed down his face. His shoulder ached. Reeling with pain, Grant pulled himself from the water's edge.

Thunder clapped at the horizon, its blasts increasing the throbbing inside his skull. In the auto lights, he saw Selena on the ground. Beyond her, Thurmond staggered through shrubs and climbed a terrace of the heiau. The killer limped after him.

Grant released the sling wrapped around his waist. He retrieved three lead balls from his pouch.

The killer caught the news editor, tripping him to the ground. A knife gleamed in his hand.

Grant whirled his sling cords, flinging the almond-shaped missile. In rapid succession, he hurled the other lead balls. The assassin's hands flew up, and he fell to the ground. Thurmond crawled away. Grant hurried to Selena's side, pulled her up, and held her to his heart.

"The killer is Sato," Selena said. "He is the son of the Japanese who was lynched."

"He's the five-year-old boy. I guessed he might be the murderer. That's why I came to this place, but I still find it hard to believe. He saved me at the Moana and was so friendly."

"Yeah, friendly like a snake. Oh my God, he is getting up."

Out of lead balls, Grant grabbed the *kusarigama* that lay near Selena. He shuffled across the rock-strewn ground, Selena beside him. Thurmond had risen to his feet. He wobbled at the edge of the auto headlights. Sato found his knife. He limped toward the editor.

Grant swung the haft of the ninja weapon. The chained ball struck Sato on his arm. The knife fell. But the killer grasped the chain and pulled Grant from his feet and into him. The fighters grappled. Sato turned his body, swinging his hip into Grant's belly. Pulling Grant's shirt, he flipped him over his shoulder.

Heavy rain poured onto the peninsula. Water ran in little waterfalls from the three terraces of Ku'ilioloa. Grant rolled onto his back, slapping his hands against the smooth earth of the heiau, breaking his fall. Sato followed up on his judo throw reaching to grip Grant's hand. Grant pulled away from his grasp, bending back and leaping onto his feet. Relentlessly, the assassin came after him, his hands moving in rapid strikes.

Like a fencer blocking the stabbing epee of an opponent, Grant blocked the blows with his arms and elbows. Sato attempted to clap his ears. Grant dropped low and slammed a fist into the killer's belly. The man's ridged stomach muscles deflected the blow. Sato's closed hands struck Grant on his back, bringing him to his knees. The killer raised his clenched fists, ready to bury a final blow into Grant's exposed neck.

The scythe at one end of the *kusarigama* plunged into Sato's side. Selena yanked its handle, ripping flesh. She followed her attack with a rock-filled fist that pounded Sato's ear. Selena twisted and whipped a leg across his back.

Sato staggered among the rocks of the terraces. Selena pursued him. They came to an edge of the heiau that jutted above the ocean. Waves rolled into the narrow tip of Ku'ilioloa. Plumes of foaming water flew up and onto the boulders that formed an edge of the temple.

Exhausted, his body a mass of hurts, Grant stumbled toward the battle. Sato's shroud and mask had fallen, his face marred with hatred. "You will not cheat me of my revenge," he said. His fist smashed into Selena, knocking her to the ground.

Grant kicked Sato's knee. The murderer fell. A great wave showered salt water over the combatants. Before Grant could react, Sato lifted from the ground, balancing on one leg like a crane, his injured leg drawn up. High winds flung stinging rain into them. The howling storm muted Selena's moans.

"Give it up," Grant said.

"No. I swore to avenge my mother. Thurmond must die."

"Why?" Grant asked, watching Sato's foot, balancing on a flat rock. Despite his crippling injury, Grant believed Sato to be more dangerous than ever. He needed to focus on his enemy. To watch for that momentary tension when muscles bunched and, like an unwound spring, the assassin strikes.

Sato stretched his arms. He pursed his lips, fighting his pain. With an effort he said, "Thurmond is the one who stirred Mills, Nolan, and your grandfather into hurting Japanese who left the plantations to start businesses. He is the one who said the killers of my father should not be put on trial. He is the one who secured their freedom from punishment."

"And you must kill him and us?" Grant said as he made his move toward Sato, his eyes on the man's good leg planted on the rock. There it is. The leg bent, then the foot springing upward. Grant stepped to the side. The kick missed. Grant's open palm smashed into the murderer's nose, crunching cartilage, driving bone into his skull.

Blood flowed. Sato fell backward. His back hit the boulders at the edge of the temple. A wave swept over him. Sato slid into the sea. The receding water took his body and dragged the killer over the rocks and into the deep.

Grant could do nothing to save him. Weary, he stumbled to Selena. He gathered her into his arms. Together they walked toward the autos. Through the howling wind Grant heard sirens wailing.

CHAPTER 46

GRANT SURVEYED HIMSELF in the mirror. The expertly tailored dark suit no longer wrapped him like a vise. He inserted his finger between his neck and bow tie, satisfied that he had enough breathing room to make it through a long evening.

In the foyer of the mansion, James Kingsley stood at the entryway table, his face wreathed in a broad smile. Grant hobbled down the stairwell, his steps slow. He still hurt from cracked ribs and a puncture wound on his side. "You look great, son. A few days' rest has brought you back."

Grant stepped toward his father, his heart tripping as he saw the white envelope on the table. He knew it contained the results of blood testing. Should he spoil this special evening by learning the truth? He loved James Kingsley. He was more than a father to him. He was a mentor and friend. But Grant would not hide behind the law. He would learn the answer and resolve his paternity, whatever the consequences.

James Kingsley beamed as he folded Grant into his arms. He said, "I am so proud of you. You have accomplished extraordinary things in a few weeks." He gripped Grant's shoulders, his blue eyes searching his face. "Your mother is a wonderful woman. Her beauty is beyond compare. I loved her very much.

"There was a slight stain on her impeccable reputation, when an unfinished note was discovered in your mother's room. I was distraught. My heart's choice was dying. I did not guard my dear wife's personal thoughts that were meant for you. I made the mistake of sharing the note with Sheila. She always hated your mother. With the deathbed discovery,

Sheila was intent on destroying my Leinani's reputation and your right to an inheritance." Kingsley's eyes misted and he closed them to stem the tears that poured down his cheek.

Grant hugged his father. The two men clasped each other in a tight embrace, remembering the goodness of a wife and mother that they both loved. Grant took out the white handkerchief from his left coat pocket. Wiping his tears, he said, "Mother could have taken her secret to the grave and never raised these doubts."

"Yes, but she dared not face the maker if she hadn't made her confession. But one indiscretion proves nothing." James Kingsley walked to the table, took the envelope, and tore it. He took a letter from his coat and said, "This is your mother's last note. Only Sheila Grant and I have ever read it. It proves nothing. You are my son, and you will always be my son."

Kingsley took the torn envelope and letter to a hallway brazier. He lit a match and burned the documents. Smiling, he said, "Let's go to your party."

***

Charles drove the family limousine around the circular driveway of the Moana Hotel, stopping at the marble steps of the entryway. Men in white coats, gloves, and ties greeted the Kingsleys and escorted them into the lobby of the hotel. Asing saw Grant first, saying, "Good work. Your hunch paid off and all murders solved. Rudy Tang and his men will be tried for attempted murder. You saved them from the hangman."

Hitchcock came up and said, "Nice job at that temple. Say, if you want to be a police detective the force could use a man like you."

Grant smiled. He knew that the lieutenant would never admit that he had made a mistake. But he didn't want an apology, only the admission that he was no longer a suspect. He felt a clap on his back and turned to see the smiling faces of Pahoa and David Kamaka.

"You did a great job," Pahoa said, his face beaming. "You cleared Hawaiians of blame for the murders."

"All of us with native blood are indebted to you. The fallout from the murders, if the kahuna nui was Hawaiian, would have been enormous for our people," David Kamaka added.

There it was. David had put it to him. Agree that you are one of us. Say you are not part of the ruling class established by the missionaries who had come to Christianize the Hawaiians. Kamaka placed him on the fence of choice between power and poverty.

Before he could answer, Thurmond, Ritter, and his father interrupted the conversation. Ritter said, "I want to congratulate you for your excellent recommendations on labor issues. Several of our HSPA directors were considering the same proposals as you so clearly outlined in your report. We will support and adopt them. Thurmond has agreed to editorialize for 'plantation paternalism.'"

Thurmond nodded. His face, neck, and hands showed no effects of the ordeal he had undergone the week before. "Yes, that is a great phrase that you coined. It actually was what plantations used to practice, until the boom years of sugar after the Reciprocity Treaty. Then the pursuit of money replaced good Christian values." A kind expression replaced the usual sternness of his face. "I haven't properly thanked you for saving my life. I also apologize for calling you a traitor. I have spoken with Captain Trask. He has explained the important work you have done for our country. We cannot publicly acknowledge your service, but the word will spread that you are helping Hawai'i withstand whatever ill fortune may come from the east."

"But I hope you understand that there are thousands of Japanese living and working in Hawai'i, loyal to the United States," Grant said, gripping Thurmond's shoulder to emphasize the point. "This is especially true of the second generation, the Nisei. They love Hawai'i. Treat them well, and you will find they are excellent citizens. Do not repeat the same mistake that led to the lynching of Mr. Agato. All it produced was a desire for revenge. Treat these young men and women of Japanese ancestry, born in Hawai'i, with respect. You will find that they will serve these islands and our nation with loyalty and devotion."

Thurmond nodded. "I spoke at length with Selena Choy. She explained Sato's motivations for his actions. I realize that sowing hatred as I have done has produced nothing but animosity and a desire for revenge. I am not too old to learn. There is no excuse for killing, but neither is there any good reason to push for reprisals against a group of people who are blameless. I almost paid with my life for my bigotry. I will not make that mistake again."

***

Selena sat by his side at the banquet table, her father, Dan Choy, next to her. The magnificent Banyan Court of the Moana Hotel held more than a hundred well-wishers. The elite of Honolulu were present. The speeches covered Grant's heroism in World War I and his accomplishments since returning to Hawai'i. It came time for him to acknowledge the good wishes of those who had assembled to do him honor.

Grant squeezed Selena's hand and took the podium. He thanked all the people who had helped him in his quest to solve the murders. As to labor issues, he repeated what he had expressed in his recommendations. He begged for tolerance of the multiple racial groups that had come to Hawai'i to work in the sugar fields. As he moved toward closure of his remarks, he reached his hand to Selena and drew her to him.

"This is my partner. She helped me in every way she could to prove my innocence. There were times when others doubted me, but Selena was steadfast in her belief in me. At great risk to herself, she fought to save my life. I would not be here today, but for her. Tonight, let me announce to all of you that this Hawaiian-American will marry this Chinese-Caucasian, whom I treasure above all other women."

There, he had done it. He had told the power brokers that he had crossed the color line. If they thought him worthy, they would accept his belief that the skin's whiteness had no special meaning. The worth of a man or a woman should be decided by their deeds.

In a throaty voice filled with promises of future pleasure, Selena said, "To hell with the blue laws." She kissed Grant with passion. Applause thundered in the Banyan Court. The orchestra beneath the great tree began to play a Hawaiian melody, "My Heart's Choice."

The End

ABOUT THE AUTHOR

BILL FERNANDEZ GREW up on tiny Kaua'i Island, Hawai'i and attended Kamehameha Schools, Stanford University, and Stanford Law School. After serving as a judge in Santa Clara County, California, he retired to his hometown and turned to writing. This is his first work of fiction after three memoirs which chronicle the years of chaotic change from isolation to the impact of World War Two and its aftermath. An avid spear fisherman, his beautiful underwater descriptions create a welcome respite from his teen years of trying to make sense of it all.

Other Works

Rainbows Over Kapa'a
Kaua'i in Peace and War
Hawai'i in War and Peace
John Tana, An Adventure Tale of Old Hawaii, available 2016

www.kauaibillfernandez.com
facebook: Bill Fernandez Hawaiian Author

Made in the USA
San Bernardino, CA
12 January 2018